THE PINEBOX VENDETTA

JEFF BOND

At the junction of Queen Street and von Cresswell's Alley, Jonas Pruitt and Ephraim Gallagher were observed quarreling over a pinebox of unknown import. The one-tyme associates swore in the public square and vowed their clans should ne'er again make common cause.

Constable Q. A. Kincaid reports two horses were lamed in the incident and one wrist shattered, and speculates the dispositions of many bystanders were surely spoilt.

— Excerpt from *Kerryford's Boston Gazetteer*, November 4, 1769

PART I

CHAPTER 1

JAMIE GALLAGHER STOOD BESIDE THE PIRATE AT THE SKIFF'S RAIL, the African sea thick on his skin. Neither man could see the other in the moonless night, but Jamie smelled the khat the Somali never stopped chewing—sweetly sharp, a scent that made Jamie feel part cleansed and part crazed.

"The money is ready," said the pirate named Abdi. "My men have packed the briefcase."

"*Wanaagsan.*" Jamie ducked his head in gratitude. "You believe the general will accept a briefcase?"

"This is the usual way, yes. It will be checked for explosives with X-ray and IMS swabs."

"Of course."

"Also, the general will insist on verifying the amount before the release occurs."

"His men are going to count ten million dollars?" Jamie asked.

The Somali spat khat leaves into the sea. "He has machines. The machines check by weight."

Jamie exhaled, pushing his own breath into the hot, still air. The money would weigh out.

The money wasn't the trick.

Abdi continued, "Once the amount is verified, the general will call his people in the jungle by satphone, and they will free your journalist."

"Immediately? I'll need confirmation from HD before we leave the yacht."

"That is the arrangement."

Jamie mopped his brow. Acting wasn't his strength, and he hoped his insistence on this procedural point was convincing. In fact, Humanitarian Dialogue (HD) knew nothing about tomorrow. There would be no representative at the hand-off spot, and the French journalist—whose reporting on minority suffrage truly had opened the world's eyes—would not be freed.

This was a regret. But Jamie Gallagher had lived with worse.

He said, "I'll be X-rayed, too?"

"Yes."

"Strip-searched?"

"At a minimum. You should expect a body cavity search."

"Fine." In his years advocating for peace and public health around sub-Saharan Africa, Jamie had had his cheeks probed, his neck magnetically combed, and the arches of his feet flayed. "I suppose the general's in no position to be trusting."

The pirate took a while to respond. Was he eyeing Jamie in the dark? Signaling to his men back on the mothership? Jamie's statement had been obvious and shouldn't have invoked offense.

Since joining the pirates at Merca, a white beach paradise down the coast from Mogadishu, Jamie had detected hostility—even after paying their exorbitant convoy fee. Abdi himself had been civil enough, but his three young lieutenants, after pointedly using their left hands to shake Jamie's, had glared at him with undisguised contempt.

He understood this. A westerner waltzes onto their ship with unimaginable stores of cash—cash that, in a matter of hours, will bring them into contact with the most wanted war criminal on the planet. Naturally, they resented him.

He was what, five years older than them? With his bandanna and dishwater-blond hair?

Abdi said, "This is a great risk for us. We have earned the general's esteem. We do not wish to squander it."

Jamie heard the clench in the man's jaw. "I assure you, I will comply with every procedure he or you tell me to follow."

General Mahad and these Somali pirates fought on the same side of many issues. Both wanted the ruling Muslims out of Puntland. They didn't care that the Muslims had remade the conflict-ravaged region into a prosperous enclave, introducing compulsory education and a foodstuff-based living wage.

For the pirates, the problem was their strict, Islam-centric brand of law and order, which had made the coastal waters harder to pillage.

General Mahad's beef was simple: the Muslims had replaced him in power.

He'd ruled Puntland for a decade, enriching himself and his cronies using any resource available—khat, guns, people. When word of his atrocities leaked, international pressure mounted for a free election. The general agreed after a period of stonewalling, believing he could manipulate the results. When Al Jama-ah won anyway, the general stole all he could in the weeks before yielding control.

According to a local guide Jamie trusted, the general toured polling stations his last day with a machete, taking three fingers from each precinct leader.

"If I lose next time," he told them, "you lose the rest."

Though he retained a few loyalist strongholds like the one holding the French journalist, General Mahad himself lived on a yacht, moving constantly to evade capture. The Hague had convicted him last year in absentia.

Now Jamie asked, "Who'll be coming aboard with me?"

"Me and Josef," Abdi said. "We are known to the general."

"Will you be armed?"

"No. He will search us, too."

Jamie shuffled in place, the skiff feeling suddenly unsteady beneath him. "I—er, I hope it'll be okay that I bring a gift. Akpeteshie. I was told it is the general's favorite liquor?"

The pirate groaned pleasurably. "Akpeteshie, yes."

"I thought we might share a drink as a token of good faith."

"The bottle is factory-sealed?"

"Yes."

"The general will like this. The general believes in courtesy."

Several retorts came to mind at the ludicrous idea this butcher had any claim on civility, but Jamie swallowed them. He removed a pair of night-vision goggles from his rucksack. Before looking himself, he offered them to Abdi. Abdi waved them off as though the technology were frivolous.

Jamie scanned the horizon, right to left, left to right. The skiff's sway seemed to increase. The eye cups stuck to his sweaty forehead.

The smell of khat, which hadn't bothered him before, grated now, like sugar grit needling into his nose and eardrums. He felt the pressure of this place keenly. Every actor—man, woman, or child—who entered this stretch of ocean would be girded to fight. They must be. Choice never came into it.

A shape appeared on the horizon. Jamie thumbed his focus wheel until red blurs resolved to running lights.

"The general," Abdi said.

Adrenaline jolted through Jamie. Here was a ghost vessel—a vessel many militaries of the world would board on sight, and one the United States wouldn't think twice about blasting to smithereens with a drone strike.

The yacht grew larger in the greenish display. Jamie screwed on a bulky magnifier lens and was able to make out guards on the gunwale, ambling, AK-47s on their shoulders. The yacht was perhaps twenty meters. Several figures were sprawled out on deck, sleeping in the open for the heat.

Jamie raised the goggles, thinking to find the general on the bridge. The cockpit windows were smoked—opaque from outside and surely bulletproof.

He panned back down. The craft made a leeward turn, and he glimpsed new figures at the base of the pilothouse. These were prone like the others but smaller—a dozen in a line, little pulled-apart commas. Most of them were still, but one squirmed restlessly.

Children.

Jamie's stomach shrank to a cold fist.

⚜

He barely slept. Long after rowing back to the mothership and helping Abdi loosely tie up the skiff, and bedding down in the holds beside crates of ammunition and rocket-propelled grenades, Jamie lay awake thinking of those children.

He'd known the general had kids, twenty or thirty that he acknowledged. And it shouldn't have been surprising such a monster would keep family members near, in the cross-hairs of danger. Still, the concrete knowledge of these innocents shook Jamie. His moral clarity waned, like a tower of blocks losing its crosspiece.

How will the general's children move on? What if they fall into the arms of the pirates or the next warlord up?

From here, it was no leap at all to obsess about the French journalist. When the exchange was revealed as phony, would the general's men execute her on the spot? They would blame her, despite the fact that she had played no role whatsoever in the ruse.

Renée Auteuil had been raised by a jobless father in Roubaix, the post-industrial husk of a city. She'd worked sixty-hour weeks as a line cook to support them. She'd defied dictators on three continents to achieve the eminence and audience that had prompted General Mahad to snatch her last spring.

Now Jamie was putting her in jeopardy, and for what?

So that he could feel better about himself? So he could feel absolved?

Jamie had chosen Puntland precisely because it was neutral territory in the feud between his family, the Gallaghers, and their conservative arch-enemies, the Pruitts.

The two clans had been fighting for nearly three centuries—and while there was hardly a facet of American political, corporate, or philanthropic life their battles hadn't touched, neither family had much connection to Puntland. As president, Jonathan Pruitt hadn't carried out any significant dealings with the territory during his term. (His *only* term, thankfully.) The Gallaghers facilitated relief missions all over Africa, but nothing specially in Puntland.

Jamie's action tomorrow wouldn't be interpreted as having grown out of the feud, or impacted the feud, or given the Gallaghers some edge in the next midterm elections.

This was separate. This was good, a thing nobody could spin or debate.

That had been the plan, at least.

Now doubts roared in Jamie's mind. He dug at the roots of his hair, flopping about the damp, creaking boards. The Somalis snored in the adjacent room. Their arsenal reeked of grease and sulfur. Jamie crunched his eyes and pulled his rucksack, which he'd been toting around since freshman year at Yale, down over his head.

The thoughts still came, and the guilt.

His emotions spiraled and sickened and fought, and finally came to a head. He growled, disgusted by himself, then tore through his rucksack for the shoe that contained, wedged up in the toes, a newsprint photo of a mass grave discovered in northeast Puntland.

By penlight, he stared at the image. He seared it into his brain. The open trench of dusted gray bodies. The overlapping femurs. The fleshless faces.

The photo was merely one of dozens. Jamie knew the general was well-positioned to continue the slaughter once the collective international eye moved along.

"That's it," he whispered aloud. "Not one more thought."

❧

The meeting was to take place twenty minutes after sunrise. Jamie woke, having finally fallen asleep around four a.m., to the Somalis chatting in their native tongue over pieces of flatbread. He dragged himself aboveboard, feeling at once languid and jittery.

"Bread?" Abdi offered, tearing a piece from a slab.

"Thanks, no." Jamie reached into his rucksack instead for a piece of biltong, the wildebeest jerky he'd grown fond of. "Has the general been about?"

"Yes, Josef saw him. The hat." Abdi made a sifting gesture above his head to indicate the general's beret.

The day was already scorching, the sky's blue brilliance broken only by the boiling disk of the sun. The general's yacht rocked softly in the west, appearing quite large now, its bow sleek and spear-like.

"They're within gun range," Jamie observed.

"Oh yes. We are in their scopes."

As if to prove the point, Abdi raised a hand in the yacht's direction and laughed. Nobody joined him.

The pirate named Josef, taller and broader in the chest than Abdi, loaded the ten-million-dollar briefcase into the first of three skiffs. Jamie stepped in after, fitting his rucksack into the hull—careful of the Akpeteshie inside—and tying back his hair.

Abdi took a minute instructing the two men staying back on

the mothership. Was he arranging a distress signal? Telling them what to do if shots were fired?

Coordinating a double-cross?

There was no use worrying. Jamie had placed himself between dangerous people, but dangerous people performed the same calculations benign ones did. The pirates would keep up their end so long as the benefits remained clear: not only cash, but stronger ties with the general and the establishment of a new back-channel to the powerful Gallaghers.

The skiff loaded, Adbi yanked the outboard motor's cord. The engine sputtered alive and settled to a rumbling purr. Josef untied them, flashing a grim thumbs-up to the men staying behind.

They charted a course for the general's yacht. The sea felt choppier on the smaller craft, which didn't bother Jamie—a lifelong boater and varsity swimmer in college—but did compel him to pull the rucksack protectively into his lap. If the Akpeteshie somehow ruptured against the hull, the mission would be lost.

As they neared the general's yacht, the faces of his guards became visible—wary, textured faces. The carry-straps of AK-47s sawed their necks.

Abdi cut the motor and drifted in.

A section of railing was unclipped, and a ramp extended from the yacht's stern. After helping Josef tie up, Jamie slipped the rucksack onto his back and boarded. The Somalis trailed him with the briefcase.

"*Halkan, ku siin!*" said one of the general's men.

Abdi shook his head forcefully at the request—to hand over the briefcase. The guards backpedaled, their formation hemming Jamie and the pirates into a corner of the aft deck. Abdi and Josef walked with their bodies shielding the case as if it contained plutonium.

With these uneasy field positions established, the general's men conferred briefly and parted to form an aisle to the pilothouse. General Mahad emerged.

The general wore his full dress uniform: navy blue, epaulets, ribboned medals. He lumbered forward with a mild limp, said to have originated during the Simba rebellion of 1964.

He raised his chin to Abdi, then spoke to Jamie. "Welcome to the one and true seat of Puntland, Mr. Gallagher."

Jamie felt the man's deep, scarred voice in his bowels. "That's none of my concern. I'm here for Renée."

The general smiled, his lips fat and sly. "How fortunate she is. You are the white knight, eh? Sir Jamie?"

The characterization stung, but Jamie pushed on. "I've been in touch with Humanitarian Dialogue—their helicopter is ready. Give me a latitude and longitude for the exchange and let's get this over."

"Your friends have the money?"

Every eye on the yacht turned to Abdi, whose knuckles tightened on the briefcase handle.

"Ten million," Jamie said. "Count it if you like."

The general crooked a finger at one of his men, who disappeared to the pilothouse. The man returned with a machine resembling a fax with bill-sized trays.

Abdi stepped forward with the briefcase. The man with the counting machine passed a handheld X-ray scanner around the case and swabbed a cloth along each edge.

He started for the pilothouse with the cloth, likely to perform a residue test for explosives, but the general stopped him. Then gestured for Abdi to go ahead.

When Abdi undid the clasp, the lip snapped open—ten million was a squeeze, even with an oversize case—and a few packets spilled out.

The counting began.

Now Jamie reached into his rucksack for the Akpeteshie.

"I've heard tell around campfires," he began, gathering himself, "that you enjoy a certain Ghanaian beverage."

The general grinned when he saw the bottle, squat, the neck's glass bowed in the distinctive shape of a baobab tree.

"This is true."

"Shall we drink together?" Jamie said. "It's early, but I find a day started well nearly always ends well."

The general palmed his jaw. There was a risk he would set the gift aside, but Jamie was counting on this subtle challenge to his manhood—in front of his crew, in front of Abdi and Josef. People like the general didn't back down from such dares.

Jamie thought of his old classmate Rock Pruitt who'd downed a fifth of whiskey disproving a frat brother's claim that prep-schoolers only drank martinis and smoked reefer.

"I would quite enjoy that," the general said. "After the bottle is checked."

Jamie raised a shoulder, feigning indifference as two men seized the Akpeteshie and held it sideways up to the sun, testing its feel in their hands, poking fingernails along the dripped-wax seal.

They would find nothing. Jamie's sister Charlotte Gallagher, founder of internet-of-things giant SmartWidget and the eighteenth-richest person in the world, owned 45 percent of the local distillery that produced Akpeteshie. She had allowed Jamie to follow this lone bottle through the factory. At the final step, just before corking, he'd poured out 150 milliliters of liquor and replaced it with an equal amount of king cobra venom.

For fifteen months, Jamie had been inoculating himself with increasingly larger doses of the venom. He had started, after discussing the strategy at length with a Sudanese shaman, with a pinprick diluted in a pint of water. Last week, he had managed eight milliliters of venom—the amount a shot from the spiked Akpeteshie would deliver, depending on the pour—and suffered only dizziness, blurred vision, and severe cottonmouth.

When his men were satisfied the bottle was unaltered, the general took a pair of tumblers from the yacht's fiberglass sideboard.

Tumblers, not shot glasses. Eight ounces at least.

"To finding a middle, eh?" The general poured each tumbler to the brim. "Two parties can start from opposite ends and, with good sense, find a common understanding."

Jamie's teeth pulverized each other in the back of his mouth. He'd always found the rhetoric of compromise disingenuous, whether it came from television pundits or the North Carolina Gallaghers exhorting the clan to give ground at the fringes of the abortion debate.

To hear it from the mouth of a man like Mahad? Revolting.

"*To the middle*," he spat.

He raised the tumbler to his lips. Calculations whipped around his brain. Eight ounces divided by one point five…

Equaled six times the amount of venom his body had previously endured.

The liquid was amber, almost orange. As the glass tilted, Jamie imagined he saw currents of venom slithering among the palm wine. His fingers trembled. Some sloshed over the side, but not nearly enough.

In his periphery, Jamie became aware of Abdi and Josef arguing with the general's men. Abdi slapped one empty well of the briefcase. The general's men shouted. More rushed to the deck from below board.

The general balked at Jamie's tone. "You do not like my toast. That is your right. You are the guest, so make your own." He smirked about. "We are democratic here, aren't we?"

Jamie ignored the low hoots. "To justice." He regripped his tumbler. "To justice, and fair treatment for all living things."

The general guffawed, big and toothy. "For ten million, yes. Why in hell not?"

Their eyes locked over the tumblers' rims. Jamie perceived

something in the man's look, some hustler's instinct, and knew if he faltered now—even for a moment—the trap would be blown.

Jamie stared into the lethal brew, waited for bright madness to rise, and drank. The Akpeteshie burned his throat. His jaw felt weak and daggers pressed into his eardrums from inside. Still, he kept his head tipped back and drank it all.

The general and several of his men goggled at the feat. When their eyes turned to him, the war criminal downed his, too.

"…no, *the release!*" Jamie heard behind him. "No money before release!"

"We will keep it."

"No, us! We will hold the money."

A guard wearing ripped denim leveled his rifle at Abdi. Josef stepped forward to push aside the muzzle. Another guard drove the butt of his rifle into Josef's back, crumpling the pirate.

Jamie didn't know how long he and the general had. During his inoculation, the symptoms would begin in about a minute, but he'd never ingested this large a dose.

His heartrate zoomed and breath pumped through his chest like air from a bellows—still, this could be the effects of anticipation.

"So, um…the release," he said, feeling a vague duty toward Abdi. "If you…so I'll call HD and be sure Renée, er…s'all okay with the money…"

Words were deserting him. The scuffle on deck was intensifying. Josef had recovered to pounce on the man in denim. Abdi was buried in a furious tangle of fists and churning hips.

Jamie didn't understand the fight. Let them have the money— who cared?

He began to feel disconnected from his body, Abdi and Josef blending into other people he'd known in life, Gallaghers and Pruitts, senators and reporters, grad students and business titans, all fighting without reason, finding joy and enemies, grinding their life into the larger sausage.

The general unleashed a thunderous whistle and raised his hand for calm. The struggle paused. Every eye turned his way. He began to lower his hand but suddenly couldn't.

His arm convulsed and became some bucking stick-animal beyond his control. His fingers twitched unnaturally. He grasped his throat, staggering back. Froth bubbled in his nostrils.

The man who'd retrieved the money scale from the pilothouse pointed at Jamie.

"What is this?"

Jamie tried answering, but his tongue would not obey, dead and heavy in his mouth. Pain gored his brain. Sweat screamed from his pores, a thousand beads altogether.

This wasn't the outcome Jamie had wanted, but neither was it wholly unexpected. He thought now of life's best moments. In Burundi, feeling that boy's skeletal hand squeeze as he sucked a tab of enriched peanut butter. On the vineyard, fourteen years old, swinging his cousins round and round in celebration after his mother—the senior senator from Connecticut and Democratic National Committee chairperson—had succeeded in her long-shot campaign to retake majority control of the Senate.

Above all, though, he remembered kissing Sam. Seniors on their last night at Yale, about to go conquer the world, standing together in an entryway. Emotions spiked to the heavens. Their mouths came together in the gentlest, deepest touch he'd known before or since.

Samantha Lessing. God, she was it. The life he missed.

Half the general's men were swarming the Somali pirates while the other half moved on Jamie. There was a gap between the two, but it was closing.

Jamie willed his tongue back into service.

"This was right," he croaked. "Here, today. This was not a waste."

And he believed this—dashing across the deck through grasping hands, over the gunwale, into the black ocean.

TEN YEARS LATER

CHAPTER 2

S AM SLIPPED OUT OF THE WNYC STUDIOS AT FOUR THIRTY, waving off cheers of "Have fun!" and "Take me with you!", hurrying through the lobby, jogging a short block to catch the uptown C. She needed to pick up a daughter and possibly husband in Brooklyn, then be back in Manhattan for the 5:41 p.m. train to New Haven. Reunion check-in closed at eight. If the train arrived on time, she'd make it easy.

If not? If any of the dizzying array of pitfalls inherent in teenagers and public transit popped up? Sam guessed they were sleeping on the street.

Half an hour later, she hiked three flights of stairs with key at the ready. The apartment was unlocked.

"Joss?" she called. "You are packed, yes?"

Her daughter's door was closed, but guitar chords thwanged through. Sam stepped around French bread pizza and a stack of indie music magazines to pound twice.

"Not telling you what to wear," she yelled, "but I suggest a dress or dress-like garment for Saturday night."

The music inside dulled, indicating Sam had been heard. The warning bell had been sounded. She found an oversize duffel bag in the hall closet and tossed in her stuff: toiletries, three-odd outfits for the weekend, Zoom audio recorder.

About outfits: Sam both cared and didn't care. She was forty-three. Her classmates were forty-three, give or take. Nobody should go rocking a prom dress, but they weren't dead yet either. She brought dark-red sleeveless, plus yellow floral in case of glorious weather.

"Leaving twelve minutes!" she said through Joss's door. "Zero wiggle situation."

Tight timelines didn't bother Sam—the studio commonly dropped post-production on her for shows that were airing in mere hours. Packing now, she thought pleasurably of the friends she'd see at the reunion. Laurel in from San Francisco. Jen Pereido. Naomi, even though she was still recovering from the birth of her fourth(!) child.

From her own daughter's room came a squeal, streaked with joy. The noise pinched Sam's heart. Her husband Abe was in there—they'd probably harmonized on some new melody. Which was awesome. Truly. Except that it was 4:48.

She opened the door. "I hate to be Yoko, but the time's come to break up. Leaving in five minutes."

Fourteen-year-old Joss looked up from fingering the neck of her guitar, still grinning. Abe sat cross-legged on the floor with the Yamaha across his knees, a kind of strung-out, hipster Dalai Lama. Both appeared stumped.

Sam said, "Yale? My alma mater, where you've been dying to go for months?"

Joss's grin vanished. "Dad said you were leaving whenever! Isn't it like an all-weekend thing? Today's only Thursday."

"Yes, but in order to check in Thursday night, as I hope to," Sam said, patiently as she could, "we need to arrive on campus by eight o'clock."

"That's ridiculous, I've barely even looked at clothes."

"Then look quickly. I'm winging it myself."

Joss shot upright, dropping her guitar with a *clang* against the bed. "I'm not going to Yale on, like, zero notice. You can't just spring this on me."

"I sprung no thing on no body. We discussed timing last night, and this afternoon I sent your father four texts—every hour, on the hour—reminding him."

"But those go to *his* phone," Joss said. "Remember, I don't have one? Because you won't let me?"

Sam stretched one arm laboriously toward the ceiling, focusing on good breaths. Apparently, they were skimming right over Abe's not passing along the messages. His long-running campaign to absolve himself of any and all responsibility—waged by a steady pattern of never giving a crap for anyone but himself—had succeeded at last.

"Look, we can argue about phones again or we can try to make this train. Otherwise, we basically miss half the reunion. We might as well skip."

This genuinely spooked Joss. Her face hollowed even more deeply than usual. (She'd grown three inches this year, causing Sam to marvel at this moody, suddenly supermodel whose laundry she washed every week.) They'd been talking about the reunion forever, what architecture couldn't be missed, whether student activists would be around for Joss to connect with.

Sam hated to use fear, that blunt-force instrument of the parenting arsenal, but she knew a reasoned argument would produce nothing but gridlock.

Joss started packing.

Abe, who'd disappeared to the bathroom, emerged now with drawstrings dangling from his sweats. He nodded to a pair of shiny heels in Sam's duffel.

"Somebody's dressing to impress."

"I haven't seen these people in twenty years," she said. "I'm erring on the side of adequate."

Her husband snorted, seeming to take the comment

personally. Twelve years older than Sam, he'd been an already-aging rocker when she had met him in her late twenties. Between drugs and alcohol, and having nowhere in particular to be for the last twenty years—no office or classroom mores to adhere to—Abe had aged poorly. His leatherette skin belonged to a person decades older, and beige hair had fled the top of his head for his ears and nostrils.

"You're more than welcome to join," Sam said, stuffing in a toothbrush. "But we are leaving *mucho rapido,* so…"

He ambled a step away, picked up Joss's guitar and set it in its case.

She heaved the duffel's halves together to make the zipper zip. "You're passing, correct? I just want to confirm with a verbal yes or no answer."

Sam knew with four hundred percent certainty that some future argument would hinge on this point—whether or not Abe had been invited. They would be sniping back and forth about Yale, how phony or not phony her friends were, what first-world problems they were finding themselves crippled by, and he would break out his trump card.

You were embarrassed. You didn't want me there, dragging you down.

And here it came, earlier than expected.

"You don't have to faux-invite me," Abe said. "You prefer to go alone. Oh, you'll tolerate Joss. Joss is an acceptable accessory. Perfectly cool, I get it. I won't ruin your triumphant return."

Sam again focused on respiration.

In, out. In, out.

"This is a real invitation," she said. "Just like the one I offered in April, and in May. You are absolutely welcome at my reunion. Come. Please. Joss would love having you there. Maybe you could jam with Thom—he's supposed to be playing Toad's."

As convincingly as Sam delivered these words, her husband was right. The invitation wasn't real. Abe thought Thom's music was derivative and had zero interest in strumming out tired chords while Activist Boy preened at the mic for the ladies. If Abe went, he would grump and sulk and criticize, and ruin the whole thing.

"Pass," Abe said. "Thom can play 'Better Man' solo. That is where he opens, isn't it? Pearl Jam? Or is it the first encore?"

Sam chuckled with relief. Complicity with ragging on her own friends? Fine. Fine, she'd do it—so long as he stayed home.

Their daughter's voice came through the wall, "What's the formality situation for Saturday night dinner?"

"Less stuffy than a cotillion," Sam called back, "but expect mosh-pitting to be frowned upon."

As she waited on her daughter, Sam kept tabs on a few text conversations by phone. People were arriving into New Haven and wondering where Demery's had gone, or at the airport dreaming of hugs on the quad, or annoyed because they had to work tomorrow which *royally sucked*!

Sam grinned at this last but didn't tap back a response. Abe was watching her, surely guessing what the rapid-fire chimes were about. For Sam to actively join in would risk an argument or, worse, a change of heart.

She didn't think her husband was capable of attending the reunion for spite, enduring a rotten weekend just to play the killjoy. But why push him?

Finally, Joss emerged. She had changed into a clingy ankle-length skirt and carried a backpack.

"Thank you for hurrying," Sam said. "Excited?"

Joss rolled her eyes but couldn't completely suppress a smile. Sam clutched her hand. After double-checking the cat dish had food, she slipped on her jacket and pulled her cell charger out of the wall, jamming it into the side of her bag.

Abe tilted his head. "Why're you taking the Zoom?"

Shoot. Sam inwardly punched her brain for not packing last night.

"Ah…I'm kicking around this audio doc. Just ideas. Might record some clips."

"Topic?"

She hated how he asked, all aggressive and pedantic.

"I doubt I'll have time." She considered lying outright. Joss was watching, though, and the idea of cowering in front of her daughter—who was learning how to relate to others and respond to adversity and be an assertive female—repulsed her. "It's about pinebox. How it affected our class, et cetera. Of course the vendetta's been done—this would try to get at it through the lens of our class at Yale. We had one Pruitt, one Gallagher, that death freshman year. Kind of the whole feud in miniature."

She shrugged, pretending to be flip, and started for the door. It was 4:32.

Abe asked, "Is Rock Pruitt going to the reunion?"

"Dunno," Sam said. "We didn't exactly run in the same circles."

"Really? That seems disingenuous given you were bosom buddies there with the immortal Jamie Gallagher."

Sam felt her chest constrict. *Let it go*, she told herself. *Let it go like Elsa. Turn yourself to ice, and everything slides right off.*

Except she couldn't.

"Jamie despised Rock. You could walk the earth and never find two people with more diametrically-opposed worldviews than Rock and Jamie."

Abe huffed. "Those beautiful people and their worldviews. What rarefied air you'll be breathing again."

Sam opened her mouth hotly to speak. At the last moment, she stopped and finished zipping her bag instead. She stood tall-shouldered, smiled, and invited Joss to lead the way out.

"The audio doc does sound right out of *This American Life*," said Abe, evidently unsatisfied with the fight's resolution. "Who produces that? Must be one of those Yale ninety-sixers working there you could pitch."

She felt like asking how he could possibly believe in mythical

Ivy League connections after this life of theirs: Sam's twelve years bouncing around the periphery of pseudo-academic film, hustling after grants, performing peon tasks in job after job to bulk up a CV so it could sit on her Patreon page getting a half-dozen page views per month. She had finally risen to prominence at WNYC but almost in spite of Yale, which carried significant prima donna baggage in the field.

Again, though, Sam restrained herself in front of Joss.

"Hey, quick Zoom question," she said. "You think forty-eight/twenty-four-bit, or forty-four/sixteen is better? It'll be mostly outdoor clips."

Abe tipped his balding head left, then right. "Forty-eight. File sizes won't be that different, and at sixteen, the Zoom gets super noisy."

Sam crinkled her nose. "Yeah. Yeah, I guess that's right. Thanks."

Mother and daughter both pecked Abe goodbye and bounded off to catch a train.

Joss seemed to study Sam down the stairs, and she wondered momentarily if her ruse had failed—if Joss understood that Mom had forgotten more about sampling rates than Dad had ever known—and had only made this final query to escape the apartment on a positive note.

Other fictions existed between the couple. That Abe respected her managerial position at WNYC. That she believed his vow to start playing shows again—that those freelance audio-tech Fiverr gigs he'd parlayed fairly successfully into income were just temporary and not his professional endgame. That reuniting each night for dinner, they asked about the other's day with anything like genuine interest.

Sometimes Joss would make comments indicating she knew. "Gee, Dad, bitter much?" or, "I'd rather not be involved in *this*," swirling her hand as though over a cesspool. Other times, she seemed oblivious, just a regular kid consumed by regular kid stuff.

Either possibility broke Sam's heart.

The L train was late. As Joss practiced pirouettes idly on the platform, Sam stared up the track, squeezing the handle of her bag, her toes nudging over the yellow stripe. Her phone had continued its chiming, Laurel and Terri texting about meal times, shoe choices, whether Naples still served pitchers.

Joss caught her checking her screen. "*What?* What're they saying?"

Sam stashed the phone in her jacket. "Oh, just blabbing about how I'm missing out."

"Which one, Naomi—the one who's writing a novel? Or the famous blogger?"

Laurel had written some for HuffPost, but "famous" was pushing it. Sam was okay with Joss idealizing her alma mater. Joss's academics were solid, dance extracurriculars would help, but she hadn't yet shown the kind of passion that propels kids to big-time achievement. Maybe meeting Laurel and others, and being exposed to Yale's vibrant undergrad activism, would spark it.

And if not? There were worse fates.

"All of them," Sam answered. "It's a grand conspiracy to make me jealous."

She peered up the track again. Still no train.

Next to her on the platform, a young guy in bikewear groaned. He flashed his phone around to his group, and they trudged off for the stairs.

"Excuse me," Sam said. "Sorry to bother you, but did you—er, is something up with this train?"

Bike Guy raised his screen for her to see. Sam squinted. Some app she had no idea even existed reported a forty-three-minute wait for the L line with the reason *Signal malfunction*.

Joss said, "Can we just get an Uber?"

"No. Uber all the way to Manhattan is way expensive."

"It's like ten dollars."

"It is *not* like ten dollars," Sam said, starting for street level, pulling up her mental city transit map. "More like thirty or thirty-five, and given the reunion fees pretty much wiped our bank account, we need to economize."

Joss dragged a step behind. "Dad said he got two new gigs today. That's like a hundred fifty dollars right there."

Sam bit her lip. How to explain to a teenager about budgets, and debt, and the way expenses keep coming at you like luggage off an airport carousel—only you have to grab every last one?

She decided to keep it simple. "We live in Brooklyn. Brooklyn is expensive."

She could've added *So are private ballet lessons*.

"Dad said he'd buy me new guitar strings," Joss said. "Can we not even get those? They're twenty dollars, basically how much an Uber would be."

They were crossing Willoughby Avenue now, Sam hurrying to enter the intersection ahead of the next traffic wave—which gave her cover to ignore her daughter's niggling response.

Abe never joined Sam on the financial-responsibility front, content to shower Joss with records and music goodies, reaping all the credit, making Sam the spoilsport. In fairness, he never spent a dime on clothes or gadgets for himself. He simply loved seeing Joss happy.

In a marriage chock-full of grievances, Sam found this one hard to prosecute. Abe's gig income from Fiverr roughly equaled hers from WNYC. The money was no more hers than his. He poured himself into Joss. Music instructor, English tutor, after-school snack chef: Abe was all these and more.

Maybe he'd lost interest in Sam, but for Joss? Anything.

The next best route to Penn Station was via the crosstown Fifty-four. Sam caught her mopey teenager by the wrist and urged her down Willoughby, shortcutting through Maria Hernandez Park, bags bumping thighs. Her friends' texts continued furiously, each *ding* bright and fun and begging to be read.

If they missed this 5:41 train to New Haven…ugh. Just thinking about it soured Sam's stomach. Missing the first night on campus. Limping back to the apartment. (They couldn't actually sleep on the street.)

At last, they reached the corner of Myrtle and Hart—the bus stop.

The Fifty-four had pulled away from the curb and was nosing into the center lane.

"No way!" Joss stamped her clog on the sidewalk. "We're totally missing this reunion, aren't we?"

Sam tuned out her own accelerating panic. "Nope. We are not freaking, got it? We shall not freak."

After briefly considering whether the Visa could support the Uber charge—in case she decided to cave, ceding all standing in the eyes of her only child—Sam consulted the posted schedules. There was a third transit route: the M.

She hitched the duffel bag securely up her shoulder, oriented herself as necessary to the map's colorful lines, and headed them for their new waypoint. A faint throb above her left heel heralded the start of a blister.

The station was a straight shot up Myrtle. They needed to hustle.

They needed that next M train.

As her subcortex steered them past strollers and idling taxis, Sam's larger thoughts were on Yale. Those sunny, blanket-lined quads where she and Laurel and Jamie Gallagher had discussed Nietzsche and taught each other linear algebra. Where Thom had founded the Razorlicks. Where ideas were big and you didn't have to sweat signal malfunctions or feign ignorance about sampling rates.

Sam knew forty-three-year-olds wouldn't have the same conversations as twenty-two-year-olds. Once you've changed diapers or dealt with a rotten boss, you can't go back to debating abstract versus figurative art. Not with a straight face.

Still, she wondered if some core magic might remain. New ventures hatching over hors d'oeuvres. Common struggles discovered over a second glass of Chardonnay. She imagined the delights coming not from her closest friends, whose stories she knew from Facebook, but from refreshed acquaintances. Some boy she'd argued with in English 120. One of the food services workers she used to scoop shepherd's pie alongside.

Maybe she would connect with no one particularly but find the spark inside. Maybe this pinebox documentary could be it.

Sam didn't know quite where the project would go. She'd conceived it partly in memory of Jamie, whose life had been consumed by the Gallagher-Pruitt feud. Whatever had happened in Africa, she felt sure it traced back to the feud somehow. But maybe there was some greater underlying truth to be surfaced. Maybe as she talked to classmates about this conflict that played out across all their newsfeeds and televisions, something more would emerge—some comment on the way they lived.

In another five minutes, Sam lugged her duffel bag onto the platform of the Myrtle Ave station and got her first break of the afternoon: a westbound M train, easing up to the curb.

She exhaled, standing aside for Joss to board. Her daughter dumped her backpack and collapsed into the first seat by the door, forehead damp with sweat.

She asked, "Are we gonna make it?"

Sam wedged both their bags underneath the bench seat, careful of the Zoom. "Yes. We're absolutely making it."

CHAPTER 3

ROCK PRUITT IGNORED SIGNS FOR *REUNION PARKING*, LEAVING HIS Maserati in front of Silliman College—the residential quad designated for Yale '96 this weekend—and tossing his keychain at the first uniform he saw.

The kid protested, "I'm campus laundry—I just pick up towels."

"So do it in style," Rock said.

Deciding to officially check in later, he strode west through campus. Yale inhabited New Haven like a bitchy swan inhabits some polluted lagoon. Her Gothic towers rose above the urban blight, fine stonework facades alternating with vacant storefronts. Rock walked College Street, gazing up the grand pillars of Woolsey Hall, over the odd hive-like cube that was Beinecke Library, into the baronial classrooms of Harkness Hall where professors had tried convincing him to be embarrassed of Western civilization. Memories sharp and big. With each step, his anger grew.

New Haven had few taxis. He flagged one immediately.

"Mory's," he said.

The driver asked, "Little early for the hard stuff, no?"

"No." Rock boomed shut the door. "There's fifty bucks in it for every faculty member you mow down."

Oh, Rock had enjoyed Yale. College was college. Friends, sex, beer. Painting nipples on old Nathan Hale. But the place seethed hostility toward him and anybody like him. From man-hating "consent forums" to indigenous peoples-worshiping curriculum in freshman history, to Yale Debate rejecting him out of hand despite national championships in high school, to the dean of his residential college warning that "Branford is an inclusive space, and must remain so" his first day on campus—the crusty, washed-up poet knew exactly who Rock Pruitt was.

Really, it was the clan's own fault. He'd been a seventeen-year-old idiot—he went where his dad told him to go. And for the Pruitts, just like for Bushes and Clintons and Gallaghers, it had to be Yale. Generation after generation, they shipped off for that Eli cred, that imprimatur of class—no matter that the place had been rabidly anti-conservative since the sixties.

They just kept sending their boys and girls and astronomical tuition check like it was 1795, and cigars and porters would be provided at orientation.

Did they not know? Or care? Maybe the elders figured serving four years as a liberal punching bag toughened your hide, inoculation in case you chose a profession dominated by "the Effetes and Elites," as standard-bearer Jonathan Pruitt used to quip.

Well, Rock had punched back. He'd pissed in the debate team headquarters—sprayed that file cabinet top to bottom, turned their prissy white notecards yellow.

And he wasn't done punching.

The taxi dropped him at Mory's. Entering the taproom, with its mahogany paneling and Depression-era portraits, Rock felt at ease. He sat on a burgundy stool and propped his elbow upon the solid-feeling bar. The portraits showed football, baseball, lacrosse teams. Faces like his own—but in black-and-white and under neat center parts—stared back.

1795 was exactly the idea here.

"Rock Pruitt," a raspy voice called over the bar.

Rock couldn't have been more pleased if a dozen Playboy playmates had appeared. "Johnston! Holy hell. I figured you'd be six feet under by now."

Johnston hobbled over, draping a towel over his starch-white jacket, and offered his hand.

"Guess I should be."

In the shake, Rock felt the man's gnarled skin like a rawhide ball glove. "What do you know, sir?"

The bartender scowled outside. "Eh, lot of crap. Same as ever."

"I hear that. Amazing they keep you around, right? Shriveled-up white face like yours. You're a walking, talking billboard for the patriarchy."

"What I am is cheap." Johnston shakily unstopped a bottle of Pappy Van Winkle's. "Besides, they can't fire me. Get in trouble for age discrimination."

"There you go. Finally found yourself a minority."

Rock tossed back his bourbon in one gulp. Johnston gassed him back up and began putting the bottle away but Rock swiped it, pouring a second glass for the bartender. They drank to protected classes.

Leading up to the reunion, Rock hadn't corresponded with friends. He made new ones easily. Casting about for possibilities, he spotted a pair of coeds sitting near the fireplace.

One had metal junk in her face. The other kept dragging her toe up the opposite calf under the table, making Rock absolutely crazy.

Undergrads. Yum.

Mory's was founded in 1849. Most Yalies only ever went to the stodgy club-restaurant for Cups, the giant handled trophies you ordered by color—the tastiest being Purple, made with champagne and Chambord—and passed around a group, drinking until the last man could turn the cup upside-down on his head and stay dry.

Rock had gone his first weekend at Yale with his freshman roommate, Derek Dickerson. They'd taken their whole dorm floor, a ragtag collection of dweebs and hicks and first-chair New Jersey violinists. Dickerson said he would order everything off his fake ID, recently obtained in Canada, but the old (even then) barkeep Johnston recognized Rock—having waited on many a Pruitt—and served them without question.

Rock and Derek Dickerson became best bros. They bonded over a shared—and godlike—capacity for alcohol and willingness to go ugly early. They took all the same courses, large survey guts that left their social calendars free, and both pledged DKE.

Wherever one yelled, "Are the proprietors aware this party *sucks?*" the other was sure to follow a short distance behind with grain alcohol to liven up the punch.

Until March 12, 1993, when Derek died.

Now Rock asked, "When is the naming ceremony?"

Johnston rubbed his rag hard into a scuff on the bar. "Sunday. Unless they find a slaveholder in the Gallagher family tree before then."

"Don't joke, someone might," Rock said, finishing his third drink.

The barman retrieved the bourbon again. The undergraduate girls by the fireplace were beckoning. He raised an unsteady finger their way.

"You know the *Gallaghers*"—Johnston spat the name—"will have insulated themselves. Paid people off. Whitewashed anything embarrassing."

Rock shrugged. "Sometimes you miss a spot."

Yale was christening its newest residential college "Gallagher College" over reunion weekend. These namings had become tricky business in recent years, as protests had forced administrators to wipe the dedication plates of various buildings and monuments due to their honorees' less-than-enlightened histories. The Gallagher name surely felt safe, that bastion of public service whose progressive roots stretched back to Revolutionary times.

Charlotte Gallagher's occasional twenty-million-dollar endowment gifts couldn't have hurt either.

"I hear Owen Gallagher might make an appearance," Johnston said.

"No kidding? There's a guy I can't wait to see exposed for a blithering dumbass," Rock said of the Gallaghers' presumed entry into the next presidential race. "Who else? How about Foxy Charlotte? Something about a woman rich enough to buy Norway makes me hard."

Johnston hadn't heard anything about Charlotte Gallagher.

Rock continued, "Tell you one Gallagher who won't be there: her brother. Unless they move the event to the bottom of the Indian Ocean."

Johnston chortled as Rock cupped his hands over his cheeks like gills.

Eight drinks in, he was finally buzzing. He felt confident. His anger had matured to a kind of generalized desire to take, to possess. Energy sparked through him. The burgundy stool seemed taller. He felt bigger in the pants.

He glanced at the undergrads. "I should go introduce myself to the new generation of thought leaders. Put their next three cups on my tab, aye? Be sure they get a little kicker too."

The fossil of a bartender smiled.

❧

He bagged the pretty one. The friend, Ms. Pierced-Up Sourpuss, tried pulling her back to the dorms, but Rock talked her into staying with the help of (a) much alcohol, and (b) the tried-and-true technique of acting like the friend-protector is wiser and more mature—"Listen to Skyler, Skyler's got a good head on her shoulders"—until vanity kicked in.

He took her in the Mory's staff bathroom. Her weight in his hands, pinned against the porcelain sink, felt like steak. He lasted forever with all the booze in his system. He talked hard in her ear. She laughed thinking they were jokes, so he gave more. Plumbing rattled below and she whimpered at the end.

Rock felt great walking out of Mory's. The fact that her backpack had had a Greenpeace patch was a tasty cherry on top, but his satisfaction ran deeper.

Twenty-three years ago, Yale had taken from Rock Pruitt. He'd arrived with astronomical expectations. Handsome. Self-assured. Articulate. An athletic standout and champion debater from one of the two most powerful families on the planet, who'd been elected a town alderman *as a high school junior.*

Four years later, he'd left not as the future face of the Pruitts, as all had expected, but as a black mark on the clan.

Yale had taken his legacy. Now he was taking back—with interest.

Exiting to York Street, Rock beheld Sterling Library. The Gothic spires topping New Haven's skyline. The mottled stone inset with statuary of knights and monks and angels, eagles, Latin script. High, narrow windows of stained glass—the sort of craftsmanship nobody bothered with nowadays. A breathtaking building full of books.

Dead, dusty books.

Rock circled around its backside, gazing up the south face. Were the balconies wider here? Nearer the roof?

Hmm.

This very land had actually belonged to the Pruitts in 1927, when construction of Sterling had begun. Rock's great-grandfather Frederick had operated a repeating-rifle factory here, quite profitably, and refused to sell to the university. For close to a year, Yale excavated the site, digging right up to the Pruitt Riflery gate with no agreement in place. Finally, forced by various municipal tentacles brandishing "the public good" like a riding crop, Frederick accepted the university's terms. And the liberals got their book altar.

Now, Rock walked to a hardware store on Orange Street and bought a sledgehammer.

Checking into the reunion formally, he stowed the sledgehammer in his assigned dorm room. It was four o'clock. Not dark, like he needed for tonight's main event, so Rock wandered into the Silliman courtyard to mingle. Old classmates were streaming through the sun-streaked quad, picking up packets and Y96 tote bags, heaving suitcases up stairs, shooing their brats off to play on the rope swing.

He ran into a DKE brother.

"Hells yeah, Rock Pruitt!" the guy said. "I knew this weekend would rule."

Rock gripped him by the shoulder, and they banged forearms. A food service worker was wheeling kegs toward a catering tent. Rock commandeered one and they drank in the entryway, two hours steady, attracting three more DKE brothers and a stray SAE. Pinheads from the first-floor suites shot them looks going in and out of the bathroom.

Rock pissed in their sink.

The SAE was an investment banker and kept fishing for tips.

"What's *next*, man?" He spread his arms, just about popping a button off his shirt. "REITs, derivatives—the value's gone. Where's it go next?"

Rock grimaced, bolting his beer. During his time at Pruitt Capital, after those bogus ethics charges ran him out of Congress, Rock had invented a complex financial instrument based on distressed medical debt. You bought it for pennies on the dollar—all these cripples or their widows who couldn't pay their bills—then went back at the states or Medicaid for unclaimed subsidies. Absolute gold. Five hundred, six hundred-percent returns.

Until the Senate Finance committee, a puppet of the Gallaghers at that point, introduced legislation banning them: the Predatory Healthcare Debt Act of 2009.

Rock began, "Frankly, Henry—"

"Harry."

"Whatever. Frankly, the value is in the same place it's been since the dawn of time. With dumb people. Dumb consumers, dumb bankers. Dumb Chinese lusting after ultra-luxury condos. Find the dumb people, you find the moola."

Harry absorbed the advice with a cocked-brow squint. On his chin was either spittle or beer foam.

Rock continued, "If you're dumb yourself—and this feels like no great stretch—that's alright. Find even dumber people."

He drank on. He donned a suit at some point. More hangers-on joined, forcing the conversation to the courtyard where it eventually joined the official reunion cocktail hour.

The crowd grew five bodies deep as Rock held court. It was like being back on the campaign trail. Confidence swelled his chest. He dispatched hecklers—hell, eighty percent disagreed with every word he said—by logic or volume or very often both.

When some dangerous topic arose, like race or gender, a revving would start in Rock's gut. Red, raging glee. And he'd say the exact thing everyone knew to be true but didn't have the balls or brains to articulate.

A few engaged him on politics or the feud. Blair Olmstead (a male "Blair," no joke), who'd served in the House too as a loony California Dem, seemed to think he'd ascended to a similar stature. Holding a champagne flute, ascot around his scrawny neck, he stepped into the ring.

"The discourse has become so productized," he mused. "You get entire ecosystems spawning around one worldview or another. Church, academia. Media of course—literally, every last news item is fundraising fodder. When politics infects every last one of our institutions, polarization becomes a fait accompli."

Faces turned from Blair to Rock, who'd been chatting up a married beauty who used to play lacrosse.

Rock dipped his head thoughtfully. "The ascot is gay."

Blair tittered—hollow, nasal.

"Not gay as in odd or merry," Rock said. "*Gay*-gay. Effeminate. Homosexual. Signaling to others that you enjoy…"

He gave examples of acts an ascot-wearer might enjoy.

Dinner was barbecue fare on Cross Campus, the large central quad, and would include all reunion classes—not just his own '96 but '86, '76, on down to the dinosaurs still hanging on from WWII and earlier. More Olmstead-esque pontification was inevitable, and Rock played his garrulous role.

The organizers had lined the quad with wine-tasting tents featuring vintages either owned or operated by classmates. Rock reached past rows of quarter-inch pours in plastic cups, taking bottles by the neck.

Questioned once, he said, "I'm supposed to invest on the basis of two measly sips? No."

As he awaited the late hour of his conquest, thinking longingly of the sledgehammer back at the room, he enjoyed himself. He gladhanded and recalled hijinks of younger days, and introduced a fresh-faced oh-sixer to the old "necking nook" of Harkness Hall. He filled up on burgers and tapenade.

He saw other Pruitts. Other Pruitts saw him. He would nod their way and even talked at length to Arnold Junior, class of seventy-six, big deal at the American Enterprise Institute. But he wasn't going out of his way.

Every so often, he would gaze across the quad to Sterling Library.

It goaded him.

He imagined the face. That smug, superior face, trained on a book. *We read, therefore our worldview trumps yours.* Rock's jaw tightened to the point where his eardrums hurt.

The liberal stranglehold here hadn't been supposed to matter. It was presumed he would float along among the privileged, tailgating with senators, sailing in Rhode Island over breaks, enlarging his already large name by charm and wit and the phenomenal talents all had observed through Rock's adolescence.

On his last day of prep school, bags packed for New Haven, an English teacher he'd frequently sparred with in class had said, "I can't say it's been a pleasure, Rock, but here we are. My grandkids will be amazed I knew you."

When Derek Dickerson had died—in the dorm room they'd shared, on a night when half the freshman class had seen them running riot over campus—the Pruitt machine had gone to work. They'd boxed out media and intimidated police, and kept Rock out of jail—but his foregone ascension to head of the clan was kaput.

No more background shots of Rock at aunts' or uncles' swearing in. No more invites to be a fly-on-the-wall at Jonathan Pruitt's cabinet meetings.

In the twenty-three years since Dickerson's death, Rock's last name had opened plenty of doors. But the toughies, the ones with gold behind them, he'd had to bust down himself. The House seat in Georgia, the dinky third district, which should've been a Pruitt lock, he had won with zero family help. When Democrats in Congress went after him—that sexy beast Charlotte Gallagher's fingerprints all over the trumped-up charges—he'd been left to fend for himself.

After losing the House seat, Rock had caught on with Pruitt Capital and made them all boatloads of cash with his distressed-medical-debt instrument. Did anyone thank him? Did Jonathan Pruitt get off his high horse to acknowledge the multitude of campaign ads and whispered slurs Rock's genius stroke had financed?

Nope.

Rock could still recall the Great Man's words when he'd inquired after the ambassadorship of Thailand, a country Rock had toured with much pleasure in his early twenties. They were sitting in the Oval Office.

"Scandal shall not tarnish the first Pruitt presidency."

That was Jonathan Pruitt. Like Robert E. Lee, the man had no vices. The Pruitt brand—upstanding, disciplined, righteous—superseded all other considerations.

The refusal had sent Rock into a tailspin, the sort of rotten downward spiral Vegas can inspire. Rock next threw himself into a series of speculative ventures, a fourth New York airport, arctic fracking, a chain of private, values-based schools in the Midwest.

Stubbornly, masochistically, he poured his time and fortune into each. The airport never found a borough. The schools went belly-up within ten months. The man running them turned out to be a pedophile—as the director who'd vetted him, Rock faced personal legal jeopardy.

Only last month, he got final word from the drillers: Baffin Island had zip, two hundred thousand square miles and not a drop of unexploited oil. He briefly entertained the idea of finding a plane and a brick of cocaine and shooting up every caribou and Arctic hare in the miserable, Godforsaken place.

Instead, he came to this reunion.

❧

The sun set over New Haven, dirtying the sky to a pink-orange blear. Rock welcomed the cooler temps as his suit had gotten stuffy. He left the barbecue with juice in his step.

Tonight's sanctioned reunion activities were scant, some lecture and a Woolsey Hall concert. He skipped them to bar hop. His wife texted at the kids' bedtime and he Skyped with them, doing his froggy face for Isabelle, threatening Rock Junior with merciless titty-twisting if he didn't score at least three goals at hockey tomorrow.

Hanging up, Rock polished off a pitcher with three junior anthropology faculty who declined his offer to snag a hotel room. "Sure? They know me at the Hyatt. I can have that jacuzzi roped off. Get those bubbles good 'n' grimy."

At eleven thirty, he returned to his dorm in Silliman College. The sledgehammer was waiting in the center of the room. He hoisted it. In his alcohol-light hands, the thing felt wild and dangerous and like a tool of justice.

He slipped into his billowy car coat and stashed the sledgehammer inside. Leaving his entryway, heading up College Street, Rock burned with anticipation.

Any number of awful outcomes might occur. Rock felt this was the correct time and place for an awful outcome, surrounded by all this nostalgia and glorification of past. There would be symmetry in ending it here, where his life had derailed.

Either Yale takes everything from me, or I cold-cock her one.

The guard working the library vestibule wore a turban and neat beard. "We close in seven minutes, sir."

Rock lifted his cellphone, elbow brushing the concealed sledgehammer. "I'll be speedy. Snapping a few pics for old time's sake."

The guard smiled and waved him forward.

Rock strode through Sterling's spectacular reading room, where students were shelving volumes and scooping up notebooks to leave. Stained-glass windows lurked at either side, lead veined, deep blues and looming magentas. A woody, vanilla odor permeated the space.

Rock, who was surely giving off aromas of his own, found it nauseating. This place, so staid and pompous, made him unwell. Bloodlust beyond anything he'd felt at Mory's or elsewhere gripped him.

At the bank of elevators leading to the stacks, another guard manned a desk. He opened his mouth to speak.

"Six minutes?" Rock preempted.

The man pushed a button under his desk. Accordion doors folded open, permitting Rock onto a rickety elevator.

The buttons numbered to twenty-three. Rock pushed for the top floor. The car clanked and wheezed, and began its groaning ascent.

Rock's heart galloped. The sledgehammer's steel was cold through his shirt. He was close—and with every screeching inch of cable, closer. He felt like a prizefighter in a stadium tunnel, the way forward narrow and sweet violence ahead.

The elevator opened at twenty-three. Rock exited to a landing, from which radiated a dozen aisles of books. A red *Exit* sign supplied the only light, casting dim crimson down one corridor.

Visitors to the stacks were supposed to flip on lights as needed, but Rock didn't want light. He headed down the center corridor, soft footsteps echoing, hundreds of yeasty books glaring at him from their dark recesses. He reached an oval window and peered through.

In the distance was the New Haven skyline, modest, spotty.

He wasn't here for the view. He was here for what lay directly below.

The balcony.

The window's brass lock was rubbed green. Rock tried thumbing it open, but the mechanism wouldn't twist. He put his hip into it, then his shoulder, then his whole body—all six-four, two hundred fifteen pounds. Nothing budged the lock.

He took out his cellphone and shined its flashlight outside. Through the oval glass, he saw an exterior bracket fixing the window to its stone casing. The bracket was bolted-on metal—a permanent, irreversible measure disabling the window.

Damn.

Rock cursed Yale's nanny-state mentality and himself for not anticipating it. During his time here, access to the Sterling roof from twenty-three had been widely known. Naturally, so long as lawyers still lived and breathed, a small, unregulated joy like this couldn't be allowed.

He slugged the window. It burbled in place. Solid three-quarter-inch glass.

Would the sledgehammer do the trick?

It didn't matter. The window was bisected by lead, and neither segment was large enough to fit through.

He backtracked to the elevators. As he was boarding, an announcement came over the public address.

"The time is now eleven forty-five. Sterling Library is closed. Please exit and bring all books to the front desk."

Rock rammed his knuckle into the button for twenty-two. The door folded shut. He rode down one flight. He burst off the car and into the center aisle, rambling, kicking books from the stacks in his wake.

He reached the oval window, which looked identical to the one a floor up, and whipped out his cell.

He looked out.

No bracket.

God bless lazy liberals. Quickly, the alcohol in his veins returning to a boil, Rock unlatched the window and stepped through onto the balcony.

The night air was brisk, black, alive. Rock felt like he could dive forward and be carried—or fly if necessary—wherever he wanted. He felt he could swipe his fist out across this railing and rip every light from the city.

He looked up. The balcony of Twenty-Three was four feet overhead, too high to reach—probably why they hadn't bothered neutering this window. The underside of the balcony was artfully scalloped, its smooth, round stone giving no grip points.

Rock thought for three seconds.

The railing. He could reach if he stood on the railing.

He rolled his shoulders forward, cracked his jaw.

It was a bad idea. Not only using the railing here, but the whole shenanigan—he understood this in a blink, the way he'd once seen himself on a TV monitor during a debate, belittling an old tax-and-spender who used a cane, and known from the image alone that the takedown was a mistake. (In the following weeks, surrogates and robo-calls had accomplished the same with no likability hit to Rock.)

Revenge against Yale would be magnificent, but wasn't this pure symbol? It wouldn't gain him a thing. It wouldn't forge a path to that Virginia Senate seat coming open next year. It was adolescent, an elaborate raising of his middle finger.

This truth was known to Rock's brain—and if Rock was a man who decided matters with his brain, he might've stopped.

Rock Pruitt was not such a man. He commonly walled off certain truths or episodes from conscious thought. Climate studies. The night of Derek Dickerson's death. Watching *Guys and Dolls* as a horny fifteen-year-old desperate to snag a cheerleader.

If the brain wasn't subjugated—fully, brutally—it betrayed you. When weak parts of you wanted a thing, your brain served up the rationale, sure as some sycophantic aide slipping you a position paper he knows mirrors your opinion perfectly.

It was what he hated about the left. When Charlotte Gallagher had struck gold with SmartWidget, flipping the money advantage the Pruitts had traditionally enjoyed, where had that Gallagher crusade for campaign-finance reform gone? Into Nantucket Sound, apparently. A cavalcade of professors had lined up to justify the hypocrisy, publishing opinion pieces explaining what overwhelming advantage the wealthy still enjoyed, academic papers measuring—by some tortured method—what outsize influence the rich had in politics, even net the boundless SmartWidget cash.

Shrugging off the insanity of his pursuit, Rock hiked up to the railing. The stone was a good four inches wide, a gymnast's beam. He stood with feet diagonal, the heels of his wingtips hanging over. His soles sent pebbles on three-hundred-foot dives. The rush constituted a new category of drug.

A gust wobbled him. Rock swung one foot back behind him, then forward, then bent his opposite knee and spread both arms wide for balance.

Better get moving.

He pivoted to face Sterling and reached high for the balcony above. He managed to gain its bottom with the fingertips of his right hand. While he was extending his left arm to firm up the grip and start pulling himself up, his jacket came open.

The sledgehammer fell.

Rock clamped his knees shut, catching its heavy head between his knees. He froze in this position, teeth grinding, the face of the sledgehammer digging into his suitpants, handle dangling in the chasm below.

Five seconds.

Ten.

His knees quavered. The sledgehammer began slipping.

He needed to reach down with a hand. Which one, though? His right must have the stronger grip. Sucking in a breath, he took his left hand from the railing, causing his body to swing momentarily above the Trumbull College courtyard below, and rolled that shoulder toward the ground, relaxing his kneecaps at the same time.

It was a lot of coordinated movement, probably too much in his state.

He missed.

The sledgehammer began a sickening, end-over-end tumble for the ground. By reflex, Rock snapped his feet together and caught the handle between his shoes. The rest dangled out over the courtyard.

Knowing this hold was even more tenuous, Rock raised both knees to his chest and transferred the sledgehammer from his feet to his hands—the motion kinking his body like a sweaty, desperate Slinky.

Terrific pressure strained the arm still holding on above, the wrist torqueing, the shoulder joint crackling.

Still, he kept his grip.

He simultaneously pulled himself up another four inches and heaved the sledgehammer up, managing to cartwheel it between two wrought-iron bars of the twenty-third-floor balcony. The impact shook the stone he was holding—the *boom* must've been audible half a mile away.

Now Rock could focus on getting himself up. Using the side of Sterling for leverage, he walked his wingtips up to a point where his body nearly paralleled the ground. Then he began working his hands up the spindles, biting his lip, feeling the effort in his armpits.

Finally, he swung over the railing onto the top balcony.

No sweat. Just like fetching the whiffle ball from Old Man Gaither's backyard.

The sledgehammer was waiting on the balcony floor. He retrieved it with glee, spinning it in his palm.

The roof was just a catwalk away. Rock bounded up the diamond-checkered steps, his shoes' *smack, smack, smack* echoing to the street—to the very land Pruitt Riflery had once occupied. He'd just sighted the first of the building's dual roof spires when lights came on inside.

They were coming for him.

He ran faster. Reaching the roof, he inhaled cold, clean air. His shoes felt spongy on the tar and gravel surface.

He heard metal on metal from below, then clattering.

Then footsteps.

He crossed the roof, circling past the spires to the west side.

There! Straddling the far edge of a lone section of peaked roof, head bowed, collared shirt greenish by the moonlight.

The reader.

Like most statues, he knew he was better than you. He wore this pensive, faux-humble expression, holding the book with one hand meekly draped over the top. The pose had a persecuted vibe.

All he asks is a place to read, a place of peace and contemplation.

Sure! Rock thought wildly. *I know just the place—how about the top of a tall building? That way you can look down on the rest of us unworthy brutes.*

He had despised this statue as an undergrad. He'd journeyed up here maybe a half dozen times with Derek Dickerson or another pal, often trashed, but never thought to do anything.

He'd been a boy then. He hadn't understood institutions were meant to be destroyed—like the wooden pyre at the end of Burning Man.

Rock took a running go at it. The sledgehammer on his shoulder, he accelerated along the tar and gravel, carrying the momentum two steps up the peaked slope and swinging, his lead foot planting on the roof's edge, his weight dropping into his hips —Rock had hit cleanup for the baseball Elis all four seasons—and unloading.

The head fractured but didn't sever. Rock took another hack. A blow to the neck sent half the collar flying to the street below. A shoulder shot made a delicious *crunch.*

He began swinging faster, barely aiming, aware that his mouth was stretched wide and grotesque hisses were coming out. *Bam, doink, crack.*

He would've liked to cleave the book, but it was carved tight against the reader's chest with too much surrounding stone. The head, though, was ready to say *sayonara.* Rock's initial barrage had left it sagging, twisted a few degrees right as though distracted by some hubbub in the periphery.

Yeah, baby, Rock thought. *I got some hubbub for ya.*

The energy spreading down his body was orgasmic. He was sweating with exertion, but his muscles weren't tired. They felt supercharged. Had his dress shirt split down its back a là the Incredible Hulk, Rock wouldn't have batted an eye.

He took his last swing. The face of the sledgehammer connected squarely, and off flew the reader's head—a gray hunk, airborne, toppling, dumb, beautiful.

He never heard it land. Sirens split the air, and an army was upon him.

❧

Rock chucked the sledgehammer in the general direction of the reader's head. He started for the north side of the roof, thinking to…well, he didn't know, but the point became moot when a door between the spires opened and two security guards emerged.

Tits.

He sprinted for the catwalk. That direction was clear—the rent-a-cops had come up by the conventional janitorial route—and Rock hurtled down the steps, his ears ringing, a dervish in the night. It was impossible that a forty-two-year-old former congressman, a member of the storied Pruitt dynasty, was so engaged, but here he was.

He reached the balcony of twenty-three. The roof banged with footsteps: they were coming for him. Hard. Rock looked out across New Haven. Police cruisers had pulled up on Elm and Wall—flashers wild, parked crookedly—but they weren't directly below on York Street.

He lowered himself over the railing, dangling momentarily as before, free over the campus, clutching, lilting. He squeezed his midsection to get swinging, out, in, out…and let go just after the apex. He landed in a heap on the balcony below.

He repeated this insanity ten more times. No two drops were the same. By the time he'd descended to the twelfth floor, both elbows had bled through his suit and his spine felt like a towel in a locker-room snap fight.

Rock picked himself up with the idea of dashing inside here, at twelve, but the lights were on inside. He could see through the stacks to the elevator bank, where a guard had just disembarked.

The guard saw him at the same time he saw the guard.

There were balconies all the way down to three, but Rock didn't feel he could keep going this way—they could run stairs or ride elevators faster than he could lower himself. He could bum-rush the guard. This appealed to Rock on many levels, but it would take too long. He'd be overrun.

There was another way down.

He turned away from the guard, who was racing toward him now, and stepped atop the railing. He was getting used to these bad boys—he flexed his knees twice, like Randy "Macho Man" Savage warming up the top ring rope at WrestleMania. Directly underneath was a sort of foliage moat, bushes and mid-sized trees. Ornamental spiked fences surrounded some Yale buildings, but he couldn't see well enough in the dark to know if one lurked here.

He emptied his lungs, emptied his mind, and jumped.

Soaring through the air, Rock lost his stomach. He'd skydived before and knew the sensation, but still it chilled him to the core. He felt his feet drifting out in front of him and realized he'd given exactly zero thought to how he should land. The ride was smooth, free, cleansing—like leaving a hooker.

Rudely, a pad of high branches and thorns met him. A hundred arrows pierced his back and butt. He tumbled through one level of branches, then another, his pants and face getting flayed and head jerking unnaturally. A limb poked him right between the eyes, stopping him for a moment before gravity insisted he resume falling.

The pinball route down slowed Rock—saved him, in fact. He landed in a sprinter's stance, his knee in some herb-smelling ground cover.

He ran pell-mell. He didn't waste a glance at traffic lights crossing Elm Street, cut east toward Old Campus, dashed up High Street.

The gate on this side of Old Campus—the double quad where most freshmen lived—was locked, but Rock's reunion badge blipped it green.

"That's him!" a cop yelled from Elm. "Go, *other way!*"

Rock banged through the gate and tore ten yards into Old Campus. Then hammer-stomped in place, thinking where to go.

Back to Silliman?

Ahead to the train station?

Every inch of his skin stung. He felt like he'd just fought a porcupine.

Cops appeared at the Elm Street gate.

More cops at High Street, the direction he'd come from.

Rock u-turned for the south gate, the only escape left. Fuzzy blue rimmed the craggy tops of Dwight Hall, McClellan Hall, Chittenden Hall—centuries-old campus icons.

Rock ran. He tripped on cobblestone and blew through a midnight couple holding hands, spinning the dude to the lawn.

Three-quarters of the way across the quad, Rock saw— unmistakably through the south gate—more blue lights.

He was surrounded.

The air became hot or busy or something, just for a snap, before they tackled him.

Rock's head bounced off cobblestone. His wrists were joined viciously, and he opened his mouth to scream where he was going to bury these *bleepity-bleeping bleeps* and their entire families when a hood closed over his head.

Quickly he was yanked to his feet and forced ahead, blind, by at least two pairs of hands in his back.

His captors said nothing, only kept shoving him. When Rock's feet dragged, they gripped him by the belt and coat and ran him forward. A card reader beeped. Rock felt himself being boosted over a step.

They were entering a building. *A building on Old Campus?*

The hood chafed the wounds on his face, and whatever was around his wrists—zip ties?—cut his skin. They were racing down a flight of stairs, now another. Rock stumbled, slamming the man in front of him. The man said nothing, only kept them hustling ahead.

The temperature plummeted. Rock smelled, what, wet earth? Vines? Rot?

Were they in some cellar or sub-basement?

Only now did the men speak. So scrambled was Rock's brain, between booze and sledgehammers and his abduction, that he only heard disconnected syllables.

"On your belly."

Rock stood dumbly.

A captor shoved him to the ground, which was indeed mud. Rock crawled on his elbows in the direction indicated by their barks and prods. He struggled through what could've been a doorway or tunnel entrance, the ground briefly stone, then mud again.

He fell repeatedly. His hood and car coat—did he still have that rag?—were caked solid. Dirt filled his teeth and nostrils. He'd possibly pissed himself.

He crawled fifteen yards before being told to stand. It was a tunnel, some sort of tunnel. Rock could feel a limestone wall with the fingertips of his left hand. Drips fell somewhere, long, tortured *plops*.

Now they walked briskly. The men permitted Rock to move by himself but never got more than a shirt-grip away.

Military.

Rock had dealt with mercenaries in various capacities, once

through Pruitt Capital, other times working for the family's darker tentacles. He knew how they operated. They didn't differentiate cruelty from efficiency.

They reached a door. Rock heard a combination lock spin and a progression of *clinks* as the mechanism disengaged. A boot clapped something solid.

Hardwood? Marble?

A walkie-talkie rattled, a sound Rock hadn't picked out of the chaos before.

"The package is in hand," said a voice near Rock.

Static made the response inaudible.

The voice said, "Caesar-One is ready for him?"

After another static-heavy response, Rock was led aboveground—or so it seemed by the air, still frigid but antiseptic now, lemony to the point of feeling astringent on his neck. These stairs were steeper and slightly spiraled. He had the sense of climbing into a fairy tale, up to the chamber of some sequestered beast or princess.

Through another door, the path leveled. Rock recognized the intermittent heat of recessed torches on his skin.

He wasn't in Old Campus.

Nowhere in Old Campus felt like this. He was entering a realm of tradition and accumulated glory, of secrets, of silence. A place that didn't apologize for greatness, too entrenched to care about Yale's recent—in its timescale—turn toward soft-headed progressivism.

Rock stood at last in the center of a room. When his captors tore off his hood, he popped his eyes and breathed, and *breathed*, feeling like he'd just escaped a tomb.

In fact, he was in a tomb—and seated in a wheelchair before him was one of the most powerful men on Earth.

CHAPTER 4

THE STARS MORE OR LESS ALIGNED FOR SAM ON PUBLIC TRANSIT, putting her and Joss into New Haven at six-thirty. It was plenty light out, so Sam decided they should economize and walk from the train station.

Joss gave the obligatory teenage groan at forced physical exertion, but her mood improved as they approached Yale. Campus was, truly, an outdoor architecture museum. Sprawling New Haven Green, the towering stone goalposts of Dwight Chapel—Sam caught her daughter's eyes swelling at the vast, effortless art.

"Mom, is this about climate change?" Joss asked, staring down at a sidewalk chalk sign.

Sam stooped to read. *YOUR WATER IS RED AND OWED BACK TO ITS PEOPLE.*

"Could be," she said. "Or Native American rights?"

Joss twisted to read from another angle. She'd recently taken an interest in politics—like many girls her age, she was all in for Owen Gallagher in the next election.

Sam remembered, as a freshman, puzzling over these obtuse slogans scribbled by various activist groups. She envied her daughter now, discovering new injustices and societal ills to care about. It made a sad contrast to Sam's own engagement level today—too busy to educate herself, taking her news from social media or late-night comics.

They arrived at Silliman College, the dorm location for the ninety-six reunion, with the sun still full over the horizon. Sam met a few classmates in the courtyard, smiling amiably at those she recognized but couldn't name, shrieking and throwing her arms around those she could.

Tape arrows labeled *Registration* marked the cobblestone path to entryway A. Sam made a halfhearted attempt to leave Joss hanging out with a group of friends—"I'll go sign us in, back quick"—but Joss broke away too. As they stepped along the arrows, Sam pointed out a corkboard of flyers for various clubs.

"Wanna just wait here, check out the flyers?"

"No, I'm good," Joss said. "I'll follow you."

Sam approached the check-in room, wringing her hands.

She hadn't paid for Joss. Probably Yale had a hardship rate, some need-based discount, but she hadn't gotten her stuff together and figured it out. She'd only registered herself.

Which was worse: lying to your daughter, or shattering the illusion that her situation—and yours—was the same as everybody else's?

Sam split the difference.

"Okay, truth time," she said. "I didn't officially register you as an attendee."

Color drained from Joss's face.

"It's no big deal," Sam insisted. "All it means is you don't get the swag."

"Swag?"

"Yeah," Sam said. "Yale pens, Yale water bottle. That stuff."

"Do I—can I still walk around?"

Is she starting to sniffle?

"Absolutely!" Sam said. "No sweat whatsoever."

"And, like, food? Can I eat meals with you, or…?"

"Of course. It's all buffets anyway, you just cruise right through with me."

"What if they want ID? Or some kind of ticket? They'll kick me out, I—"

"They will not kick you out," Sam said. "And we'll definitely get to check out all those lectures together, just like we planned. Good? Cool?"

Sam's last two claims were unverified, but at the ten-year reunion, nobody had gotten carded at the pasta salad station or before "China in the Twenty-First Century and Beyond."

"Cool," Joss said. "I guess."

She ambled over to the corkboard, looking ready to disappear into it.

Sam closed her eyes and almost wished Abe were here. Abe dealt with Joss's freak-outs better. He knew how to ride them out, how to make himself human foam that just absorbed their daughter's stress—rather than amplify it like Sam.

In the registration room, a cheery girl in a Yale nineteen cap handed Sam a tote bag, information folder, and magnetic badge attached to lanyard.

"Now it says here," the girl said, referencing a clipboard, "that your account has a balance due. Did you want to take care of that now?"

Sam leaned closer to see. "I—I thought I paid in full?"

As the girl paged forward and backward for confirming documents, Sam fished around for credit cards. Which was more likely to accept a big charge, Discover or United Visa? She thought Abe had put the amps on Discover, but Joss's ballet autopay came out of Visa…

"No."

For a moment, the girl's word hung in the air. Sam glanced out the window to the courtyard, where a group of grownups were chatting while golden-haired children chased each other around the perimeter. They looked like two or three families who knew each other from trips to Vail or Yale-Harvard tailgates.

Sam imagined one of her old friends walking into registration this very instant, stopping short at her humiliation.

Then the Yale nineteen girl looked up with a sunny frown. "Sorry, I'm wrong. I was totally looking at the line above yours!"

As Sam's heart restarted, she gathered her reunion materials. She fetched Joss—slumped, biting her nails—from the corkboard, and they headed to their room in entryway H.

The dorm was empty and stark, all plaster and heavy wood. A tremendous fireplace anchored the common room, inoperable —the flues had been boarded up during Sam's undergrad days. She and Joss took a pit stop at the bathroom shared with the suite across the hall, then dropped their bags in a corner and settled.

Joss eyed a cast-iron radiator. "You lived here, like, four years?"

"Believe it or not," Sam said. "We didn't come for the amenities."

Despite the digs, their mood was improved from the registration scare. All logistical snafus had been conquered. They were on a college campus for the next three days—no work, no school, surrounded by important architecture and thought.

Joss was reading through a listing of sample courses. "Intersecting Studies of Dance and Quantum Physics!" Her jaw literally dropped. "Can we go?"

Sam took the pamphlet, whose serifed print indicated the lecture would happen Saturday at eleven-fifteen.

"We can do anything you want to do."

Joss rose up her tiptoes as though *en pointe*, humming with excitement. It was exactly the sort of moment Sam had hoped for.

Then her phone buzzed.

She forced her eyes off the gorgeously produced pamphlet and her even more gorgeous daughter.

It was a text from Abe.

wheres the 19v charger?

Sam glanced to the left-side pocket of her duffel.

here, she wrote. *the Zoom takes 19v.*

His reply was immediate. *need it for gig, just came in. express delivery ($$$)*

Sam's head flopped back like her neck was a hinge.

When Joss looked over, she caught herself and—forcing a smile—gestured for Joss to keep reading the listings.

She texted, *can't you ask Quinn for one? or Aida?*

He didn't need it immediately. Even with the client paying for express delivery, Abe's gigs still carried a minimum four days' turnaround.

He took his time replying, and Sam could visualize him perfectly—pacing, grinding two fingers into his bare head until the knuckles bowed concavely. If he was really pissed, if the client was one of those "fantastically promising" singer-songwriters he hoped to sleep with, he might slap their ratty futon in frustration.

Nowhere in his mind, of course, was the consideration that she might need the charger for her Pruitt-Gallagher documentary.

Finally, he replied.

can't do my job without juice

Sam felt dragged down. She couldn't slog the adapter back to Brooklyn. Which he knew. There were adapters to be had, from either of the friends she'd mentioned or, absolute worst case, by heading into the city and borrowing one from WNYC. She had inflicted a minor, completely inadvertent inconvenience upon him, and now he was grilling her.

He was, basically, being an ass.

Oh, it wasn't much. Many days she endured worse. In this

moment, though, looking out on the stately brick courtyard of Silliman College, she and Joss reading descriptions of talks by world-famous scholars? The cruelty was exquisite, like some mossy boulder chucked into the middle of a pristine pool.

Five years.

Five more years of this.

In five years, Joss would leave for college—and Sam would leave Abe. She would be forty-eight years old. Regularly coloring her hair. Done having kids, staring menopause in the face.

But free.

The thought of another half decade of bickering was soul-sucking, but Joss had shown enough signs of fraying that Sam felt she had no choice. Her daughter's bond with Abe was too strong. Last spring when he'd been away six days moving his mother into an Arizona nursing home, she'd suffered. Suddenly, the sleeves of all her shirts were too long. When an ant infestation swarmed their kitchen—a thing Abe always took care of—she'd had something like a panic attack, sobbing, hyperventilating.

Sam's own parents had divorced when she was a senior in high school. The news blindsided her. She'd stopped doing her schoolwork. Her GPA nosedived. It might've even cost her Yale—her admission had been pending second semester marks—if Sam's guidance counselor hadn't called the admissions office and pleaded on her behalf.

And Sam had been seventeen then. Joss was fourteen. Losing Abe would devastate her.

If she lost Abe. Sam supposed the custody choice would be Joss's, and it seemed like no slam-dunk she would pick Sam. Joss didn't understand, couldn't understand at her age, so many of her father's shortcomings. Sam had shielded her from the worst: his infidelity, his total cowardice when it came to the tough business of telling their child no.

To Joss, her father was mellow and centered, the man who'd taught her to ride a bike and finger E minor.

Sam ignored Abe's last text.

"Let's hang our clothes, alright?" she said. "We don't want our dresses looking like elephant hide for Saturday."

Joss agreed, walking her bag toward the two bedrooms. "Which one do I sleep in?"

Sam pointed to the door whose laminated label read *Samantha Lessing (Isaacson)*. "That one. It's both of ours."

Joss's shoulders sagged and she was assuming a facial expression that conveyed just how lame she found the idea of rooming with her mother, when the common-room door burst open.

"Oh my God, Sam Lessing, you made it!"

Laurel Trowbridge rushed in, leaving her gold-buckled bag in the entryway, wrapping Sam in a hug. The two had roomed together junior and senior years, and they had arranged to room together here. Laurel looked every bit the San Franciscan she was, classic platinum hair framing her face, stud earrings, athletic slim pants ready for yoga or a hike up Mount Tamalpais.

"It's so refreshing to see you," she said. "My travel day was nuts, but it's all worth it now."

The two women looked at each other. Sam felt more emotion than she'd expected. Laurel had been such a fixture in her life, and seeing her brought that part of her youth screaming back. Laurel's eyes, that sparkly squint, were hopeful as Friday night or first rehearsal.

They also made her think of Jamie Gallagher.

Laurel, after a gushing sigh, turned to Joss. "And you! Look how stylish. Last time I saw you, you thought jeans were evil. I heard you're becoming quite the serious dancer?"

Joss kicked one foot behind the opposite heel. "I just went to five-day-a-week practice."

"Wow, good for you. Last month I was at a writer's retreat with a woman who choreographs for the ballet, NYC. Absolutely brilliant—so many interesting things to say about how dance is evolving."

"Evolving?"

"Yes, I'll tell you all about it!" Laurel ducked out to the entryway for her bag, fluttering her fingers at some other arrival, and ducked back in. "I am so excited we all get to be roomies. Won't this be fun?"

She flopped her wrists open at her chest, a cheesy gesture that, coming from Sam, would've earned Joss's best gag-me face. Sam figured she would cut Laurel some slack, possibly swell her eyes and turn slowly away—a lesser expression of disdain.

Instead, Joss did a half pirouette and said, "So fun!"

⚜

Dinner was roast turkey or veggie lasagna in the courtyard. Sam staked out a table with Laural and Joss—who thankfully got no scrutiny from the woman carving turkey onto plates—but ate most of her food on the move, finding classmates.

It was her first chance to have those conversations she'd imagined back in Brooklyn, to recover that core enthusiasm for life.

And?

There were nice moments. Keenan from the dining hall talked about loathing the advertising work he did but liking his coworkers. They both agreed that college, this Utopian situation financed by your parents or your own future insolvency, teed you up to get knocked flat by adult reality.

The wife of Sam's friend Sanjay shared stories of their teenager's scatter-shot choices about peer groups that made Sam struggle to keep wine from shooting out her nose.

Still, there was too much resume. *You went* where *from grad school? Into private equity?*

Well, I did a summer in finance too...

It was also Sam's first chance to record audio for the pinebox documentary.

She took about an hour warming up to it, deciding whom to interview. She found herself not wanting to do it in hearing range of Laurel, who'd been telling everybody how she was "growing her brand" by publishing short opinion pieces around the web.

Finally, with Laurel at the bar station and Joss having found a group of other teens—as teens will—Sam broached the topic with Eliana Rowe.

"How the feud *affected* me?" Eliana said, as though Sam's opening question had a grammar error.

"Right," Sam said. "You were political back then. Did it motivate you, being near two people whose families were so influential?"

Eliana's face only pinched more.

Sam added, "Or did it turn you off, all the drama?"

Because she sure looked turned off. Sam had picked Eliana assuming her background as a UNICEF director would make her a cooperative source.

Bad assumption.

"I was aware of the dynamic, vaguely," Eliana said. "I was busy with Shelter House. It wasn't something I thought much about."

She glanced down at the recorder in Sam's hand—disdainfully, it seemed to Sam. Sam asked a throwaway follow-up about whether she recalled her first time crossing paths with Rock Pruitt or Jamie Gallagher—"Not especially, no"—then switched off the Zoom.

Maybe Eliana was right. Maybe this was petty, sticking a mic in people's faces at a reunion. Small-minded. Sensational.

She decided to try again. Eliana had been kind of a downer during college—her opinion alone shouldn't decide this.

Gabe Navarro was hovering nearby. Gabe hadn't been politically involved at Yale, but he'd been in that same social set

Rock and—to a lesser extent—Jamie had. Plus, he was standing right here.

She gave her opening spiel.

Gabe said, "You mean that old rusty dagger? Or the coffin buried on Thomas Jefferson's farm?"

"No," Sam said. "Well, sure—if that's what you associate with the feud."

And here was the other problem: "pinebox vendetta" meant different things to different people.

Sam thought of it as a catchall reference to the families' long-running feud, this Hatfield-McCoy fight writ large. But there was also Gabe's conception of "pinebox," this dark mythology of the feud's origin. Some claimed it traced back to an ancient double-cross involving the Declaration of Independence. Others said a dagger bearing the Pruitt crest had killed an important Gallagher heir.

The clans' leaders downplayed this talk. When Jonathan Pruitt had been running for president, he'd famously joked, "I pledge to keep the family pentagrams out of the White House, locked up safe in my attic."

Rumors persisted, though. CNN still dusted off its five-part *Secrets, Relics, Betrayal: Unpacking the Pinebox Legend* every so often, stoking the intrigue.

Gabe said, "I dunno. If it was real, don't you think it would've come out by now? Two-hundred-however-many years?"

"Probably," Sam said. "Now that we have Instagram."

Gabe laughed, swaying a little. He'd had a cocktail or three. "Is your documentary going to go into Rock Pruitt and his roommate, that whole 'accident' deal?"

"Depends. I'm just planning to talk to people, see what comes out of conversations—conversations like the one we're having now."

Gabe stood up taller, seeming flattered. Sam felt a little guilty —she'd mentioned her WNYC affiliation in passing earlier. He probably thought this was some network project green-lighted to air next month.

Which it definitely wasn't.

He said, "I was around that night, you know. When Dickerson died? I saw them both, him and Rock."

"Really? What do you remember?"

"I remember they were outta-their-heads drunk. Standard operating procedure for them, of course."

"Of course." Sam shifted, moving the Zoom's mic closer. "The story was they'd argued, right?"

"More than argued."

Sam felt spider feet on her spine.

"You…and you saw it?"

"Yeah, I saw. It was at this party on Old Campus. Dickerson shoved Rock into an aquarium."

"Like a fish tank?"

"Uh-huh. I forget whose party it was, but they had this aquarium? Uh, what a mess. All their fish and water, and these little purple pebbles. Rock got drenched."

"He was mad?"

"He was livid," Gabe said. "They almost came to blows *right there.*"

Implying with his voice that later on, as they both understood, it had come to even worse.

Sam asked if he'd ever told this to the police.

"Sure, the police knew. They interviewed a bunch of us from the party." Gabe made a dubious face. "But they knew what answer they were coming back with. They were in the tank from the start."

An ex-teammate of Gabe's approached for a loud, back-slapping hug—effectively ending the interview.

Sam packed the Zoom away in its case and went looking for Joss.

Wow. Gabe had been infinitely more helpful than Eliana. She

would have to Google it later, but Sam felt confident the shattered aquarium had never gotten into the public record in ninety-three.

Which meant one of two things: either the Pruitts had suppressed the incident, or the police had decided on their own to be discreet with the investigation's details.

What other details were out there about Derek Dickerson's death? How many other witness testimonies had been swept under the rug?

The official cause of death had been "Undetermined." Dickerson's head had displayed evidence of blunt-force trauma, but the coroner hadn't been able to rule out alcohol poisoning as the fatal factor—with any wounds coming after the fact, perhaps in a fall. Rock Pruitt's story was that he'd returned to his Branford College dorm at two o'clock in the morning and found the body.

Was it possible somebody—*somebody at this reunion*—had seen Rock getting back to Branford? Who could verify that two o'clock claim?

Or refute it?

How about somebody who'd seen the next phase of the roommates' quarrel—after the busted aquarium?

Sam hadn't come expecting to investigate a cold-case murder this weekend. She hadn't even come with the idea of damaging the Pruitts. She didn't mind the Pruitts generally. She'd never voted for Jonathan Pruitt, but she felt like he'd been a reasonable president and actually preferred the clan's upright discipline to the many flavors of crazy populating today's right wing.

Rock Pruitt wasn't just any Pruitt, though. Rock was different. A known megalomaniac. A proud misogynist.

Sam wasn't sure quite how this fit into "recovering core enthusiasm for life," but she felt pretty confident it was worth doing.

Sam woke at six forty-five the next morning. She'd arranged beforehand to run East Rock with Laurel—the route they used to jog as undergrads on those preciously free afternoons, just because the sky was blue and their muscles called them to.

Slipping quietly from bed to the common room so she wouldn't rouse Joss, Sam dug running shoes out of her bag. She hadn't worn them in months and the laces felt weirdly tight across the bones of her foot. Shoes, spandex, sports bra—she geared up, tapped some Grapenuts into her mouth from a baggie, and sat on the couch waiting for Laurel.

She felt, eh, decent. She should've gone to bed an hour earlier and drunk less wine, but the night had been too full of possibility —especially after what Gabe Navarro had told her.

Though nobody had quite topped Gabe's aquarium nugget, other classmates had been willing to talk about Rock Pruitt on tape, like Kim Jaffe who remembered him laying "it" on a friend's shoulder in the dining hall.

Now, as noises started coming through Laurel's door, Sam imagined how she might describe the project to her former roommate. They'd gone all last night without talking about it, but Sam would have to today. It would be weird to keep keeping it from her.

It was going to be weird telling Laurel, too.

Sam figured she'd just do it now. Get it over before the run, push past any weirdness, carry on with the day. What she didn't figure was that her own door might open first.

"Mom, did you pack any white socks?" Joss asked, shuffling out with sneakers and fuzzy eyes.

Sam did a doubletake. Joss was athletic enough but just didn't...run. Recreationally. When Sam had mentioned her and Laurel's East Rock plan on the train yesterday, she'd shown no interest. Apparently, all Laurel's talk about marathons and Big Sur fun-runs had opened her mind.

"I did," Sam said, digging a pair from her bag. "Sure? I'm happy to bring you—thrilled, in fact—but you're in no way obligated."

"No, I'll go. It'll be refreshing."

Soon Laurel emerged in shorts and a Davenport College T-shirt, and Joss had cobbled together runnable clothes, and they headed out.

And, again, Sam had failed to mention her documentary.

Laurel held them up in the entryway when she remembered she needed to briefly confirm a timeline with her editor. "Sorry, they're rabid to get my next draft," she explained, tapping out a reply, then stashing her phone inside and leading them out by the College Street gate.

The morning was clear but not yet hot, the sun nudging into a white-wisped sky. Sam hopped from foot to foot, a bit chilly, eager to move.

Laurel held a button on her Fitbit. "What sort of pace are we thinking?"

Sam chuckled in Joss's direction. "We aren't what you'd call regular runners. Be gentle."

Joss huffed at her as they spread out three abreast on the sidewalk.

The run was spectacular. They had Whitney Avenue all to themselves at this hour, not a car in sight. Crisp air swelled Sam's lungs as they headed due north up Science Hill, passing Victorian homes repurposed into graduate department buildings. Sam's legs stretched out pleasurably before her, each step like the first off a crowded train. She didn't give a single thought to breathing or heel strike or arm motion, just going, pavement zooming by underfoot.

Maybe exercise should be a cornerstone of these next five years. Clarissa from WNYC ran—they could be run buds. Sam could take up tennis or join that ultimate Frisbee game, Saturday mornings in Prospect Park.

They were on Science Hill, so why not do some math? Exercise plus more substantial friendships, plus Joss. Could that equal a life? A life worthy of years forty-three to forty-eight, arguably the tail end of her prime?

Once they had settled into a pace, Sam asked, "Still loving San Francisco?"

"Immensely," Laurel said. "No way I could go back." She'd grown up around Boston. "All the causes I'm involved in, my professional network…the Bay Area's home now."

"Makes sense." They passed the bronze horned dinosaur of Peabody Museum on their left. "You're still seeing that civil rights lawyer?"

"He didn't work out," Laurel said. "It got strange—he ended up being very jealous of my critique partner, who I've been friends with forever, way before him."

"Guys can be like that."

"But, you know, I'm out there. Dating." Laurel glanced left then right at a cross-street. "How's Abe?"

Sam thought her tone contained a hint of gloat, but she might've just been reading into it.

"Jamming along," she said with a glance at Joss.

"He was doing those Fiverr gigs."

"Right. He actually does well there. I thought it was kind of bogus at first, honestly, but I guess enough people need these freelance music services."

"And you're still happy at WNYC?"

"Most days," Sam said. "We produced this piece on the exotic bird trade in Nicaragua. God—it's awful, from every possible angle. Ninety percent of the animals die in transit."

"That is awful. What was your distro strategy? Just on the network or something like VOD or direct sale?"

"Just our network."

Laurel made an ambiguous noise as they passed into East Rock Park proper, leaving behind Victorian buildings for tree-rimmed meadows.

"I know people," she said. "People in serious film, who could help expose it to a broader audience. If that interests you."

Sam wondered who these West Coast people were and how their "serious" films differed from the ones she and her colleagues in New York had been producing for decades.

"Thanks. Yeah, I'll let you know."

Soon they reached the summit. Laurel cruised to a stop at their traditional break point, where two coin-operated binoculars overlooked New Haven. Sam slowed in the last ten yards to let Joss catch up. Her daughter had managed admirably but fallen back as the grade had increased. They huffed together into a line with Laurel.

Laurel unstuck two reusable bottles from the small of her back. "Water?"

Sam accepted one and twisted off the cap. She took a swallow and handed it to Joss, who drank hard.

As they took in the view—distant New Haven Harbor, the bright bricks of Kline Biology tower looming over the leafy campus quads—Sam was keenly aware that she *still* hadn't filled Laurel in on the pinebox documentary.

Every time she opened her mouth to do it, she felt her whole body clench against what she knew would come next.

The murmured *"Oh really?"* The commentary about the piece's marketability. And laced like some gummy preservative through every word, the comparison—implied if not explicit—to Laurel's own achievements.

Why does it have to feel like this?

She didn't want friendship with Laurel to be a chore. She didn't want to engage in passive-aggressive quibbling. Part of her had figured this weekend would be different, that fortysomethings were past the subtle digs and one-upping. Another part of her, though, had known they weren't.

Sam found it occasionally unbelievable two people who'd lived together as long as she and Laurel had—two years here, plus another six months in the city before Laurel headed west—could have so much latent tension between them.

The factors that'd placed and kept them together in college had always been superficial: politics, gender sensibilities, shared interests in the arts. Their personalities fit imperfectly at best. Sam admired Laurel's spirit and desire to improve herself—and others' selves—but just couldn't join in without feeling silly.

At Yale, the dynamic had benefited from the presence of Jamie Gallagher—the third leg of Sam's primary social triangle. Jamie had Laurel's same earnestness, and belonging to the first family of American Liberalism raised him above the pissing contests that had so turned off Sam.

The triangle held marvelously until the very end. There'd always been something in Sam and Jamie's bond, an easy depth that threatened to tilt the triangle. They would end up on stone steps at two in the morning, or wasting some rainy afternoon across a table at the Daily Cafe, Jamie's rucksack between them.

Jamie had serious demons stemming from his family situation, which explained—and took the edge off, in Sam's mind —his extreme idealism. He had some deep wound or need, and the mystery of that void drew Sam to him. Here was a guy with the means to possess anything in the world except what he wanted: purity.

Moral and intellectual purity.

Sam had seen it coming in the spring—Jamie's feelings growing beyond friendship. It was a completely natural and predictable phenomenon, pairing up as college wound down. Sam felt the urge too but resisted. Jamie was headed to the Peace Corps; she was headed to New York to cut her teeth on minor Chekhov productions. What was the point? Why bother?

Remembering now, as she took in the vista once more before starting the run back down to Silliman, Sam ached at her twenty-two-year-old idiocy.

Despite Sam's restraint with Jamie, Laurel had picked up on the new vibe. The last couple months in their suite were chippy. They bickered over laundry and computer time—Sam didn't have one and had always shared Laurel's laptop, a practice Laurel ended without explanation.

They did have one moment, she and Jamie. That final night at Yale, when people had danced and toasted and told stories and been bowled over by emotion—longing, hope.

Sam had gotten swept along, too. She'd celebrated with old castmates at Mory's and sat around the Davenport courtyard talking, crying, gaping at all that was behind and ahead. Nobody wanted to give up and sleep. They headed up to their rooms at one or three or four-thirty a.m.

Sam had been sitting beside Jamie from about midnight on. Their bodies angled toward each other. Their knees touched. They were sitting on a cobblestone ledge.

Then, with no clear impetus, her leg was draped over his—or maybe the other way around—and her fingers had found his palm.

They kissed in the entryway. Once, and just a kiss—but it was the best she'd had before or since. Soft and full and savoring, carried along by months of tension and expectation.

Sam went to bed feeling close to perfect, like she'd stolen air from a balloon without it deflating.

Her disappointment had been mild when Jamie didn't write as he'd pledged to in the entryway. She had only sent a single postcard herself, and who knew if mail addressed "c/o Peace Corps Macedonia" even got delivered?

Sam never imagined a future in the Gallagher clan. A month bumming through Europe together, a long weekend hiking the

Appalachian Trail? These could've been cool. They just weren't to be.

The run down went quickly, though Sam's blister flared up and Joss kept grimacing in a way that suggested inner-thigh chafing. (Sam knew better than to ask in front of Laurel.) Things were busier back on campus. Despite herself, Sam felt good slipping through crowds in trim-fit running duds.

At the gate, Laurel nodded to the event schedule. "What's this on Saturday morning, 'Candle ceremony?'"

"The memorial," Sam said. "For classmates who died."

Laurel shrank from the schedule. "Is that…I wonder how many that is."

"There were something like fifteen."

Suspicion flashed in Laurel's face. She took only a second puzzling out Sam's inside information. "Are they doing one for Jamie?"

Sam nodded. "We decided to."

She'd said nothing but the truth—and not meant it as any sort of brag—but Laurel seemed to infer one. Her lips folded back into her mouth, the skin going white.

Sam was about to pooh-pooh the incidental disclosure, to explain the reunion chairperson also lived in Brooklyn and that was probably why they'd consulted her, when Laurel perked back up.

"Speaking of politics," she said, laying her key card against the gate reader, "how thrilling is Sayed's campaign? I'm in his Circle of Champions fundraisers. He'd be such an important voice on Capitol Hill…"

And like that, they were onto Laurel's contributions across a range of bodies—Bay Area zoning boards, Sausalito artist co-ops. She recapped her relationships with prominent class of ninety-six influencers, people who wrote for Slate or led alumni ex-pat groups overseas.

Listening, Sam felt suddenly tired.

Is something wrong with me? The two most extensive relationships in her life, with Abe and with Laurel—the only adults she had cohabited with—didn't provide joy. In fact, they were train wrecks. Sam didn't *think* she was uncaring or a serially dissatisfied person, but maybe from an objective point of view, she was.

"Mom's working on a documentary about the pinebox vendetta."

The words jolted Sam from her thoughts. She and Laurel both whirled to the speaker: Joss.

The trio had passed through the courtyard and nearly reached their entryway.

"Right, Mom?" Joss said. "It's going to be *This American Life*-ish, about the feud and how it impacted your guys' class."

She fanned her dancer's fingers, seeming to try enlarging the description—and Sam in the process.

Sam felt a rush of warmth. She'd barely mentioned last night's interviews to Joss, just in passing while tucking her into bed. Joss didn't know about Rock and the aquarium. She simply wanted Laurel to think her mother was doing important stuff.

Sam breathed out her nose. *Time to quit being meek and own this.*

"Right, I have this idea," she said, and gave the gist of the project.

Laurel observed, "That's a big hunk of source material."

Sam nodded. "I'll have to wrestle it down, find a focus."

"You could talk about Jamie and Africa…" Laurel had just let them into the room. She pulled her key from the lock and unlaced her shoes. "…or Rock Pruitt, all the controversy with his roommate. Are you leaning a particular way?"

Joss was watching with unblinking eyes, eager to hear her mother's answer.

Okay, Samantha. Own it means own it.

"Actually, I am," Sam said. "I heard something last night about Rock. Something new."

She told them about Gabe Navarro and the aquarium. When Joss asked what had happened to Derek Dickerson, Laurel looked hesitant. It occurred to Sam she had no frame of reference on children and didn't know what could be discussed in front of a fourteen-year-old.

"I think I've mentioned it before," Sam said. "Derek Dickerson, he died in an accident? Or maybe a not-accident?"

As Joss considered this, she dug at her inseam—an unflattering gesture she'd had for years. Sam crooked a finger for her to stop, but she didn't see.

"So maybe your research would actually *solve the case*?" Joss said. "Like the Innocence Project?"

Sam weighed different answers as she stripped out of sweaty clothes. She knew she should temper Joss's expectations, but the run up East Rock had her blood pumping.

"I'm gonna poke around," she said. "Maybe there's more out there. Maybe there's a way to surface the truth."

CHAPTER 5

ROCK'S HEAD FELT LIKE IT WAS INSIDE AN OIL DRUM, SOAKING IN viscous, sticky crude. Muscles behind his eyes hurt. His tongue and the roof of his mouth were fused cotton.

The last time he could remember waking up like this, he'd been in a Thai brothel. Two girls sleeping across his face and his scrotum in a leather cinch-bag.

Today? In his reunion dorm room.

Man-alive, what a ride.

Rock had hung out occasionally in the Skull and Bones tomb as an undergraduate—and of course he knew his family had had Bonesmen dating back to the mid-1800s. But finding Marshall Pruitt there was a shock. The old man, who'd led the clan's off-books paramilitary operations for the better part of a half century, had said he was in the area for the Pruitt event on Long Island.

"Right, but what're you doing *here?*" Rock had said.

New Haven sucked, and the secret society's tomb—dank, built half out of limestone—wasn't exactly the Ritz.

Marshall sat back in his wheelchair and frowned. His face was like the sepia-stained leaves of an ancient book.

"Keeping an eye on you," he said. "Which, it would appear, was a wise deployment of resources."

Rock hung his head. His name was already sludge among the family elites. If word of this stunt got out? It'd be toxic sludge.

As if reading his mind, Marshall said, "Rock, Rock. Of all the reckless pursuits…"

They sat across a pocked wooden table, flanked by stone busts and a broad ivory mantle. Group shots of the first classes of Bonesmen—a dozen suits standing over an actual skull and crossbones—adorned the walls.

Rock's eyes stung. The lighting was weak, from wan yellow candles set deep in the walls. He could barely make out the corners of the tomb. In one, there seemed to be a jagged artifact of some kind.

Hey. That wasn't—

"In the bushes below," Marshall said, reading Rock's eyes as easily as his mind. "My men beat the police to the spot."

Rock stalked over to see the Sterling Library reader's severed head. Its neck had cleaved in wild Z shapes. Both ears had chipped off, and its eyes were dumb voids from Rock's sledgehammer blows.

Rock, recalling the orgasmic feeling of battering the thing, had an urge to punch it anew with his bare fist.

"Brilliant," he said.

Marshall Pruitt kept a stern expression. He swiveled his chair, thumbs shaky on a black joystick, to face Rock. "If people knew about this, they would question your mental fitness."

"Those would be damn fair questions."

Finally, the old man couldn't hold back. A grin busted across his seamed face—a grin that said if he weren't stuck in that cursed chair, he would've been right up on that roof with Rock last night, hacking away. He wheeled over for an embrace.

Marshall Pruitt had a man's grip, working legs or not. Above all else, he was that: a man.

Marshall had brought down Central American governments. He'd stolen elections in the South, bold as a bandit in a bandanna, and exacted capital revenge for offenses a lesser man would've laughed off.

And when some thorny issue had landed on Jonathan Pruitt's Oval Office desk, who had he turned to? Where had that upright, pristine brand of his gone?

Out the window. The president had called Marshall, his older brother, and ridden him and his Black-Ops teams like thoroughbreds over a muddy track.

"Sterling Library does have cameras," Rock said. "To be safe, someone probably ought to—"

"Done. The tapes reside with me."

Rock exhaled with relief, but noted the distinction between "reside with me" and "were destroyed." The old man was a collector of leverage.

"And as far as the Saint goes," Rock said, "this isn't the sort of business he'd care to know about. Don't you think?"

Marshall Pruitt smiled thinly at the nickname. "Jonathan just had a stent placed in his right coronary artery. Let's do spare him the aggravation."

Although Jonathan Pruitt was the unquestioned leader of the clan, there existed other power centers. There were Michigan Pruitts, rougher, ideologically libertarian. There was Pruitt Capital, which just wanted to keep collecting its bags of money and stay out of the newspaper. There was legendary Coach Pruitt, whom Mississippians had been begging to claim their governorship for a decade.

And of course Marshall and his spooks.

These factions toed the line with many of the former president's conventions—ties or female-equivalent dress on TV, no Twitter, all that—but otherwise made their own ethics.

Rock asked, "Is he on Long Island for the event? Or has he delegated the judging?"

"No, he is judging—he's already arrived in the Hamptons. The Virginia Senate seat is heady stuff. Quite winnable. Rest assured, Jonathan will handpick a candidate of unassailable moral fiber."

Disdain dripped off the words. The aforementioned event was a Pruitt tradition widely known as the Choosing. Rock hated the name—it sounded like some dystopian young-adult turd.

At its base, a Choosing was an audition for whoever wanted the clan's backing in an upcoming race. Jonathan and other greybeards would gauge the hopefuls' command of a room, see how well they glad-handed donors. There were wonky candidate v. candidate issue debates, and murder boards where you were forced to explain every last vote and misdemeanor. The person who emerged with the fewest warts won the clan's blessing and full support.

Choosings weren't staged for every election. Only the biggies —and the Virginia Senate was certainly a biggie.

"Velasquez?" Rock asked.

"She will be formidable."

"More than formidable—she'd have to lay an egg to lose. Pro-life female. Latina. Military service. *You kidding me?* Peel back that brown skin, ten to one says she's a cyborg."

Marshall wheeled over to a mahogany sideboard and poured himself. He offered nothing to Rock. "Could be room for a dark horse."

At this, Rock's heart began hammering. "How dark?"

Marshall gave another thin smile. "Tell me, what else do you have planned for reunion weekend? Besides nearly falling twenty-three stories to your death."

He wasn't about to give Rock a straight answer on Virginia. No surprise there.

"Ah, drink. Spread the Pruitt seed far and wide."

The skeletal man took a sip, licked his lips. His eyes, deep-socketed like snake holes in a lawn, closed with a yearning air.

When he and Rock had worked on past operations together, Marshall had enjoyed hearing of the younger man's exploits.

Rock said, "Taking the chopper down to Long Island this morning?"

Marshall returned to himself. "No, I'm here today." He raised a ring that tripled the girth of his knuckle. "This is my reunion weekend, too."

"Jesus H. Christ, so it is! Fifty—is that right?"

"Fifty-five."

"Pickings must be getting slim. What do you do, go raid the thirty- and forty-year tents for tail?"

Marshall shook his head, grinning. "In fact, I have other business in New Haven this weekend. An opportunity."

He let this waft between them. With Bonesmen of centuries past looking on from pewter frames, Rock tried to imagine what coals the old man could have in the fire. Alcohol still riddled his thought processes.

It came to him anyway.

"Gallagher College."

The spymaster recoiled at the name, but nodded.

Rock said, "Surely they wouldn't let a Pruitt show his face at a Gallagher naming ceremony."

"Surely. But they can't stop us from participating by other means. They expect a laurel-wreathed coronation from the media. We can challenge that narrative."

Marshall explained the clan's coordinated push to "smudge up" the Gallagher brand ahead of the coming elections. Gallaghers in Congress would be painted as out-of-touch radicals. The outreach efforts of the Gallagher Foundation were being combed for cronyism and extremist ties. Some of this research was of the push variety, volunteers questioned aggressively or filmed responding to underage girls wanting abortions, or job applicants openly professing their love of God and desire to display this love at the office.

"We have to work twice as hard now," Marshall said. "That Charlotte Gallagher money is everywhere online, in social media. We have to make our own oxygen."

Rock winced at a crick in his side—the night's injuries were coming back as the booze wore off. "Somebody needs to take the lot of her Smart gizmos and drop 'em in bathtubs."

"Most are waterproof."

Rock grunted. "Then drop *her* into a bathtub—after a few wallops."

"I keep a notebook of options for Charlotte Gallagher—I'll add another entry," Marshall said. "The more pressing need, though, is to tarnish Owen Gallagher. The left's donor class is uniting around him. That sense of inevitability is gathering. Every day, he looks more like the nominee."

"Democrats," Rock scoffed. "They just love picking their loser ahead of time."

"Indeed. Though Owen Gallagher might not lose."

"Come off it, the guy's nothing. He was governor of New Hampshire—weakest governorship in the country. Couldn't have let himself out of a jaywalking ticket."

"He's currently polling seventy-eight percent among independents."

"They met him last Wednesday. There are Roombas smarter than this guy. All he is is hair and a throaty chuckle."

"Presidents have ascended with less."

Rock smirked. *True enough.*

He had actually spoken at length with Owen Gallagher at some bipartisan blah-blah symposium years ago, and immediately written him off. The guy thought "single-payer" meant you couldn't put kids or a spouse on your health plan—and now the Gallaghers, the self-anointed champions of thoughtful political discourse, wanted to run him for 1600?

"There must be dirt on him."

Marshall folded his veiny wrists in his lap—a pair of hairless rats. "We've looked. Thousands of dollars on oppo research. Tens of thousands. You can bet Joan Gallagher's done likewise—they wouldn't be trotting him out if he wasn't clean."

Again, the old man's analysis was on point. The coming presidential election was the Gallaghers' big shot. The Pruitts were sidelined with a Republican in office—the man who'd beaten *their* man in the last cycle.

That primary loss had been bitter. Rock's uncle, Mark Easton, had emerged from the Choosing, partly owing to his different last name—incumbent fatigue was heavy, predisposing voters against another Pruitt presidency. Mark ran a by-the-numbers campaign. He made no mistakes. Unless you counted being caught on a hot mic saying, "They want to pick a dick just to make a point? Then they'll pick a dick," which Rock didn't.

He simply lost.

In the post-mortem at the family compound in Louisiana, Jonathan Pruitt had delivered a sermon about their having lost the moral high-ground. They'd waded too deep into the muck in pursuit of victory. They should have let the dick be a dick. (Not his words.) They should've hewed close to the Pruitt brand.

Hence Theresa Velasquez being in favor. And Rock being out.

"What do you have in mind?" Rock asked now. "Plant something? Gin up a protest?"

He thought of Johnston, the Mory's bartender—that idea of finding slaveholders in the Gallagher family tree.

"Possibly," Marshall said.

"Did the boys ever dig up a transcript of those Trotsky comments Joan Gallagher made at the fundraiser in Berkeley?"

"They did," Marshall said. "We have an open dossier—it could help in the general. But accusing the Gallaghers of being socialist at Yale? They'd probably get their name on a chapel, too."

"Fair enough. What about pinebox?"

Marshall reared back in his wheelchair. "Not pinebox—not now. It's not ripe."

"Not *ripe*? We're talking about a presidential election, how much riper does it need to get?"

Rock had gotten himself worked up—defaming Gallaghers did this to him—but Marshall Pruitt was the picture of composure.

"Take the long view," he said. "Pinebox will bury the Gallaghers, once and for all. But it needs the proper stage. It needs the proper moment." He sniffed the stale tomb air. "For now, it stays in our pocket."

Rock shrugged. Marshall was the maestro—if he said pinebox needed to stay under wraps, then pinebox had better stay under wraps.

"What then?" he asked. "You're thinking of a smaller-scale scandal? Some kind of disruption?"

"This is college. Crazy things happen on college campuses." Marshall nodded toward the reader's severed head. "For the right sort of crazy, the reward could be substantial."

Rock bore into the older man's eyes. "Substantial like Virginia?"

Marshall Pruitt shifted his jaw from right to left, tapped the sharp point of his chin, and instructed his men to escort Rock back to his dorm.

☙❧

Now in boxers, flip-flops, and vintage 1992 T-shirt depicting Harvard cheerleaders orally engaged with Yale football players, Rock left his entryway for the Silliman College kitchen. Gongs clattered inside his head, and the cotton in his mouth kept swelling. He scratched himself liberally.

He stole from a perfect matrix of washed juice glasses, stuck the pilfered glass under a dining-hall OJ udder and filled it halfway. Walked the OJ to the caterer's tent and nabbed a bottle of champagne, popped the cork, and—as some administrator walked by giving him the stink-eye——filled to the brim with foamy, pink-tinged gold.

Boom. Mimosa.

What, he pondered, was Marshall Pruitt capable of? Doubtless he could put Rock's name in for consideration for Virginia. Rock felt certain he would. When the rest of the clan had shunned Rock after the death of Derek Dickerson, Marshall had stuck by him. Marshall had given Rock his start in Southeast Asia. Years later, he'd funneled soft money to Rock's House campaign when no other Pruitt had a dime for him.

Still, his sway with Johnathan Pruitt was debatable. Marshall was like the chained minotaur in the castle dungeon—they'd let him out for bacchanalia or bloodsport, but they weren't asking his opinion on peasant tax rates.

Rock thought, and drank, and drank more, and thought and drank at the same time, and finally decided sabotaging the Gallaghers' naming ceremony was a worthwhile endeavor. Even if he got zip out of it.

It just needed doing, like a pinata needs a bat to the belly.

Standing in boxers in the Silliman quad, Rock whipped out his cellphone and dialed Yanni Jovanovic. The provocateur answered on the first ring and heard out Rock's rambling foreword in full, five minutes, before saying a word.

"Slavery, you want?" he said.

"Or worker exploitation, or carbon footprint," Rock spitballed. "We're going for hypocrisy. Beyond that, I'm not picky."

There was a pause, which Rock presumed to be Yanni tapping away at one of the dozen laptops he sat among in his unkempt patch of Seattle incubator space.

Rock had seen the place once, when they were deep down in the gutter, hanging some transgender-bathroom assault story around Joan Gallagher's neck. What a hole. You needed waders if you wanted to escape without being covered in Cheez-It dust.

"Meh…first pass, I'm not seeing much," Yanni said. "If I'm going to start a fire, I need a little smoke to work with."

Rock swigged mimosa between his cheeks. "Okay. Okay, what about a more surgical strike? Any slime floating around on Owen Gallagher?"

"That guy is pretty boring. Isn't that the whole point of him?"

"That's why slime's important. Tell me some guy who brags about his manhood on tape banged a porn star? So what. But if *Owen Gallagher* bangs a porn star, Mr. Squeaky Clean? Now we're in business."

"I don't think he banged a porn star."

"Yeah, I get he hasn't banged a porn star!" A woman holding hands with a boy roughly Rock Junior's age glared—Rock tugged his crotch at her. "So we pay somebody. We find a nanny or house sitter who left on bad terms. Then she goes on *60 Minutes* and claims intimate knowledge of his genitalia."

Yanni responded with his geeky hiccup of a laugh. "Not bad. I could set some balls in motion, but the problem is time. Isn't the event Sunday?"

Rock winced. Social media had sped up the game, but Yanni was right—a fake affair would take more than two days to engineer.

"Work up some hit pieces on your side, but don't deploy. Lemme do some work here. See what I can manage on the smoke front."

He swiped away Yanni's call and dumped the last of his breakfast cocktail down his throat.

There was a pile of fat pastel chalks near the Silliman master's office. He grabbed the darkest-colored piece, donned shorts, and took out up College Street. Every ten-odd sideway panels, he stooped and scrawled a message.

DO YOU KNOW HOW MANY SLAVES OWEN GALLAGHER'S GREAT-GRANDFATHER OWNED?

(Rock didn't.)

Then:

RESOLVED: POLITICAL DYNASTIES = PATRIARCHY.

He considered calling that one good but decided subtlety was not his friend now and added, THEREFORE "GALLAGHER" COLLEGE = PATRIARCHY.

Rock took special joy in channeling and manipulating the far left, in turning their jaw-quivering outrage back against itself. Nobody could ever be as pure as them, least of all privileged folks like the Gallaghers.

Once he had graffitied a good swath of campus, Rock hit a copy store. He slopped up a few flavors of inflammatory flyers using their anonymous computers and printed three hundred each. He roused several homeless men along Chapel Street with twenty dollar bills, instructing them to paper every bulletin board in sight.

The indigent were an agile, capable workforce. Rock had used them variously before and enjoyed their give-and-take now, carrying two dozen donuts into a bar and splurging for pitchers once the job was done. The homeless stank, but they had spirit. They were beyond kowtowing to authority and couldn't be bullied like regular members of society. Rock respected that.

From the bar, Rock hiked out to the new college—soon to be Gallagher College—on the edge of campus. The construction was a striking mix of Gothic and modern, white stucco with fine stonework and chunky, character-rich windows. Naturally it hit all the "green" checkboxes, solar panels on the roof, low-flow faucets. If you tried throwing a plastic straw in the trash, Rock figured a robotic arm descended from the ceiling and swatted you in the face with pictures of asphyxiated sea turtles.

He approached the gate. He tried his reunion badge on the card reader, but it flashed red.

A maintenance man inside was carrying an armful of extension cords.

"Hey!" Rock called. "I need in."

The man looked behind him as if Rock had been talking to someone else. "Can I—er, help you?"

"For your sake, let's hope," Rock said. "I need to check things over for Sunday. Now the ceremony is occurring in the main courtyard, that correct?"

The man flubbed an answer, re-gripping his cords.

"Forget it," Rock said. "Just lemme in, I'll figure it out."

He shifted from foot to foot, exuding impatience.

The man walked over with a thick expression and pushed open the gate. "Your, um, event badge should've worked on—"

But Rock was past him, breezing through a fifteen-foot archway, striding over clipboards and safety goggles to the courtyard.

The space, bounded by dorms up all four sides, was majestic—as though the architect had squeezed two city blocks into one. Decorations for Sunday's ceremony were underway. White folding chairs. Bunting featuring the new college crest, a female figure holding black and white scales. At the sight of it, Rock laughed and gagged in the same breath.

A podium stood atop a temporary stage in one corner of the courtyard. Rock saw from ten yards out that it was no schmoe podium.

Here was a broad, substantial piece of equipment. Its build quality was exceptional, big honking microphone and some alloy made to resemble wood for the cameras.

Rock walked up the stage to examine it. The interior of the podium, the inclined surface you looked at while speaking, resembled the deck of the USS Enterprise: teleprompter screen, thumb-stick control, various dials, gauges, and buttons.

Across the top, a placard read *SmartPodium*.

Of course.

Rock tapped the teleprompter, and the screen changed from a screensaver to a document titled *Schedule of Events*.

3:00 — Kalifa Babajide

3:10 — Lisa Vance
3:20 — Joan Gallagher
3:30 — Owen Gallagher

Rock felt his gut jump and instinctively uppercut the air in front of him.

The dumb-ass is speaking.

This definitely raised the mischief quotient. Thinking this smarty-pants gizmo might even have Owen Gallagher's speech preloaded, Rock tapped the screen again—right on the dumbass's name.

A dialog appeared asking for his username and password.

Rock filled his cheeks and looked skyward. *If I had the IQ of a carrot like Owen, what would I pick for a password—*

"Who let you in here?"

The voice yanked Rock from his musings. He turned and lo and behold, there she was: the Queen of the Universe.

"Why, Charlotte. Lovely to see you."

"Who let you in?"

He raised his badge. "I'm a Yalie, same as you. Remember? Jamie and I were classmates?"

Charlotte Gallagher didn't flinch at the mention of her dead brother. Ice-faced, she blew by Rock to examine the SmartPodium. She traipsed her fingers protectively over its screen, as though worried he might have left some bodily secretion.

What a wildcat. Chic, chin-length roan hair. Cheekbones that could've cut diamond. Smarter than any three people you could name, and knew it.

"I was here four years after you and Jamie," she said. "They wouldn't have graduated you then—or now. Different times, different sensibilities. Progress."

"Yep, Yale's all about progress. Now there's #metoo, right? How fun this campus must be."

"I'm sure it's a downer for prolific abusers like yourself."

Rock grinned. Damn, was he hard. One long step forward and it'd poke her in the belly button.

"That's one tight ship you're running." He nodded to the SmartPodium display. "Ten-minute blocks? Shouldn't you leave a little space for that renowned Gallagher flair?"

He caught her sighing and remembered that *New Yorker* profile about her efforts to impose discipline on her clan. Whereas the Pruitts tightly coordinated their message and efforts, the Gallaghers were known for going off-script and making reckless mistakes. No fewer than five recent Gallagher candidacies had ended in scandal.

To be fair, the Pruitts had played a role in a few.

"Speaking of clan norms, shouldn't you be wearing pants?" Charlotte crinkled her nose without looking at his shorts. "What would Jonathan Pruitt say?"

"Jonathan says nothing to me, if he can help it."

The billionaire—sixth on last year's *Forbes* list—grinned herself now. They were standing very close. Her tongue shifted behind her lip, and she pivoted in a way that made her shirt's stiff white fabric stretch across her breasts.

Is she doing this to me on purpose?

Rock was absolutely out of his head. He glanced around to see where the maintenance man was. Could they sneak down to the boiler room? Commandeer an empty dorm?

"Ugh, don't even think it," Charlotte said, looking green. "I shouldn't have let you this close. Now I need a shower."

Apparently not on purpose.

She continued, "What are you doing here, Rock? What sort of foulness are you cooking up?"

Shower. Foulness. Rock would be lucky if it didn't happen right now in his shorts.

He said, "I'm just curious what profound thoughts the Gallaghers plan to share with the larger Yale and New Haven communities. For example, will the allegations of slaveholding be addressed?"

Charlotte's face went from nauseous to bored. "That dog's not going to hunt."

"Why? Because all your Smart devices will suppress the story in their owners' newsfeeds?"

It was well understood that SmartWidget—which had started with internet-of-things devices and grown into watches, personal assistants, everything—filtered the news it presented to its massive user base. "Unvarnished, personalized intelligence," they called it, but of course, it was hyper-varnished. Anything the Southern Poverty Law Center pooped out got through, but never a byline from the Heritage Foundation or AEI.

"Go. Now." Charlotte swiped her podium's screen, some intricate pattern that turned it off. "Find some dark, wet place with spores of mold and decomposing bacteria, and just sort of melt in."

She began walking away.

Rock called, "Please keep talking—*please*?" He laid a fingertip on the screen. Nothing happened. "Well, have a great weekend! I'm in Silliman College, room 321 if you need company. Must get lonely at the top…"

She twisted back with an expression like a vegan being force-fed sirloin steak, and disappeared.

Rock felt revived walking out of the new college. It was nearly noon, the sun straight overhead, and his forty-two-year-old bones had new life.

Direct engagement with the Gallaghers did this—made him feel fine and mighty and healthy, no matter what he'd been putting in his body in the hours before.

He winked at girls walking with boyfriends. He saw a kid in a beret staple a theater flyer over one of his, and promptly ripped it off and threw the crumpled pulp into the street.

He called Yanni.

"Find any smoke?" asked the provocateur.

"Forget smoke," Rock said. "Owen Gallagher is giving a speech here, Sunday. I want it carried by as many livestreams as you can call in. I want steelworkers in Pennsylvania to see it. I want the Pope to see it. Everybody."

CHAPTER 6

T HE CANDLE CEREMONY WAS EARLY, EIGHT O'CLOCK SATURDAY morning. Sam confirmed the Zoom was good on batteries, then slipped away without waking Joss to find a seat in the courtyard.

The grass was matted from all the foot traffic of the last days. A few stray forks and red cups had eluded the cleanup crew, dotting the shrubs.

Sam felt good, having run yesterday and mostly skipped the bar station last night. She'd been too busy, splitting her time between catching up and recording documentary clips. She'd found two more witnesses to the aquarium story, including one who said Rock had promised to *"put Derek through a frickin' wall"* when they got back to their dorm. A third said she'd seen Rock and Derek so drunk that night they'd wandered into traffic arm in arm and nearly been hit by passing cars. It wasn't clear if this had happened before or after the aquarium, but either way, it was solid footage.

The catching up had been successful, too. With everyone arrived now, the reunion had a far-flung festival vibe. Every time she turned around, Sam was discovering a forgotten pal or reliving some seminal moment.

She had learned that Naomi Burroughs had gotten divorced. She'd cooed and given Naomi a long hug, but been surprised by how happy she seemed. Naomi talked about how she and her husband had adapted to passing in the halls without a word, how the pattern of stifling indifference had held for years until the affair broke it open—and she'd told all this *smiling*. Because, as she said, it was "over. Finally."

Sam had come right to the brink of divulging her own situation…then stopped.

What if Joss had ambled up?

Now Sam pulled a chair over to a group of friends sitting quietly, waiting for the ceremony to start.

"*Hi!*" she whispered, and they waved or mouthed back likewise.

Fifteen candles were arranged on a linen-covered table. Behind each stood a photograph and cream card identifying the deceased classmate. A microphone sat unattended on the table. A woman Sam recognized as a ninety-sixer stood nearby with her hands folded solemnly.

Sam took the Zoom from her purse and set it on the next chair.

At the stroke of eight, the woman leading the ceremony lit all fifteen candles from a taper. Blowing out the taper, she turned to those gathered—between thirty and forty, grouped in bunches like Sam's Davenport crew—and gave a subdued smile.

"Thanks for coming to honor our classmates, these friends who were taken too soon."

She briefly acknowledged those who'd played a role in coordinating and read the name on the first card. Penelope Gutierrez had rowed and majored in chemistry.

"Would anyone like to say a word about Penelope?"

A woman in slacks strode to the table and described Penelope as kind, shy at praise, and committed to her family in Oregon, where she'd returned to teach and coach softball after

Yale. Her death on vacation in Peru had shaken their circle of friends.

Other speakers cracked jokes, sobbed, and gave information for memorial funds. Twice, there was a sort of race between friends to speak about their classmate, a meeting at the microphone, then a falling over one another to say the other had known him or her best.

Once, nobody answered the call. Sam's heart crunched as the organizer scanned the crowd in vain on Todd Nixon's behalf.

The fifth candle was for Derek Dickerson, Rock Pruitt's freshman roommate. As a man with a puffy pink neck stood, Sam pressed record on the Zoom.

"Honestly? This sucks," the puffy man began. "Derek should be here. He should be here this weekend, lighting it up with me, with Nicky. With our whole pledge class."

From behind his back, the man produced a frosted bottle of vodka and two glasses. He fumbled placing one before Derek's photo—his bloodshot eyes made Sam feel good about her own restraint last night—then poured each full.

"To you, Dicks. Think about you every day. I, uh…and even though he's not here"—the speaker glanced around the courtyard —"believe me, he's drinking for you, too."

The puffy man downed one shot, then, after feinting like he might dump it on the lawn, smirked and downed the second.

A buzz passed through the courtyard at this clumsy—but unmistakable—reference to Rock Pruitt.

Sam shifted the Zoom to clear its mic path, to ensure it caught the full eulogy. Naturally, it was all glory and praise. How generous Derek had been at the keg tap, what a loyal shoulder to cry on he'd been after the speaker's high school girlfriend had dumped him over the phone.

The truth poked through, barely disguised. When the speaker mentioned Dickerson's being "popular with the fairer sex, one might say," Sam tasted bile in her throat.

The rumors about Derek Dickerson had been grotesque. He would troll early-morning parties for women, recklessly drunk five nights out of seven, sidling up to women on frat-house couches and starting neck massages unasked. He played no sports at Yale but swung his preppy, chestnut hair and chuck-roast shoulders around with an athlete's swagger.

It came out later that in Dickerson's brief time on campus, just six months, he'd amassed no less than eight sexual misconduct complaints. They had been bubbling up through various disciplinary panels at the time of his death.

This was partly what Sam found so intriguing about the incident. About his death. It wasn't some down-the-middle tragedy like Ted Kennedy and Mary Jo Kopechne. Derek Dickerson's accidental death had the dual impact of stopping a serial rapist, and the career of Rock Pruitt—which even in the early days, everyone around understood was burgeoning. Rock had bulled his way to Congress anyhow, but who knew how high he might've risen with a clean past?

The DKE brother finished his macho ode and sat back down to grave fist bumps from his friends. Sam switched off the Zoom.

It occurred to her she would need the puffy man's consent to use his audio. Really, she should interview him. The thought repulsed her—with no husband around, he'd be all joshing and hitting on her.

Other classmates had died of disease, overdose, one trying to save his parents' dog down an abandoned well. Sam cried for people she'd never met and felt chastened by the smallness of her own problems.

Stacked up against these hardships, a failed marriage was nothing. A flat tire on the way to work. She had health and decades of life ahead, and resolved to kick herself in the butt next time she felt self-pity.

The third-to-last candle was for Jamie Gallagher. His picture, which Sam had pried out of a collage frame in her apartment, showed a nineteen-year-old boy with preternaturally light eyes, surprise blooming in his face. They'd just returned from watching Yale women's hockey to find an *Equality for All: We Did It!* banner stretched across the courtyard: a celebration of the landmark anti-discrimination bill his mother had spearheaded through the Senate.

He looked so, *so* young—the corners of his mouth loose, one arm unfurling toward the frame's edge with spiraling ease.

Nobody had seen Jamie much after college, even before Puntland, so in a way, he'd been fixed in all their minds. Earnest. Idealistic. Troubled. Forever dissatisfied with himself and the world.

Sam had chosen this picture precisely to combat that conception of Jamie. Because Jamie hadn't always been that way—not as a freshman, and not in those lovely moments when he'd forgotten himself with her.

When the woman directing the ceremony asked who would speak for Jamie, Sam found her legs carrying her forward. She bumped the Zoom, and it clattered to the ground. She didn't pick it up.

"Hello, I'm Sam," she began. "Jamie and I shared a bathroom senior year, and believe it or not, we were still friends by the end." Chuckles relaxed her. "I wanted to say a bit about Jamie. Not Jamie Gallagher, but just Jamie—the person we all knew in Davenport, lugging his rucksack into the dining hall or sitting waiting for a laundry machine to free up.

"Jamie came to Yale with a lot on his shoulders. He took that burden seriously—the service part—but individual people were what fired him up. If he saw you struggling with a problem set, or getting a sofa upstairs? He always helped. He had to. It was his passion, making things easier for others to bear."

As Sam continued giving examples, Laurel and others nodded along and dabbed their cheeks. Sam cringed at the inadequacy of words, though. Words couldn't capture Jamie. The two of them had even talked about this—how malleable language was, how easily you could deceive with it, bend it to your own purpose.

What else can I do? she thought. *Stomp? Jump up and down?*

Across the quad, Joss emerged from their entryway. She held coffee two-handed at her chin.

Sam continued, "The feud—or vendetta, whatever people call it now—was hard on Jamie. He…it got in the way of what he wanted." To quell a weakness in her jaw, she summoned anger. "Because just look at our class, right? You basically took two promising people—Jamie and Rock Pruitt, who I'm told people think has merits—and made them into these barely human figures, doing insane things. The rest of us are dealing with in-laws and exams, and they're stuck in some otherworldly mortal combat. I guess it's fun for us. I guess we like watching."

Sam petered out. She stood before the crowd feeling hot, drained, and a little embarrassed. She hadn't meant to speak ill of Rock or sermonize with some blanket social critique.

Leaning on her film training, she decided to come back to the personal—to focus her audience on what mattered.

"Jamie only took time out for himself to do one thing: mountain biking." She smiled, thinking of those forearms streaked with road rash. "Otherwise, he was one hundred percent about helping others. Just look how he died—sacrificing his own life to end atrocities. That was Jamie to the core.

"He was kind, and maybe naive, and I wish he'd been born to schoolteachers in the middle of Ohio or someplace. I wish he could've just been that kid whose Frisbee hit me our first day of school, and that's it."

❧

Joss took one step out of the entryway. When a head turned her way, she stopped. Probably the head's owner—some guy sitting at the ceremony in jeans—was just shifting to get comfortable or stretch his back, but she felt awkward.

Which seat should I take? Mom's?

What if she sees me and it messes up her speech?

Joss stepped back into the entryway, deciding not to decide.

She had been awake for an hour. For half of that, she'd lain in bed—hearing Mom and Laurel leave for the memorial, knowing they were trying to sneak out without waking her up.

Maybe Mom didn't want her around so much death talk. Maybe they worried it would drag her down, or they just wanted to think about the friend they'd lost without her around to distract.

Whatever. When she'd been sure they were gone, Joss had wandered into the common room and watched from the window, nibbling the stale granola Mom had packed.

She hadn't decided what to think about Yale. Campus was amazing—the architecture, all the stone statues. The people, too. The students didn't seem like vapid, binge-drinking characters from movies. Just walking along the sidewalk, she'd overheard debates about colonialism and casual discussions of dialectical materialism.

Which was cool, but kinda weird.

Also weird? How perfectly Mom fit into the scene.

Now, standing at the table of white candles, she looked ten feet tall. She made these firm, commanding gestures. She spoke with conviction. Joss had heard her speak well at WNYC events, but this was a totally different level.

Joss tried another step away from the entryway, drawn to her mother's confidence. It felt like she was watching a TED talk. She'd known she had an awesome mom—friends who visited Joss in Brooklyn loved hanging with her—but seeing her with her college friends showed Joss more. She realized Mom had been a standout here: the center of her scene, liked by everybody.

This didn't exactly surprise Joss. It was just...well, again, weird. She was used to seeing Mom arguing with Dad about toilet repair or "some realistic assumptions about how we're going to pay for college."

Mom talked about Jamie Gallagher for five minutes. Stories, wishes, her opinions about the feud. *Did she write this out ahead of time?*

It didn't feel like it. It felt spontaneous. Although the subject obviously made her sad, energy radiated from her face. She had things to say about Jamie, and she was going to say them—and they were going to be heard.

When his name had come up at home, Mom had always downplayed their friendship, probably because of Dad's jealous jokes about "your princely classmate." Hearing Mom now, though, Joss felt the full significance of the friendship—and wondered if it might've been something more at college.

Joss was so captivated by her mother that it took her several moments to hear the murmurs.

Laurel, sitting in the back row, stood and squinted.

Somebody else was pointing to the gate, whisper-shouting to all around.

"Hey, look!"

"*What?* No, that—there's no way…"

Peeling her eyes off Mom, Joss turned to see what people were staring at.

Laurel cried, "Oh my God!"

The man was lanky, and approached the ceremony on freaky-thin legs that boosted him up at the end of each stride—a sorta quick, hopeful walk. He had a beard. Blond, flowy hair trailed back from his face like streamers off a kid's bike handles. Joss was twenty yards away but still noticed his cracked, weathered skin— which could've been the same material as that rucksack he was carrying.

The courtyard was going crazy. People rushed forward to hug

him or slap his back. A woman held up her cellphone to snap a pic.

Joss forgot her own anxieties and started for the candle table, where Mom stood holding the microphone—the only person in the courtyard who hadn't moved.

The tall flats of her face were frozen, but her eyes and mouth were swirling—three perfect circles of shock.

Joss instinctively went to her, feeling like she might need an arm or hand to steady herself with. But she didn't.

Mom's mouth kept its circle shape for one second, for two. Then turned into a giant smile.

PART II

Jamie Gallagher had come a long way to see Samantha Lessing. From the bustling streets of Juba, by van over rutted roads through the Ethiopian countryside, waiting twelve hours at Addis Ababa for the flight to Khartoum—herds of bushbucks grazing outside the airport's plate glass—and finally the overnight flight to JFK. He'd had plenty of downtime to think and embellish a mental image of Sam.

He had teased every small charm forward, the playful chin and full lips, that expressive brow whose crimps and angles used to send his emotions six ways at once. Reality might've easily fallen short of this idealized version—which, after all, benefited from two decades of yearning and glorified memory.

But it didn't.

Sam was everything he'd dreamed. Standing on tiptoes, he peered over his buzzing classmates and saw a revelation in jeans and a black blazer. Her eyes bright and curious. Her head tipped to one side, just barely—questions and concern and (maybe?) a flirt all at once.

When the person beside her—*is that Laurel Trowbridge?*—

staggered over a chair, Sam caught her arm to stop the fall—an effortless, instinctive good—then resumed looking.

Everyone was looking. Jamie knew this feeling well from stepping off trains at African stations unaccustomed to Westerners. People were hugging him. Cheering him. Smacking him on the back, jostling his rucksack. He hugged back and mumbled answers to shouted questions, using a kind of second-level consciousness while keeping his main focus on Sam.

And now he was drifting farther into the courtyard...and Sam was drifting nearer...and they were coming together as though totally alone, like one magnet to its mate.

She said, "How?"

Jamie shook his head, *not now*, and they embraced. Her body filled every hollow of his. The second thoughts he'd been having —saying farewell to his Juban friends, bouncing in the back of a rickety van—all winked out.

His eyes stayed closed a long while. When he felt her face pulling away from his shoulder, he sensed her apprehension and quickly drew back.

A teenage girl stood watching them—tall, inky-haired. She had to be Sam's daughter.

Jamie waved at the girl. Her face didn't change.

To the broader courtyard, he said, "Well, this is over the top— sorry. I literally got back on U.S. soil this morning, and then the train from JFK was delayed..."

He glanced at the table of candles and saw that two remained. When he'd approached the Silliman gate and heard what was going on, he'd paused, not wanting to interrupt a speech memorializing another classmate. Then Sam had stepped forward to discuss *him*, and he'd felt compelled to show himself.

Now he gestured to the last candles. "Perhaps we could all sit again? I think we should honor the rest of our fallen classmates. The ones who actually fell."

His quip pierced the unreality of the situation, and now

everyone did return to their chairs. The murmurs never died out entirely, but things quieted enough for the memorial to resume.

Jamie found a place in back. Sam sat beside the teenage girl—definitely her daughter, the eye shapes were identical—in a small group of Davenporters.

He focused on the last two classmates, listening to their friends tell about favorite poems and remembered kindnesses. Though he hadn't known either, Jamie tried to inhabit their lives, to shed his own skin and imagine choices he might've made—which fates could have changed, which would've been inevitable.

Jamie's father used to remind him when Jamie got angry with Republicans, Pruitt or otherwise, "Their experiences are different from yours. If you haven't grieved their sorrows or cheered their triumphs, you have no right to judge."

Jamie's mother used to roll her eyes.

After the ceremony, Jamie's classmates mobbed him again. He'd had the morning of travel to reorient to the Western way of relating—quick, without the silences he had come to appreciate in Africa—but still found conversations disorienting.

Where was he staying? Where'd he gotten those scars? Had Owen Gallagher gotten him released? (From where, exactly? Jamie wondered.)

Oh, people were nice. He recognized joy in their eyes—a dead man come back alive. But he also saw, in some, something beyond joy. The old titillation.

Unused to posturing or saying what he didn't mean, Jamie revealed he'd been living in East Africa the entire decade. Only two people from his family had known: his mother and sister. Had he killed that war-criminal general on purpose?

Yes. Absolutely.

And when after a whirlwind of exchanges he found Sam Lessing in front of him, he almost said, *I came to see you, and that's all. For no other reason.*

Except that her daughter was standing right behind her—and Sam was wearing a wedding ring.

Jamie had known about both. They had internet in Juba, of course, and he wasn't above Googling her using his friend Muneeb's Facebook account to see photos.

The fact that Sam Lessing had a family and established life was almost beside the point. He'd come to see her and confirm those noble qualities he'd ascribed to her all these years in absentia were valid. To confirm the exalted place he'd given those college memories was deserved.

He *had* been part of something wonderful—and it had nothing to do with his family or the Pruitts.

It just was. Wonderful.

Jamie had no intention of disrupting a marriage or confusing a daughter, or making Sam feel even the slightest bit awkward.

Do no harm.

She asked, "How are you?"

Jamie returned to the moment—he'd been staring—and laughed softly at the anticlimax.

"I'm well!" he said. "I love the air here. It's like the flowers pull you around campus by the nose."

Juba used to smell great, too, before the oil drilling began on the outskirts. Jamie decided not to share this. He didn't want to come off as the Great White Shaman dispensing wisdom on the Dark Continent.

Sam pointed to a welt on his forearm. "That's new. Is it... stable? Does it require treatment?"

"No, no," Jamie said. "It's just from a sugarcane stalk. If your machete angle is off, they can..."

He trailed off. *Nice one, Shaman.*

Sam bobbed her head. "I have no response for that."

"You shouldn't, yeah. My situation is totally unbelievable and requires no response." He pointedly wiped his hands, one off the other. "So what about you? Happy?"

"More or less."

"East Coast?"

"Right. Brooklyn."

"Are you at all active in film, still?"

"I am," Sam said, "though not acting anymore. I'm on the production side. WNYC, in the city?"

"Sure! That's exciting!" Jamie winced at the falseness of his own reaction—he'd known exactly where she worked. "How do you find the studio?"

"It has its moments," Sam said. "It's primarily a job, and occasionally inspiring. Like parenting."

She glanced wryly to her daughter, who passed a hand down her face in embarrassment. Even this—how the girl flattened her nose—was an echo of her mother.

Jamie asked, "Are you in touch with many Davenporters? I saw Laurel."

"Here and there. I keep up with Laurel's stuff, but in general I'm terrible. Most people probably assume I dropped off the face of the earth after school."

Now it was Sam's turn to feel sheepish. She blushed and added, "Not to equate my lack of emailing with your, you know, actual ordeal."

He grinned. "Not at all. I deserve some scorn. We've been graduated twenty years and the sum-total of my correspondence has been what, a postcard? One postcard?"

Sam's face changed at this, a troubled twitch by the eyes. "You mean, er—that postcard I sent the first summer?"

"Right. That, and then the one I sent back from Macedonia."

"I never got a postcard."

Jamie straightened up and looked behind, as though for pranksters. "I sent it to that Manhattan address, something like Eighth Ave. Started with a seven-two-eight, right? Seven-two-eight something?"

He worried this could be construed as obsessive, but Sam's squinting eyes were focused inward.

"Right, right: seven-two-eight-four. Laurel and I lived in that apartment…"

A moment later, her searching expression moved onto Jamie and they shared a long, complex look. He had assumed the mechanics of their drift apart for so long—a brief exchange of postcards, her interest fading due to geographical separation and other options in NYC—that he was struggling to place this new information.

His head was spinning.

Sam's must have been, too. Her teeth gritted in what Jamie took for indignation—at the world, at circumstance.

She said, "Star-crossed by the postal system. How rotten is that?"

"Rotten," he agreed, regaining his breath. "But I think I understand why I survived now."

Sam blinked. "Excuse me?"

"*Juju.*"

When her confusion didn't clear, he said, "An African term for karma. West African, really, though the Sudanese use it quite often."

"I see, but…still not getting the connection to postcards."

He smiled at her easy comebacks. "You started to ask before, how. How I survived. It was a miracle—about six miracles, one stacked on top of the next. For ten years, I've wondered what I did to deserve it."

He launched into the story of his escape from General Mahad's yacht. His long-cultured immunity to King Cobra venom. The general's tumblers, which had pushed this immunity to its very limits. Struggling through the Indian Ocean to one of the pirates' skiffs, gasping, convulsing, his body on fire. Being nursed from his coma by rural Somali who assumed he'd been thrown off a slaver ship, his appearance was so thin and waxy.

By the end of the story, Sam and her daughter both stared at him with an extra quarter-inch of forehead.

The daughter said, "All that actually, like, happened?"

"There are times when I doubt it myself," Jamie said, "but yes. Unless the venom fried my memory."

"And afterward," Sam began, ducking gingerly as though scared of triggering some flashback, "were you hiding? From that butcher-guy's friends, or loyalists?"

"Not really," Jamie said. "Maybe for a few months. But after that, staying out of sight had nothing to do with General Mahad."

Sam immediately understood. "The feud. You were keeping your distance from the feud."

He nodded.

She said, "Your mom and sister kept it secret, that you were alive?"

"Right."

"Did you ever get to see them?"

"Here and there, if business took them to Africa. Always in disguise, away from the press."

"Wasn't it hard being cut off like that from everybody else?"

"Some days," Jamie admitted. "When the rainy season got bad, or if I hit a setback with my work there—after the Murle radicals burned our childhood literacy center to the ground? I thought about coming back. But then I'd think about the feud, and all the schemes and power plays, and I just…couldn't."

Sam gave an empathetic wince. "Why now?"

He considered blurting out the truth—*Because I knew you'd be here*—but thought better of it. "The twenty-year reunion seemed like, I dunno, a nice round number."

Boy, that sounded dopey.

He continued, "I guess I started to worry I was waiting too long, that it would be weird reconnecting. But then the longer I waited, the weirder it got—and this reunion felt like maybe the point of no return."

Sam smiled. "From a weirdness perspective?"

Jamie smiled, too. "Exactly."

Their eyes locked for several beats. The straps of Jamie's rucksack began to feel tight.

To fill the void, he said, "How's your family? Your parents are…one upstate New York, one in Philly?"

It was a lame subject change, but Sam fielded it straight, relating that her mother had passed away but Dad was healthy and busy and refused to drive a foreign car—same as ever.

They talked another ten minutes. Jamie asked whether Sam knew anything of his old hallmate Norah Fowler. She didn't. She asked him about life in Juba. They chuckled remembering the band they'd "formed" (six practices in the Trumbull basement) junior year. Sam introduced her daughter, Joss, and somehow managed to make her the focus of every anecdote.

I've managed to learn all about plie and rond de jambe, haven't I?

Even through these unexciting exchanges, Jamie felt his admiration for Sam growing—or reconstituting, more accurately. She was so attuned to others, so ready to pause a story when another person approached, so quick to deflect credit.

Sam had been the same at Yale. Not necessarily making a splash in campus activism, but helping others in small but meaningful ways: covering a dining hall worker's shift, seeking out the artist to compliment her at one of the many gallery shows they'd attended together. Never saccharine or showy. Just humane.

It was this grace that made Jamie want to help Samantha Lessing. Because she needed help.

Jamie had experience with people whose facade clashed with their true situation—the villager who smiles in gratitude for rations but lives in constant fear of tribal violence. They're happy, but happy within bounds. They can smile but not with all their heart.

He doubted Sam's situation was life or death like those

Africans', but something was off. Some kink was holding her back, some plastic overwrap mistakenly left over a sunny window.

The daughter, Joss, kept tugging her mother's blazer.

Sam muttered, "Not now, okay?"

But the girl kept tugging and bulging her eyes—whatever it was couldn't wait.

"*But you should,*" the girl whispered. "*Mom, if you—*"

"Joss, please." Sam turned to Jamie with an apologetic shrug.

"She can ask," he said. "I don't mind—I'm strange, this whole morning is strange. Go ahead. Ask anything."

The girl beamed, boosting up on her toes. Sam shook her head in defeat.

"Fine," she said. "Joss is bugging me to tell you about this documentary I'm working on. It's about the pinebox vendetta, how it affected our class. I'm kinda looking into what the Pruitts did freshman year, how they hushed up Derek Dickerson's death."

Jamie felt all the warmth that'd bloomed over the last hour—during this magical reuniting with Sam—die. The buildings of the quad around him felt suddenly taller, and like they were rimmed with steel pikes.

Clearly noticing his reaction, she said, "It started before I knew you were...well, alive. And I completely wouldn't want to exploit your situation if you felt—"

"It's cool," Jamie recovered to say. "I mean, I know you—I know you'd do it in a classy way. Sounds like an interesting project."

Sam's mouth pinched. She didn't trust his blessing.

She was right not to trust.

Jamie did have objections. Just watching the daughter now, how her jaw set, how her stringy arms flexed. He knew exactly what was happening in that young mind. She imagined her mother landing a blow on the Pruitts—damaging them, exposing their dirty dealings. Justice would be served. The needle would tip incrementally their way.

Jamie knew this yearning, this bottomless thirst, better than anyone. It fueled you. It drove you to heights you didn't know you were capable of. It sustained you like food.

But if you let it, it could also eat you from inside.

CHAPTER 8

ROCK HEARD ABOUT JAMIE GALLAGHER'S RESURRECTION FROM Topher, his former DKE brother, as he and a third brother were hoovering lines of coke off a mirror. He assumed it was a joke at first.

"Jamie Gallagher? Did he have fins and carry a triton?"

"Nah," Topher said. "He walked right in during that memorial. They said it was like a ghost drifting through the gates of Silliman."

Rock flexed the inside of his face, enlarging his sinuses, trying at once to speed the drug's uptake and bring the wacko scene to mind.

Jamie Gallagher had never made sense. The Gallaghers were loose and carefree, not just liberals but liber*tines*—but Jamie'd been wound tighter than a Tijuana rod-ring. He was completely feckless, a namby-pamby. At Yale, people had always grouped him and Rock together because of the feud, but in fact they'd interacted little. Jamie had always acted vaguely scared of him, shying away at parties, turning away mumbling if Rock tried engaging.

"I gotta see," he said now. "I wonder if he went full native.

Dreadlocks and syphilis. I'll bet so. I'll bet he wipes ass with his left hand."

Rock asked the room at large what the next official reunion event was. He'd been crafting his own schedule, a manic circuit of bars, hotel rooms, and dive food-joints he and his buds used to frequent.

Topher said, "Whiffenpoofs concert, Old Campus."

Rock smacked his hands together. All-male singing groups made him want to stab his own eyes out, but he didn't figure on doing much listening.

He pointed at the last line of coke and said to his companion, "Halfsies?"

The frat brother nodded.

Rock covered one nostril, started at the base of the white-powder row, and mowed it down. Every speck.

"Raincheck," he promised, and headed for the door.

Rock's strides stretched out before him, devouring sidewalk panels. Dangerous thoughts sloshed through his well-greased brain. He wasn't sure what to do with—or to—Jamie Gallagher, like a jackal circling an indeterminate animal, collecting scents, weighing strategies.

Who was he walking over with? Rock had only a hazy idea. Topher he saw, oafing ahead with no flex in his trapezoids. Rock felt like Ross Jakes was in the mix, that horsey laugh honking intermittently from behind. Beyond that he had no clue.

Rock's notions of time were likewise murky. He knew only that he needed to be at New Haven Harbor by six o'clock when Marshall Pruitt's chopper was to depart for Long Island and the Choosing. Nobody had solicited his attendance at the Choosing, but Marshall had assured him he would be admitted: any Pruitt, by blood or marriage, was eligible.

Rock had asked what time Theresa Velasquez was arriving.

"Already there," the spymaster had said. "The favored few receive early access to Jonathan."

Now, thinking of Theresa sucking up to the ex-president with some BS ruminations on civility or fact-driven policies, Rock kicked the head of a street-planted sunflower clean off its stalk.

He arrived at Old Campus and initially couldn't find Jamie Gallagher. People kept holding him up, wanting his take on some issue or to share a toast.

The toasts he accepted; the takes he refused; and the Whiffenpoofs' warm-up scales he plugged his ears against.

Finally, he spotted the dirt-yellow hair of Jamie Gallagher. (No dreadlocks yet.) He was standing around a table of sculpted fruit, mercifully far from the stage.

Jamie stood with two females. One was a hot bohemian chick Rock found vaguely familiar. The other was younger. Also hot.

Didn't waste any time getting back in the game, did he?

Rock walked over, legs wide and obliterating space. He had three inches over the group.

The bohemian chick noticed him first. Her face—which had a pinkish pluck as Rock approached—turned black.

Jamie Gallagher, who was hanging on the chick's every word, noticed the change and turned. At the sight of Rock, he flinched half out of his Birkenstocks.

"Jamie. Freaking. Gallagher." Rock shook his head, marveling. "Not shark bait after all?"

He thrust his hand forward, daring Gallagher not to shake. He did—with surprising strength.

"Whoa now!" Rock said. "What've you been putting in your Wheaties, tiger semen? We should box."

Jamie pulled his hand back. "I'm out. I'm not your enemy—I'm not here for that." He shook his head. "I'm out. All the way."

Rock chuckled. "Out, huh? Man. How long were you unconscious for, down there at the bottom of the ocean? Just curious."

The bohemian chick stepped between them, her shoulder roughly brushing Rock's.

"Excuse me. I'm sure you don't care, but we were having a conversation." She squinted in the direction of his nose. "Maybe you ought to go find a glass of water. Check yourself into a clinic."

Again, Gallagher watched her like a lost man tracking the sun.

Rock ignored the chick. "Tell me what you hear about Owen Gallagher. They're running him out for a speech tomorrow, what's he going to say?"

"I'm out," Jamie said again. "I don't know one thing about Owen Gallagher or his plans. I've never even met him."

"I guess that'd be right. He came on the scene in 2012, you were still..." Rock made the gills motion over his cheeks. "How about your sis? Foxy Charlotte must have some coal in the fire, some Smart gizmo ready to take over the planet."

"I haven't seen her since I got back."

"No kidding? That's harsh. You're off chasing tail"—Rock raised his eyebrows flatteringly at the chick—"before you even hook up with your *family*?"

Gallagher seemed to be considering this—maybe Rock had hit a nerve—but the chick jumped in.

"Don't even engage with this...this oddity," she said, gently pushing Gallagher away. "There's no point."

"It's a reunion," Rock said. "What're reunions for? Reflecting, connecting, engaging. Engage me." He spread his arms wide in a show of forthrightness. "Engage!"

"You're disgusting."

Rock glanced to the side at the new speaker, the younger chick. Wrapping a strand of her own black hair around a slim finger.

"You say that now," he said with a rogue's grin, "but give me an hour, forty-five minutes minimum, and I'll convince you otherwise."

The older chick shoved him. "You should be locked up. People shouldn't have to walk around and share air with you."

The tough talk stirred Rock's loins. "'Share air.' I like that, lady. I like where you're taking us."

The three tried to relocate, moving away from the fruit table toward the shade of a towering maple tree.

Rock followed, calling, "Jamie, let's talk. We're the same. You and me are two peas in a pod. Screw our families, right? Screw their agendas."

The chick tried pushing him ahead, but Jamie answered over her head, "I already told you, I'm out. You can get all ginned up yourself, but I won't. I won't waste any more years. I'm just going to live."

And stood there with chin raised, like some band was about to strike up "The Battle Hymn of the Republic."

The man was, clearly, a moron. There was no such thing as "out" of the pinebox vendetta, short of winding up in a pinebox yourself. Even if you could disentangle yourself from the chits and alliances and outside expectation, you still had that inner need. That will to *fight*.

You could study philosophy. You could walk the earth like Jamie Gallagher. You could boink everything in sight—Rock had tried—but nothing matched the raw rush of power. The feud put it in your bones.

"Hey, I respect that." Rock was using every ounce of restraint to not laugh in Jamie Gallagher's face—the cocaine wasn't making it easy. "Don't think I haven't paid a price, too."

Something flashed across Gallagher's face that might've been the start, a faint precursor, of sympathy.

Rock thought, *I can use a moron.*

❧

Marshall Pruitt didn't hold his chopper for Rock, which was infuriating. Rock asked the helipad operator what time the old man had gone wheels up.

"One minute after six," said the ballcapped official.

It was 6:13.

Well, tits.

Rock gripped the nape of his neck and looked around. The helipad was part of the Port of New Haven, which was lucky. From where he and the operator stood, he could see a number of yachts—sleek, white wedges bobbing softly in the ash-blue water.

Most were covered or seemed empty, but aboard one, maybe a fifty-five-footer, a man in linens walked about loosing dock lines.

"Yo there, guvnor!" Rock called, starting that way. "A moment of your time?"

The man paused in a stoop. His hair was curly gray, his skin tanned to deep gold. A similar-aged woman carried two glasses of wine.

"Out for a sunset cruise, aye? Atta way to keep the fires stoked." Rock shook both their hands. "Rock Pruitt. Fine dinghy you got here."

The man accepted a glass from his wife, keeping his distance from Rock. "Are you—that is, can I help you find somebody?"

"Nope," Rock said. "But you can take me to Long Island and meet the former President of the United States."

Thirty minutes later, Rock and his new friends were putting into Amagansett, the yacht's wine cellar two bottles lighter. George Nagourney tied up to one of three piers on the Pruitt shoreline.

Though the family kept this Long Island retreat out of media reports—ties to the New York Metro area were a liability among its core constituencies—it was among their most impressive real estate holdings. The house was baronial, forty thousand sprawling square feet of brick and Italian stone. The grounds featured a perimeter of lush forest, ensuring privacy.

Rock hopped out to an empty dock. "You're kidding—nobody else boated here? This clan's headed downhill fast."

George and Sandra picked their way over sand after him, under a purple-tinged twilight. They'd spent the ride refilling his glass, watching and listening to him like some exotic parrot who'd alighted on their boat.

Rock led them to a side entrance, where two plainclothes guards recognized him immediately. Their faces emerged from shadows with broad grins.

"Gentlemen!" Rock clutched each by the elbow, these men with whom he'd done a deed or two for Marshall.

One unlocked a heavy door, permitting Rock and his new friends inside.

The other said, "We're rooting for you. Knock 'em dead."

Rock bumped fists. "I may have to."

He breezed through the mansion's service wing, grabbing a handful of bacon-wrapped scallops en route, tossing a pair back to the Nagourneys, who scrambled to keep pace. Starting in the third kitchen, he heard the din from the Grand Hall, mingled voices and glass tinkles rising over strains of Beethoven.

Everybody was here.

At the threshold, Rock pulled a fingernail across his top gums —what genius put poppy seeds on the beef tongue sliders?—and surveyed the scene. Here was Coach Pruitt up from Mississippi in his sweater vest. Karl Peoples representing the Michigan wing. Neither had an obvious connection to the Virginia seat.

Were they just sightseeing? Positioning themselves for the presidential cycle after next?

The Choosing seemed to be either between sessions or in a glad-handing period, where the contenders were supposed to circulate and demonstrate their skill pressing the flesh. In an adjoining dining room, folding chairs and a half-dozen lecterns were being arranged.

Yes. He hadn't missed the debate.

Rock found Jonathan Pruitt on the far side of the Grand Hall, before a towering wall of windows overlooking the sea. His suit was charcoal. The blue of fresh-shorn sideburns could be seen twenty yards away.

Glued to his side was Theresa Velasquez.

"Hey, ho!" Rock butted his way through the crowd, bumping ambassadors and junior House members. "You two must be discussing how to win over those Reagan Democrats in Norfolk, right?"

Theresa looked at Rock like he was mold on her smear of Brie.

But Rock didn't care about that.

He cared about Jonathan Pruitt—and there was a crinkle in the former president's face, the merest hint of amusement.

You gotta start someplace.

Jonathan looked past him to George Nagourney. "Did you bring your own pollster?"

Rock pulled the man forward by his lapel. "A supporter of yours, gave you a couple votes!" The two men shook. "George gave me a berth over from New Haven."

Jonathan hadn't the foggiest what that meant—Rock could tell from his mouth angle—but asked cordially, "And how is my alma mater?"

"Myopic beyond belief," Rock said.

Jonathan smiled perfunctorily and pivoted to Theresa, no doubt eager to resume their euphoric discussion of Northern Virginia's changing demographics and her unique ability to capitalize, when an opportunity occurred to Rock.

"They're christening Gallagher College tomorrow, you know," he said. "I have an operation underway...I think we can land a stiff body blow on Owen Gallagher."

Jonathan's stance stayed toward Theresa, but interest flickered in his face. "We've not had much luck getting to that one."

"Right, because you've had the B team on the field." Rock

opened his palm to Theresa. "No offense, but affirmative action weakens the Pruitts. Like it weakens the country."

Theresa scoffed. The flag pin on her breast glinted in a chandelier's light. "I'm not running against Owen Gallagher. I've been out on my campaign bus listening to the people of Virginia."

"Yeah? What do they say, that they're itching for a bland waffler who advocates cop killing and is soft on immigration?"

Theresa glanced to Jonathan to see whether the former president would intervene. He didn't, only clasped his hands at his waist and watched. This was part of the Choosing—sparring, responding when you got scratched.

"I've been on the front lines in Iraq and Afghanistan," Theresa said, her voice steely and sure. "When you've faced IEDs and shoulder-fired rockets, when you've been up against *real* grenades, Rock? You don't get rattled by the conversational kind."

She finished with a sip of what looked like water. Jonathan smiled his approval—and, it seemed to Rock, his relief.

Jonathan Pruitt was a man who hated risk, an odd trait for one who'd ascended to such heights. In Rock's opinion, it had been his downfall as president. The Gallaghers had effectively ousted him with their investigation of a pay-to-play pardon, which everyone in the town's political class knew to be nonsense.

Jonathan had pardoned a man serving forty years in jail for insider trading. The guy, Ian Poeskey, had gotten railroaded— weak testimony from bitter underlings, the prosecutor dropping his Polish-Russian ties like blood in the jury pool. Poeskey's wife petitioned Jonathan directly, bringing their three daughters into the Roosevelt Room.

Her husband was innocent. They were nearly destitute. *Would he help?*

Jonathan believed her, his conviction buoyed by disturbing journalism about the trial and Poeskey's apparent guilelessness at disclosing his full fortune to the court.

Within days of the pardon, Gallagher-led Democrats were

pushing media accounts of Poeskey associates making large contributions to the Pruitts' political PAC. There was rumored to be some shady fixer living in a Capitol Hill basement apartment who had documents proving a coordinated effort to curry Jonathan's favor. They even smeared the wife and daughters, suggesting they'd offered unsavory favors.

Rock remembered the girls' headshots—absolutely smoking, blond, the stuff of oligarchs' arm candy. For the Gallaghers, it must've looked like fish in a barrel.

Marshall went to his younger brother in the scandal's early days and suggested a counter-move. His men had a bead on the fixer. The sleaze was lawyering up, angling for maximum payout for his "incriminating" documents.

We can extract them. The documents can disappear with zero footprint from my people.

Jonathan Pruitt refused. He'd done nothing wrong. He had listened to an honest woman, reviewed all facts, and exercised the powers of his office for good.

He realized the Gallaghers had no interest in truth and would keep attacking, but he believed his innocence would win out. He refused to risk a cover-up, to instigate actual crimes in order to insulate himself against non-crimes.

The Democrats grandstanded their way through hearings, Joan Gallagher thundering away about "the staggering perpetuation of privilege," and nominated an anti-Wall Street candidate to oppose his reelection. Jonathan maintained his innocence. The economy was booming. He'd steered the country out of two wars and around a third.

No way could he lose.

He was innocent.

"The American people know better."

He said this at debates; he said it in the maelstrom after the October-surprise reveal of the fixer's documents, as his lead was disappearing; and he said it to aides on election night, as the cable networks were calling Ohio—and with it, the election—for the challenger.

Now Rock feigned looking behind Theresa. "Where are you hiding your husband? He's the reason you're on this gravy train, after all. You didn't leave him back in Hicksville, did you?"

Theresa glanced down, a reflex that told Rock he'd found softness. "He was in the smoking lounge. Perhaps you'll want to catch up. I understand you two used to scrum together in the summers?"

"Against, usually. I knocked out three of his teeth in ninety-four."

Rock had another hour until the debate started. He used the time to tick off to-dos. He reconnected with his supervisor at Pruitt Capital, Kim Stricker, a potential source of campaign funds. He made two phone calls: to his wife, confirming her availability for photo ops next week, and to a certain service provider in Manhattan who assured him she could get the requested resources to the Amagansett address by ten.

Rock won the debate, easy. This was a given. Beyond the high school trophies, he had routinely obliterated opponents in previous races—his last primary foe famously bowed out of the race after Rock wielded his logic scalpel on the man's farm subsidy position. (Non-position, more accurately.)

Tonight, he wittily batted off character digs. He veered from party orthodox—"Confederate monuments, why? Gimme a hardhat and bulldozer"—and when challenged, dodged aside and scored points on rebuttal. The drugs in his system were at just the proper ebb.

The rapt crowd fueled him, reminding him why he wanted the Virginia seat at all, rather than raking in seven figures with Pruitt Capital or another of the clan's lucrative private arms.

Power.

Adulation.

He stood tall, spoke evenly, and dominated.

As with all debates, though, this one was judged against expectations—and by that standard, Theresa Velasquez fared well. She varied her delivery of talking points and worked in anecdotes from her upbringing in a Charleston foster home. (Rock resisted the urge to start humming violin chords.) Her answers on social issues were clunky, but she gripped her lectern with two hands and emoted.

She concluded, "I pledge to fight for what I believe is right, and to fight for the families of Virginia."

Puke.

As great as his performance had been, Rock received conspicuously few congratulations. A few passing smiles and one hearty pounding between the shoulder blades from William Pruitt the Third—Billy, who owed his gerrymandered House seat to Rock's nifty subterfuge.

Then nada.

Rock was standing in the Grand Hall, chest full in the face of the collective cricket chirps, when Marshall Pruitt wheeled up with two drinks in his lap.

He handed Rock one. "I took the liberty. Gin and tonic."

"Much obliged," Rock said. "How'd it play with Jonathan?"

The spymaster inhaled through tight teeth. Rock was reminded of that Van Gogh of the skull with a cigarette. "He understands what you bring to the table."

"But?"

"You walked in ten runs down."

Rock growled, a rising primal noise starting from his heart.

For the millionth time, he cursed the Derek Dickerson thing. Over the years, his reputation had suffered plenty of self-inflicted damage, fine, but it was that original stain he kept bumping up against. Jonathan refused to see past it.

What could Rock do?

Bump harder.

Now he and Marshall worked the room, greeting donors and

media influencers against the vast, restless backdrop of Long Island Sound. Though Marshall was respected and facile with civilians, Rock still felt strange standing off his left wheel, like the pet human of some lethal reptile. He supposed he couldn't complain. Marshall was the only high-placed member of the clan willing to be seen with him.

They had some fun. Karl Peoples, the former governor of Michigan who'd made his fortune in carnivals, was absolutely on fire talking about the legalization of marijuana.

"We oughta get behind it, federal, nationwide!" said the man, who stood a good six-six and talked so loudly, every flounder in the Sound must've heard. "It's the right thing to do. Everyone knows it's coming anyhow. Why not take the votes?"

"That's all true." Rock didn't believe this, but he liked Karl. "But have you met Jonathan Pruitt? Used to be president? How's he going to feel when *The New Yorker* runs a cartoon of him in a ponytail, holding a bong and empty bag of Doritos?"

Karl boomed out a laugh. The Michigan Pruitts had always chafed at Jonathan's orthodoxy. Karl—the son of Rock's great uncle, who'd moved them to the Midwest on becoming CEO of General Motors—campaigned in open-collared shirts at the county fairs his carnival traveled to, downplaying the clan's social positions whenever possible.

Occasionally the rift flared and there would be talk of dissolving the Pruitt caucus, but cooler heads always prevailed. Apart, the two factions' power would be diffused, lost in the mix of nationalists and budget hawks, evangelicals and Tea Party holdouts. Together, they had the muscle—and votes—to seize the horns of the Republican bull and steer.

"Fair enough," Karl said, "but it's a lost opportunity. Owen Gallagher won't take a position. He's being cautious, see. Thinks he's the frontrunner. If we go first, we look like the future."

Rock eyed the man suspiciously. "What're you here for?"

Karl Peoples made a defensive sound like an *oink*.

Rock said, "You want to run, don't you? For president?"

Karl said no, no, he was only—

"You *do*," Rock cut in. "Holy hell. Jonathan's not going to run anybody against the dick. We're sitting this one out, didn't you get the memo?"

Karl spluttered about circumstances being fluid, *never could tell, could ya?* and various other evasions that all added up to *oh, yes.*

He wanted to seize the Republican nomination from a sitting president.

"Karl, you've got ideas, I grant you that," Rock said to the taller man. "But I think you've ridden that tilt-a-whirl of yours one too many times."

❧

Jonathan Pruitt addressed the room at nine o'clock. He mounted one of two arcing stairwells to a demi-balcony, resting his hands on a parapet of obsidian oakwood—straight out of *Titanic.*

"Please accept our most cordial thanks," he began. "Virginia is a crucial seat, and all your efforts tonight help ensure we put forth the very best candidate. At this point, formal events are over. I'll open up the hall to glad-handing now. Myself and the senior leadership will be out on the floor, in the mix.

"Please treat this as an opportunity. We're looking for women and men of action. If we've learned anything in the last few races, it's that we are no longer in a world where candidates are anointed—where discussions in shady backrooms land you in power. We need candidates who ignite passion, who're capable of shaping events around them."

Listening, Rock felt his insides rev. He bounced between the balls of his feet like an MMA fighter during intros.

He's cracking the door. He's signaling to the others I'm back in the conversation.

Rock eyed Theresa across the room. She was already busy working the crowd, flashing her pensive smile in a circle with media firebrand Zoe Pruitt. Hovering nearby were the oil-magnate Gibsons, the husband-wife pair who'd endorsed the dick in the last presidential primary, and some Heritage Foundation folks.

The only person who *didn't* seem to desperately want an audience with Theresa Velasquez?

Her husband.

Rock found Bryce Pruitt in the smoking lounge.

"Ruck and roll, baby!" Rock called. "Bring your scrum cap?"

Bryce was chatting with a pair of pals, who took off now.

"Rock Pruitt," he said. "It's been forever. How are you?"

"Damn good. You?"

The man had ballooned into a clone of his father, who'd been chief justice of the Louisiana Supreme Court before succumbing to a massive heart attack. "Alright."

"Alright?" Rock poured forward into the lounge, the noxious air stinging his eyes and throat. "We're surrounded by untold privilege—booze, Cubans"—nodding to his cigar—"ladies who'd boff us for nothing. And all you are is *alright?*"

Bryce took another puff. He picked at a button of a chaise lounge.

Rock wondered how he felt about joining the Senate husbands' club. "You'll make four, correct? Almost enough for a sewing circle."

"Real funny."

"Not at all. Congressional spouses wield huge power. Did you know Trent Lott's wife designed the Senate curtains? They used to be blinds. Can you believe that, *blinds?*"

Bryce looked up with bright hate.

Rock said, "I made that up. Who knows, though? She could have."

During his presidency, Jonathan Pruitt had tried installing

Bryce on the Eleventh Circuit Court of Appeals. Bryce had been a successful enough corporate lawyer in Baton Rouge with powerful clients—having a father who adjudicates the law of the land surely helped—but his confirmation hearings had been a disaster.

His credentials were belittled. Aides testified that Bryce had used state funds on blowout LSU football tailgates. That he'd forwarded anti-Muslim emails and pursued women in the office. Pretty mild stuff. Jonathan had figured he could sneak a Pruitt onto the Eleventh, down south in Atlanta, not as important as the Fourth in DC or Ninth Circuit out in nut-ball San Fran. But the other side had different ideas.

Bryce said, "I'll probably stay back in Charlottesville."

"Oh?"

"I'm active with the foundation, Children's Mercy. It'd be hard to walk away from all my work there."

Rock took a long swig of whatever was in his tumbler.

He caught Bryce's drift, loud and clear. Bryce Pruitt was his own man, with his own dealings, and his own staff, and surrounded by his own posse of volunteer housewives clawing their way up the nonprofit ladder while their husbands slaved away in corner offices.

"What say we take a walk?" Rock suggested. The lounge exited to a winding footpath, which led to the beach. "It stinks in here."

Bryce hesitated. Of course he knew that Rock wanted what his wife had, or nearly had.

"Aw, she's got it in the bag," Rock said. "I don't care. I'm just auditioning for the next one, North Carolina. Did you know their governor's mansion sits on *nine acres*?"

Eventually, after appeals to blood being thicker than marriage and all this politics rigmarole being garbage, Bryce agreed to join him for a walk.

They stripped off shoes and socks, and Rock pocketed a fifth of brandy. The beach felt brave on his bare feet, gritty and cold.

The air truly was a boon, fluid, almost sweet after the foul lounge. Nearing the water, Rock felt a swelling anticipation, as though some leviathan might rise out of the frothy surf.

Bryce walked on the mansion side, Rock beside the Sound.

The former said, "This is warped."

Rock skipped over a deep-crashing wave. "Why can't two cousins have a little walk 'n' talk—"

"The whole thing," Bryce cut in hoarsely. "The Choosing. Ridiculous. It's all just a power trip for the elders."

Rock was surprised at the gripe—at such easy intimacy. He wasn't about to discourage it. "They do love watching us on their hamster wheel."

They walked several paces in silence. Bryce's thick body didn't suit the sand; his feet seemed to bury themselves fresh with each stride.

"I never asked for that judgeship," Bryce said. "Do you think they even checked to see if I wanted it? If I wanted to uproot my family, move to Atlanta?"

"Thought you divorced that wife."

"We still had kids—I saw them every weekend!" Bryce kicked the beach. "He didn't care, Jonathan. His people. They wanted a friendly vote on the appellates, and it was worth the gamble. So they lost. So what."

Rock took the rare step of holding his tongue. *Just how worked up did he want this one?* This fat, whiny weakling.

How much bitterness do I need?

Bryce continued, "Those emails were in my Junk folder—I never even opened them."

"I hate email," Rock said. "I'm ready to nuke my computer and go back to parchment."

Behind them came a giggle. Then a high shriek, riding moist shoots of wind to their ears.

Rock pivoted casually but kept walking. Bryce twisted around, squinting down the beach.

There were two women. One blond. One redhead. Their smiles hung when they saw Rock and Bryce. They were walking waist-deep in the Sound, clutching each other by the wrist and forearm.

The blond whispered to the redhead.

Rock took a step back their way. "Brandy?" He waved the bottle. "We're good sharers."

They giggled again and stepped out of the water. As the ocean sheeted off them, two flawless bodies glinted in the moonlight. They wore swimsuits and silk wraps around their chests.

Bryce was rooted to his spot. His eyes couldn't have been wider if they'd had mermaid tails.

Rock handed him the bottle.

⚜

Rock rejoined the Choosing shortly after eleven. The lobbyists and mid-level bundlers had been allowed in, and the Grand Hall chittered with the minutiae of budgetary riders, pet projects, and deregulation. Limousines appeared in the horseshoe drive to take people home. Servers pulled pewter coffee urns through the crowd.

Wonderfully spent, Rock found the liveliest conversation circle—the best chance to make waves. Several prominent donors were engaged with Zoe Pruitt and Theresa Velasquez.

"…God still matters, you can't win Virginia without Him," Zoe was saying, a phrase she uttered often to her two-million-strong cable TV audience. "It's essential that our candidate have ties to the church. Clear, authentic ties."

As the donors listened, Theresa saw Rock arrive. She took her usual tack of ignoring him, joining Zoe in a tag-team performance, pounding the stakes of the election to the money men. The governor of Virginia might have the opportunity to sign (or veto) legislation on abortion, freedom of religious expression, charter schools…Republicans couldn't afford to nominate a candidate of questionable faith.

Rock stood on the periphery, picking his spot, letting them go ahead and slam him without mentioning his name.

When Theresa used the word "authentic" herself, he struck.

"Yes, you are just *so excruciatingly authentic*," he said, stretching the words until they were see-through. "I'll bet you go to the churchiest church around, don't you? Vestry, acolyte every Sunday. Whole nine yards."

She shook her head. "I attend a small church in Charlottesville. We're humble. Maybe forty parishioners? More on holidays, of course."

"Of course."

They stared at one another.

Theresa would've been well-served to stop here, to show restraint and let Rock be the a-hole. But Rock had a unique ability in these stare-down situations to goad people. He could summon that extra obnoxiousness to his face, that flat disdain people simply couldn't leave be.

"Virginia has smart voters," she said. "They can spot a fake. They'll see right through the man who comes strolling into the capital's big downtown church six months before the election."

The donors hummed reverently. It was well-known to all that Rock hadn't seen the inside of a church since the funeral of Jonathan's mother at Washington National Cathedral.

"Voters *are* smart," Rock agreed. "They're smart—and they're sick of voting for robots. What they want are living, breathing people with relatable narratives."

This prompted more hums—fewer than for Theresa, but at least Rock was getting on the scorecard.

Zoe Pruitt jumped in, "I would argue it depends on the narrative. A godless man who's thought to have killed his college roommate? How many constituents relate to that?"

Rock bit back an impulse to push those minimalist, quarter-sized glasses right through Zoe's face. The Dickerson reference couldn't be helped. He just had to eat it. "Godless," though, he could fix.

He took a gathering breath and allowed his eyes to flutter.

"'The Lord is not slow in keeping his promise as some understand slowness. Instead he is patient with you, not wanting anyone to perish, but everyone to come to redemption.'"

The jaw of oil-magnate George Gibson fell open. Theresa Velasquez moved one hand up her hip.

Rock added, "Second book of Peter, third verse. In case anyone's rusty on their Scripture."

Zoe Pruitt centered her glasses using a middle finger. "What's your game, Rock?"

He showed his hands, palms out. "I've fallen at His feet. The drugs, the shady financial dealings, the wayward impulses—which I acknowledge and would expect to emerge during the campaign? That's all done. I've asked the Lord to show me the way."

Zoe and Theresa continued to regard him skeptically, but the donors were hanging on his words.

People always said Rock's flouting of Jonathan Pruitt's church-attendance dictate would hurt him, but Rock knew better. He knew it could be parlayed into a redemption story. Give him three minutes on the subject in a debate, and he'd have the electorate believing he fell asleep every night seeing heaven's white lights.

Zoe Pruitt's phone dinged.

Theresa Velasquez's dinged, too. And Rock's, and several phones from the conversation circles on either side.

Everybody's phone was dinging.

Rock stole a glance across the Grand Hall to Marshall Pruitt, seated near the fireplace. Their eyes hitched before moving along.

Theresa Velasquez inhaled sharply. "What? How—how did this, how could he…"

Every Pruitt had swiveled to find her, raising up in their heels or wingtips, peering between coiffed heads and jeweled ears.

Rock couldn't smile, but he was drinking it in. Here was nourishment for his grievances—for the unfairness of Dickerson, for the leg-up Velasquez's ethnicity granted her. For everything.

Heat rippled through his body.

He waited until most were looking at their phones, then checked his. When he clicked the text, an image grew to his full screen.

Marshall's man had snapped an absolute money shot. Bryce Pruitt's face was centered perfectly, sweaty, seeking. The hooker's back was arched, her skin blindingly pale and that whipping hair so red—just like Rock had insisted upon, very clearly not Theresa Velasquez.

No mistaking this for a couple's home job.

"Yowser," Rock said, putting away his phone. "I move we table politics for now. Just, you know, out of respect."

CHAPTER 9

Sam took Joss to "Intersecting Studies of Dance and Quantum Physics." Laurel came, too, the three of them sitting in metal folding chairs in an airy ballet studio as an associate professor performed *grand jetés* and explained how the ebb and flow of subatomic particles mimicked classical dance. The woman was in her late twenties and commuted up from Manhattan, hair razed at a severe angle, tossing off references to CERN and the eccentric pizza-topping preferences of Nobel laureates she collaborated with.

Sam barely heard.

Jamie Gallagher was alive. For so long he'd been a ghost, gauzy memories of goofy grins and mountain bikes and a dingy rucksack, entwined with Sam's own from youth. It took her a while to orient him back into the living, touchable world—the world of today.

Every ten minutes, she remembered and re-experienced that runaway, mind-blowing joy from the candle ceremony.

She wished he were here, sitting beside her so there was no risk he'd vanish back into the ether.

She and Laurel had offered. After catching up in the

courtyard, they'd walked Jamie to registration (in a surreal twist, his name was grayed-out in the volunteer's list) and checked him into his room.

"We're hitting this dance and physics lecture at eleven-fifteen," Sam had said. "Care to join us?"

Jamie had started to say yes, but then his eyes had flicked to Joss and he'd demurred. "I—I should make some calls…the rest of my family has probably heard by now."

Though Sam wasn't sure, she thought she had detected skittishness—at seeming too forward, at putting her in a compromising position. Something about how he kept his head slightly back in conversation.

Remembering now, that uncomfortable-looking kink in Jamie's neck, Sam was helpless against a comparison with Abe. Abe, who'd texted again about the nineteen-volt charger. Who, when he misplaced his apartment keys for more than three seconds, would scream for her to come help look regardless of what she was doing.

The lecture dismissed at noon. Joss burst from the brownstone that housed the ballet studio, arms arched gracefully overhead.

"The CERN particle accelerator, *are you serious?*" She looked between Sam and Laurel's faces. "That was amazing! I can't wait to tell Miss Moreau about how quarks swing…"

As she danced over cobblestone, dipping one shoulder and then the other like a happy airplane, both women smiled.

Laurel said, "This reunion's about fifty times more exciting than the ten-year."

Sam laughed. "Right. I can't believe about Jamie. It's…" What other word was there? "Wonderful."

"And great for your documentary, too," Laurel said. "You know there'll be gobs more media coverage now."

This dented Sam's smile. Maybe it was true, but she hated the idea of kiting press off Jamie's reemergence. When Joss had mentioned the project, Jamie had seemed downright spooked by it.

Sam hadn't decided how she felt herself. Jamie's tragedy had partly inspired the project, and now that tragedy was... diminished? Less tragic?

More complicated, for sure.

Sam decided to deflect. "Oh, I'm a disaster with marketing. I tried to pitch in promoting our Nicaraguan birds piece? Brutal. I spent twenty hours calling around to bloggers and got one mention out of it. *One*. Some guy in Florida, two thousand page views a month."

Laurel sympathized, revealing that her own blog got even less traffic—and that she was thinking of scrapping her memoir due to complete and total apathy from literary agents. She'd enrolled in a night-school law program, which she hoped would give her more career flexibility.

Sam was surprised by the disclosures. As they passed the chic boutiques of Chapel Street on their way to a reunion lunch event, she wondered about the change in tone.

Did it have to do with Jamie? Some kind of realization that life was fleeting, and that petty bragging was a poor way to spend it?

Sam got her answer at lunch, over soggy pizza slices at everybody's favorite freshman haunt, Naples.

"Listen, I need to say something to you," Laurel began once the surrounding conversations gave them a private moment. "This is hard. My stomach just—since this morning, I've felt sick..."

Sam took her friend's hand over the table. "Laurel, it's okay. No sweat, okay? Whatever it is."

Laurel inhaled deeply. "That postcard. The one Jamie told you he sent?"

Sam kept an even expression, but a tumbling started inside.

Her friend continued, "The post office didn't lose it."

Sam didn't understand at first. She had mentioned the postcard in passing to Laurel, back in the dorm room as they were getting ready for the dance-physics course.

Was Laurel making some progressive argument about government services—how easy they were to criticize, but essential in a just society?

"I guess that's, I mean, possible," Sam said. "I like the post office. I didn't mean to—"

"I threw it away. I was jealous—it was right after Willem." Laurel's eyes crunched shut. "I was just very bitter then, and I got home before you one night and there was Jamie's postcard, with his messy handwriting, with this beautiful cityscape from Macedonia…"

For a moment, everything stopped in Sam's chest.

Willem Kirk had lived in their building, an NYU grad student working on a comparative literature PhD. Laurel had been interested, inviting him to dinner at their apartment and attending his poetry readings at Nuyorican. They'd hooked up a few times, but Willem had kept his distance, claiming he was in the "wrong epoch of life" for a relationship.

One night, though, Willem had gotten blotto and professed a crush on Sam. *He'd capture the moon for her! They would hike the Italian Dolomites together—the very moment he finished this blasted dissertation!*

Sam had turned him and his black turtleneck away. Laurel had been out of town and she felt they'd both dodged a bullet— Willem seemed the type to steer clear rather than return to the scene of his embarrassment.

Weeks later, though, Laurel learned the truth from a mutual friend.

Sam might've told Laurel herself—clearly Laurel was better off without the poser—if not for the fact that it continued a hurtful pattern between the two. Jamie Gallagher had not been the only boy who'd preferred Sam to Laurel.

Now Sam mastered her shock. "No worries. Laurel, please."

Laurel had covered her face with both hands.

"Come on," Sam said, "that was how many years ago? It so doesn't matter. Not one bit."

"It was awful," Laurel gasped. "It was heinous. And now—I mean, who knows how you guys might've ended up if—"

"No." Sam wedged apart her friend's hands so she could look Laurel directly in the eye. "That's a false line of reasoning. How my life turned out, how Jamie's life did—it had nothing to do with some little square of paper."

Laurel took several shaky breaths. She didn't quite seem to believe the assurance.

Sam said, "Do not worry another second about this. Jamie and I weren't going to get together after college. We weren't like that —I had my acting, he had his family stuff. It had zero chance. Okay?"

Finally, Laurel nodded, and they embraced, Sam rubbing circles in her friend's back. In another minute, they went back to their slices.

Joss had been talking animatedly to another teen, but now turned to her mother with a question in her eyes.

Sam mouthed, *it's fine*.

For fifteen minutes, they ate and joined larger conversations. The reunion proper was halfway through and easy topics had been exhausted, giving way to touchier ones like child-rearing styles and current events.

The subject of the Pruitts and Gallaghers was bound to come up. When it did, Sam drank water and became very interested in her pizza crust.

Maybe she should've mined the moment for footage, sneaked the Zoom from her purse up onto the table. With all today's emotion, though—and now Laurel's admission, which she couldn't help but cast back over the last twenty years of her life, no matter what she had just said—Sam couldn't. She couldn't bring herself to care about a documentary.

Everybody knew about Jamie's reemergence. Troy Fickert thought it was amazing and wondered how he'd wriggled out of "that crazy Africa thing." When neither Sam nor Laurel spoke up, though, he took the cue and dropped it.

"Big news on Rock Pruitt, too," Troy said after a pause. "You guys hear?"

The friend group assembled here was mostly Democrat. Somebody said, "Do we want to?"

"Ha ha," Troy laughed. "Probably not. But I'll tell you anyway. He's running for that open Virginia Senate seat."

Laurel reared up in her chair. "How? I thought the family quit supporting him after Derek Dickerson."

"Supposedly he blew away the competition in that Choosing, you know the contest they do? I have a buddy in DKE, he told me."

Troy pulled another slice of sausage-mushroom off a tin plate.

Sam had intended to stay ten million miles away from the subject, but she couldn't help herself now.

"Wasn't Jonathan Pruitt's campaign slogan, *Returning Dignity to the White House, to Your House?*" Her teeth were grinding. "What a crock. They're really going to let that psycho represent them? A guy who probably bludgeoned his roommate to death?"

Her language chilled the group. Sitting at a corner of the table, Joss pushed bangs behind her ears.

Troy said, "Yeah, I was surprised. I guess in this day and age you can fudge past stuff. The truth's fungible, right? It happened a while ago. People forget."

A gloom settled over the table, dark as if somebody had closed every blind in the room.

They'd all read articles about—and witnessed on live television—the decay of political discourse, the coarsening of the culture. It sucked. Nobody had expected the late nineties to feel more enlightened than sixteen years into the next century.

But *this*?

The idea that Rock Pruitt, whom they'd all suffered firsthand, could be dragged up from the bottom of the swamp, slime hosed off, and made into an American leader?

Laurel nudged Sam under the table. Joss was looking at her, those fourteen-year-old eyes passionate, blistering.

Sam knew exactly what they were feeling. She felt it, too.

The reunion schedule had a gap after lunch. Sam decided to kick her cold-case research into high gear.

"Joss, you don't need to be involved," she said, packing up the Zoom. "I know you've made some friends here—you could check out the Peabody, or just hang."

Her daughter looked like it'd just been suggested she quit guitar.

"Are you kidding? I have to be involved! We have to remind people who he is."

"I'm with you there," Sam said, "but I didn't want your weekend to be about this. I wanted you focused on Yale, on seeing what a college campus was actually like."

"I *have* been." Joss was in full indignant mode, squeezing the cuffs of her shirt. "Isn't this campus all about progress? About social justice? What better way to participate than stopping Rock Pruitt?"

Sam could've said more to discourage the idea—should have, maybe—but her heart wasn't in it.

She felt the same anger Joss did. It sickened her to see Rock Pruitt ascendant while Jamie Gallagher pieced his life back together from shards.

Because even though she'd been overjoyed to learn he was alive, even though he'd seemed fulfilled from his decade in Africa, Jamie had scars. Sam had witnessed them, even in the few hours they'd had together. Certain topics flummoxed him. His sentences looked back over their shoulders, fearful of what they did or didn't imply.

Joss, clearly reading the decision in her mother's face, smiled and clapped in front of her waist. "What do we do, how do we start?"

Sam pushed into the entryway.

"You start at the start," she said over her shoulder, "like my first film studies professor used to say. And this started with Derek Dickerson."

The police had recovered Dickerson's body in his and Rock's dorm room, an exclusive suite called "The God Quad." Sam led Joss down College and Elm to Branford, the residential college that contained the God Quad. She used her phone to take a few stills of the courtyard, wide shots emphasizing the peaks' height and variegated stone.

She tried the door to J, the God Quad's entryway, but found it locked.

Too bad the undergraduates were on break—somebody might've let her in or at least answered a few questions on tape about the current student body's knowledge of the event.

Joss twisted on the ball of her foot. "Now what?"

Sam put her phone away and looked around the courtyard. Today's weather was fair, the cloudless blue sky matching the deserted dormitories here.

"Hm. I wonder if Branford has the same dean. It used to be Henrik Schumer, the poet. Maybe he's still around."

They headed for the administrative entryway, near the Branford dining hall. A heavy plank door was propped. Sam held it open for Joss, who stayed back shyly, possibly intimidated by Schumer, whose poetry still appeared on high school syllabuses.

Placards designated the left office as master's and the right as dean's.

Sam approached the latter. "Hello? Professor Schumer?"

A voice from behind answered, "Right name. Wrong office."

She whirled to find Henrik Schumer walking stiffly from his desk in the master's office.

"They moved me across the hall," he explained. "Five, six years now. Dean of students is a young person's job."

He ushered Sam and Joss into leather armchairs.

"I must apologize," he said. "I've had so many Branford ninety-sixers through today that I'm afraid my recall of names is eroding. You were…?"

"Oh, I wasn't in Branford," Sam said. "I came here hoping you might chat with me for a documentary I'm working on."

She raised the Zoom from its case and briefly described the project. She didn't know quite how the poet would take her request to be recorded. There was no question his politics leaned left, but would he feel it was appropriate to comment? A college dean is dean for all students, after all, and twenty years ago, Rock Pruitt had been a member of Branford College.

Sam need not have worried.

"By all means," he said in his starchy accent. "Bring out your recorder, have at it."

A giddy chirp escaped Joss. She quickly crossed her arms.

Sam said, "After Derek Dickerson's death, you were involved in the police investigation, correct?"

"I was. It was I who coordinated the authorities' access to the dormitories, to students they chose to interview."

"And were you contacted by members of the Pruitt family?"

Henrik Schumer took on an affronted air. "From the very first moment they became aware of the incident—the following morning—to the time the coroner declared the cause of death 'Undetermined,' essentially clearing their man, not a day passed without my hearing from either the Pruitt's legal counsel or one of their number directly."

"You were pressured?"

"Relentlessly."

"Asked to conceal things? Witnesses? The scope of a forensic investigation?"

"The witnesses had all been tampered with," Henrik said. "By the time the police came calling, the Pruitts had already spoken with anyone who'd seen Mr. Pruitt or Mr. Dickerson that evening."

"And you know that, er, because—"

"The students told me." Henrik used his arms to cross one leg over the other. "It was shameful. I registered complaints with Yale and the state police. I stopped returning the Pruitts' calls."

Sam chuckled. "How did *that* go over?"

"Not well," the poet said. "I was threatened with legal action, and at least two literary journals were compelled to stop publishing my work."

Sam could feel Joss coiling beside her, stewing, angry.

"Okay, well that's…disheartening," Sam said. "Do you mind if we talk about some of the forensic details on the record? They're all more or less public domain, but it helps—just for audio, for the documentary—to have somebody voice them."

She'd been mulling who would be best to lay out these block-and-tackle facts. She could have done it herself in voiceover, but Henrik was turning out to be such a rockstar source that she figured it was worth asking.

He agreed.

"Great—thank you, I appreciate it," Sam said, flipping through a notepad to her page of known facts.

They talked through the baseline story. The coroner's declaration. Rock being the last person to be seen with Derek Dickerson alive. His claim to have returned at two a.m. and discovered his roommate's dead body.

"*Belated* claim," Henrik said. "Initially, Mr. Pruitt said he couldn't recall returning home. He'd been too inebriated. He'd blacked out. Two weeks later, after corroborating with the Pruitt legal team, the night's events returned serendipitously into focus."

"I'll bet," Sam said. "And did he ever give any hypotheses about where Dickerson's injuries came from?"

"It was Mr. Pruitt's assertion," Henrik said, "that Mr. Dickerson must have *fallen against the corner of their coffee table.*" He slowed his words incredulously.

"Was any blood recovered from the table?"

"None."

"Was it a really, I dunno, sharp coffee table?"

Henrik Schumer dipped one shoulder, concessionary. "The table was, indeed, a rough and quite heavy concrete slab. Mr. Pruitt and Mr. Dickerson had lifted it from a campus construction site."

Sam stopped herself from saying *lovely*.

"So there's no blood on the table, despite the fact that Derek Dickerson lost significant blood from a head wound?"

"Yes."

Sam checked the Zoom's battery. *Still going strong.* It occurred to her the interview would have its greatest force if she maintained an objective stance.

"That is consistent with the official determination," she pointed out. "If Dickerson had died first from alcohol poisoning, an impact post-mortem might've created less blood."

Henrik said, "Marginally, perhaps."

"And I spoke with one witness who saw them arm in arm that night, all but incoherent. A condition that could make it difficult to pull off a murder—much less cover it up so well it stays under wraps for two decades."

The poet didn't seem to appreciate Sam's objectivity. He frowned, drawing in breath through craggy yellowed teeth.

"The cover-up was perpetrated by the entire Pruitt machine. Whatever mistakes Mr. Pruitt made that evening, his brethren whitewashed."

Sam started a follow-up but Henrik, barely pausing for breath, continued, "The police were operating under the same stresses I was. At every step of the process, the Pruitts intimidated. They did not want thoroughness. They did not want the truth to out. They wanted an expedient end."

Remembering had clearly piqued his outrage. He grimaced and drove a square fingertip into the table.

Sam thought of the stories she used to hear about Henrik Schumer, who'd cultivated a somewhat clichéd hot-blooded, important-male-artist ethos in younger days. People had said he defied the Yale administration and doled out his own discipline, that he'd even let the occasional petitioners settle their squabbles with fists.

Sam understood that a man in this state was receptive to plenty. Now she mirrored his mode, head shaking, sighing Joss's way, like she hated her child seeing the world's warts laid bare.

She gestured to a brass keyring hanging from a nail. "I don't suppose we could see the God Quad, just for a moment?"

Henrik charged out of his chair.

❧

The God Quad had a huge common room, which its inhabitants had a tacit duty to fill with revelers on Saturday nights. Branford College voted each year on which foursome—seniors, traditionally—would occupy the suite. Sam had no idea how Rock had gotten it as a freshman.

Joss stepped hesitantly to the middle of the room. "So, the coffee table would've been here." She aimed her index fingers straight down. "Where did they find the body?"

"By the fireplace," Sam said, "but who knows whether Rock moved it before the police showed up."

She circled the quad on soft, careful feet, snapping more photos. The top-floor suite featured a peaked ceiling, handsome curlicue chair rails, and a fireplace with similar detail work to those in Silliman. Sam could almost smell the dirty cleats and keg foam.

Joss asked, "Did you ever go here?"

"Not as a freshman," Sam said. "But yeah, I went to a party or two here."

"So you were in that, like, crowd?"

"It was just a few parties," Sam said, running her fingers along the walls for no apparent reason. "College isn't as socially hierarchical as high school. You do what you do."

Joss, noticing what Sam was doing, knelt and began inspecting the baseboards. "What're we looking for?"

Sam yawned. It had been an exhausting day, and she'd had only the one cup of coffee at the dance-physics lecture.

"I don't know," she admitted.

Henrik Schumer had left them—"Take whatever time you need, I will lock up later"—and they'd been poking around now for ten minutes. As the rush of her noontime conviction waned, Sam thought more deeply about the documentary. Whether the Pruitt cover-up angle made sense.

Was the aquarium story enough? Did it tell a fresh story—the kind that would make some producer shout, *THIS is why people must hear the story?*

What would she do, shade all her footage against Rock Pruitt? Leave out the testimony about him and Dickerson stumbling arm in arm that night? Layer in spooky organ music?

Also, could she accept all Henrik had said at face value? The man's animosity toward the Pruitts was clear. Deserved, sure, but clear. It was likely Henrik, as dean, would've been familiar with or even presiding over Dickerson's many sexual assault complaints. Wasn't it possible parts of the narrative in his own head were invented, like those postmodernist odes that'd launched his career in the sixties?

"One of these boards is loose."

Sam's mind was thick with doubt and barely registered her daughter's voice.

"Huh?"

Joss was bent around by the fireplace. At first, Sam thought she was using it as a barre, practicing poses.

"This board," Joss said, reaching up inside the flue, "one end is real jiggly."

"It's old wood—I remember when they closed off the fireplaces freshman year." Sam waved her down, an instinct leftover from visits to museum gift shops during the toddler years. "Leave it, Master Schumer trusted us to—"

"It's off! It came off when I touch—"

Joss's voice was muffled as she ducked into the long-dormant ash pit. A *thunk* sounded, then an "Oww!"

"That's property of the university," Sam said. "Whatever we break we'll have to pay for."

Joss was visible from the waist down, the rest of her hidden in the fireplace. Soot had fallen onto her pants.

She was saying something.

"Come on, get outta there," Sam said. "There's probably asbestos all over."

Sure enough, when Joss lowered herself, she had gray eyebrows and coughed. "Where's, *ahem*—can I have your phone flashlight? There's this, like, heavy thing behind a flap."

Sam's primary mode was still motherly annoyance, but it was pricked by something else now. Some glint of possibility.

"Joss, *out*. Right now."

"There's something up there, Mom! I saw, you have to—"

"Okay, you're getting a lungful of carcinogens," Sam said. "Out of there, please."

But Joss's eyes pulsed with excitement. She disappeared back up into the flue.

What happened to that skittish teenager of mine?

Sam walked to the fireplace. She heard crunching and creaking within. Several screws *plinked* to the ground.

"Joss, *out!*" she repeated.

Now a board was hanging down vertically into the fireplace, rotted, shedding dust. Sam's insides burned at her daughter's disobedience, at the property they were destroying.

Even as she winced at the damage, though, Sam felt a tickle of intrigue. This fireplace had surely been boarded up in the same project as all the others.

Nobody's seen up here for years.

When were these boarded up? Our freshman year, wasn't it?

Yes.

Yes, it had been freshman year. The knowledge slipped into context with Joss's discovery, with the history of this suite, and suddenly Sam was spiraling—up, high, hot.

"Listen, *Joss!*" she said. "If there actually is something important like evidence up there, we're gonna have to be careful and think—"

She stopped talking because Joss was down from the flue now, her inky hair coated gray. Her eyes were closed tight against the dust—but when she opened them, her pupils were vibrating in place. She was holding a brick.

A red brick with black splatters.

CHAPTER 10

Jamie waited in the foyer of the Latham Guest House. The inn had been booked in full for the Gallaghers, and he'd spent the last hour being hugged, toasted, and raucously celebrated by relatives both close and distant.

Now he busied himself filling a paper cone with blackberry-infused water, watching a fly buzz around a potted plant.

The fly would land on one of the plant's rubbery leaves, twitch about for a second or two, then bop airborne again, weaving left and right and left again in response to…what, nectar? Pheromones?

"Big brother."

So engrossed was Jamie in the fly's existential motives that he didn't recognize the voice. He spun from the plant, and there was Charlotte.

"Char!"

He stood for an embrace, falling into his sister's warmth and dynamism. She squeezed him ferociously and was asking six questions at once about his travel, about Juba, was he sure he preferred the dorms to a room here?

"Also," she said before he'd answered any of them, "purely for my own logistical sanity—you are coming to this dry-run, yes?"

She kept one eye on him while motioning to the doorman, seeming to convey something about cars or times or headcount.

"I dunno, I've seen just about everyone," Jamie said. "You and Mom are the ones I really wanted to catch up with so—"

"Nope, you're coming." She softened the directive with that pixie-burst of a grin he remembered from youth—from award podiums or showing him some gem she'd made from their erector set. "Besides, if you want Mom, you have to. She's meeting us there."

In the fifteen minutes before the caravan left, brother and sister filled each other in on the last six months—they'd last caught up in December, when Charlotte had been in Uganda donating education technology. She updated Jamie on their parents' health while simultaneously hassling other Gallaghers into action.

When Rory Gallagher got the bright idea to swing by Dakota J's en route for a plate of wings "in celebration of Jamie!" Charlotte barred his way.

"Not a chance, Rory." Her arm was a rod across the door. "Wings turn into pitchers, and next thing you know, I'm dealing with a Buzzfeed situation."

She turned back to Jamie. "Sorry, this weekend? I just can't. They're exasperating, worse than herding cats. I like cats, cats at least take care of themselves, have some basic instincts of self-preservation."

In a forty-second rant, Charlotte lamented that their generation of Gallaghers seemed even worse than Mom's. The clan's baggy, do-as-you-like ethos was exacerbated by phones and internet and easy media. Anytime anybody got the first random idea about...whatever, tariffs, they popped off about it, not giving the first thought to how the position fit (or, 99.99 percent of the time, didn't fit) into the brand.

Jamie and Charlotte ended up in different cars heading to the dry-run, the rehearsal for tomorrow's naming ceremony, as Charlotte was needed immediately for some site issue.

Jamie shared the backseat of a sedan with a pair of men in Secret Service-issue sunglasses and the man they must be guarding: Owen Gallagher.

"Jamie, wow!" Owen said, his mouth opening and closing. "I could not be more thrilled to see a person if they…" He cast about the plush interior for words. "If they handed me a dozen baked lobsters."

The ride was under ten minutes, the new college a straight shot east from the Latham Guest House, but even that little time was enough to convince Jamie that Owen Gallagher was a lightweight.

Owen—the nephew of Jamie's father's half-brother, the former comptroller of Los Angeles—asked a series of awestruck questions about Africa.

Did you see ivory poachers just walking down the road? If you could give one item to every child on the continent—just one item, no bigger than a toaster, say—what would you give? What would solve the most problems?

The presumed nominee gave a long, finger-snapping discourse on Ebola, which he planned to eradicate. He dwelled on the virus's gruesome symptoms, becoming excited and scrubbing his own forearms.

When Jamie cut in to explain that simple respiratory tract infections were deadlier by orders of magnitude, Owen pinched his face—which resembled Jamie's, only with the broad planes attractively lightened—and said, "Huh."

As they spilled out at Gallagher College, Jamie thought about mentioning this to Charlotte.

Charlotte was the driving force in the clan now—never mind the judges and mayors, the sitting senators and corporate titans. Charlotte had the treasure chest. She had the energy and will. If she decided to pull the plug on Owen Gallagher, his presidential candidacy was over.

A phalanx of press popped Owen and Jamie's pictures, calling questions, their flashes brilliant in Jamie's eyes.

No, he thought. *Don't get involved. The voters will see through him.*

But what if they didn't?

Jamie took advantage of the commotion surrounding Owen to slip past to the courtyard, which had been trimmed with balloon arches and poinsettia centerpieces on cloth-covered tables. Stretched across a banner backdropping the stage was the new crest: a robed woman holding black and white scales.

Charlotte and their mother stood onstage, the latter considering the podium with an expression of distrust.

"Mom…?"

Joan Gallagher looked up at her son's voice and, after a brief doubletake, bounded off the stage to him.

Jamie hadn't grown up near his mother, the senior senator from Massachusetts. He and Charlotte had been raised by nannies, and their father had kept them in Boston rather than move to DC after her election to Congress.

Still, seeing her famously furrowed brow rise and feeling her spare body against his own was terrific. She'd been a great help obtaining a passport for the trip—a detail he'd overlooked until it was almost too late—and they hadn't seen each other in person for three years.

Jamie laid his hands on the podium. "You two were looking at this." With his eyes, he brought Charlotte into the exchange. "Something wrong? What's it supposed to do?"

His mother said, "That was precisely my question, Jamie." She turned to Charlotte. "What *is* it supposed to do?"

Charlotte groaned. With an air of fast-diminishing patience, she swiveled the podium for both to see.

"Your entire speech lives right here, Mother—right in

SmartPodium. It's all loaded in memory. You can teleprompt as well if you like—they're linked by Bluetooth"—she made a twisty motion with thumb and forefinger—"but the speech is here, too."

She indicated a razor-sharp display embedded in the angled platform.

Joan Gallagher said she preferred reading speeches off paper. "Computer screens put me off, the glare." She wrinkled her nose. "They're impossible in the sun."

"No, this tech is different. This is e-ink, it's better than paper."

Jamie's mother touched the screen with her index finger and jerked back.

Charlotte said, "It's amazingly useful. Every topic is cross-linked to supporting materials. So if you go off-script, or get some nasty question from the audience? All you do is tap that passage and a slew of background facts pop up."

She demonstrated on the phrase *opioid epidemic*. A dozen bulleted facts zipped to the screen.

Jamie squinted at number four. One hundred fifteen US deaths every day? Could that be true?

Joan said, "I'm not taking questions today. And I rarely go off-script."

"Look, I was just demoing the capabilities," Charlotte said. "You don't have to use them."

Their mother continued to regard SmartPodium as though it might at any moment grow arms and strangle her.

Charlotte said, "Read the damn speech off a stone tablet if you want, Mother. I give up."

On the topic of stone tablets—an elderly woman was entering the courtyard now, walking with the help of a cane and a half-dozen aides. Her eyes scanned the stage and surrounding areas, quick, skeptical. Aides bent to hear her mutterings.

Jamie's mother rushed to greet her. "Finally!" he heard. "The festivities can officially get underway…"

As the photographers outside clambered for a shot, bulbs exploding behind the cast-iron gate, Jamie sidled up to his sister.

"I can't believe it, she looks exactly the same," he said of the elderly woman. "Maybe the hair's less brown? Not much, though."

Charlotte nodded, waving to the elderly woman, who was hooding her eyes their way now. "She's the Rock of Gibraltar. Did you follow her last campaign, when the progressives ran against her in the primary?"

"No, I missed that. She beat 'em?"

"*Annihilated* 'em." Charlotte brushed lint off her jacket. "We had testimonials from four ex-presidents running in all the major markets."

"And she survived the debates?"

"Didn't have any. We said her calendar didn't permit it. 'Too busy crafting important legislation to put Maine back to work.'"

Bernadette Gallagher ("Beetle Bern" to her friends) had voted on the Equal Rights Act of 1964 and served on JFK's Commission on the Status of Women. She was a favorite punching bag of the Pruitts—they used her in ads and fundraising mailers. "Stop Candidate X! Tell Washington you don't want another foot soldier in Bernadette Gallagher's tax-till-you're-broke war on the middle class!"

Jamie asked whether she had a speaking slot later today.

"That's a no," Charlotte said. "Last time we put her in front of the camera, she used the term *queers*—and not in the reclaimed academic form."

On Bernadette's heels came the rowdy cousins from the Pacific Northwest, then the Canadian technocrats with their Nalgene bottles, then the fiftyish rocker Lem Gallagher, sporting gray stubble and a motorcycle jacket.

Owen Gallagher fell in with the cousins, cuffing one of them at the ear, laughing at a football handed off into his gut.

Cocktails were passed around, tall-stemmed glasses garnished with fruit or olives, and Jamie felt transported to the Gallagher gatherings of his childhood. Policy chatter, opinion swaps on serious novels of the day, sumptuous food and drink—the whole rambling mess spilled from one courtyard to the next, now loud, now profound, now silly and stupid and alive.

Charlotte tried corralling the principals to the stage.

"Gather round, all," she called. "We need to get a take on the optics."

Nobody changed what they were doing.

"People, *now!*" She cupped her hands to her mouth. "When *Meet the Press* plays footage of this and we look like a third-grade talent show? We'll owe it to these moments, right here."

Jamie was beginning to understand why the Pruitts kept beating Gallaghers in elections, even with all Charlotte's Smart money.

Nonetheless, he found himself accepting an offered julep and chatting with different clan members. The cousins made a giant fuss over him. Lem—in that soulful voice that'd made him an icon of the American Rust Belt—hassled Charlotte about keeping Jamie's secret so long, then threw his arm around Jamie.

"*The beating heart is back,*" he rasped, smelling of cigarettes. "For you, sir, we are grateful. Forever grateful."

Charlotte got her dry-run, finally. Each speaker stood at the podium while her audio-visual pros blocked out cameras and chairs and shades.

Owen's speech was last. As a woman with an ear-mic positioned him by the shoulders, he looked out over the assembled Gallaghers. He burped. The cousins laughed uproariously.

Jamie frowned. Despite his initial reluctance, he found himself invested in the event now, tugged back into the family concerns. He'd grown up in this world. It was comfortable for him.

The next time Charlotte whizzed by, he mentioned the car ride over.

"I hear you, I do," she said. "What can I say? It is what it is. Owen polls better than anyone in our stable."

"But he—he's..." Jamie considered many words. "He's not a well-informed candidate."

"No," Charlotte agreed, "but he's got zero baggage, plus these superficially crossover assets—the look obviously, the fact that he's from New Hampshire, an early primary state with a reputation for fierce independence."

"How did the state do while he was governor?"

"Fine." Charlotte fluttered her lips. "State did just fine. Owen won't light up a climate change panel for you, but he won't screw up either. We can manage him, control the messaging."

Using her eyes and undertone commentary, she took Jamie around the courtyard explaining what made each alternative inferior.

Victoria Parr would draw giant crowds, but the unions wouldn't come home for her.

Giles Gallagher would be tireless on the trail and have the support of his fellow talking heads, which was part of his problem—when you've spent the last twelve years of your life on television, there are simply too many soundbites and scattershot positions to defend.

Jamie said, "The Ebola thing—Owen was almost giddy. It felt like he was describing a slasher movie."

Charlotte did not laugh, which Jamie appreciated. "Look, I'm with you. I am. And understand: if Owen gets into the White House, trust me, he will make exactly no policy decisions about Sub-Saharan Africa."

She was right, of course. Having grown up in the clan, Jamie understood the public face of campaigns didn't always—or even often—match the underlying ideas. In high school and college, he would rage at his parents about this.

"It's pure fiction!" he remembered saying. "Us, the Pruitts—we invent these conflicts so we can fundraise off them! The language and logic we pick has *nothing* to do with actual policy. That surface part is all demographics and emotion."

Thinking about Owen, seeing him yuk it up now with the cousins, Jamie felt the old disillusionment.

It all boils down to power. It's no more or less than the pursuit of power.

Charlotte was looking at him with concern. "Don't let it drag you down, the horse-trading. Things are improving. They are. Good stuff's happening."

From a pocket, she produced a plastic card—the size of a business card, same sapphire blue as the Smart logo.

"I want to give you this." Charlotte twirled the card in their shared sightline. "Encoded within are credentials for a new system we just launched called NetHuman. It's a secure system, a kind of clearinghouse for all our philanthropic and charitable projects. It encompasses political stuff too but you aren't required to—"

"No thanks," Jamie interrupted. "I appreciate it, Char, but I'm not getting involved."

"You don't have to!" She pressed the card into his retreating hand, forcing his fingers closed around it. "Use it however you want. You can log in and access presentations we're giving, or just cruise around for charities or NGOs who need support, either financial or manpower. I baked in enviros and microfinance, pretty much every org that exists."

She described the technology, how different users had different accesses. Most functions were gated from regular volunteers or online users.

"Your access is top-level, of course."

She kept trying to give him the card. Jamie kept handing it back.

"I don't want top-level access. I don't want any access to—"

"Please, Jamie," Charlotte said. "Take it. I have to tell you, I thought about you the whole time I was designing this network. About how many people want to do good, *ache* to do good, but simply don't know how. All this energy with no place to go. NetHuman solves that! It gives you the information to do good anytime you're moved to, anywhere in the world."

Her appeal was so raw and earnest, Jamie didn't feel he could refuse. It was just a plastic card, after all.

"I'll take it," he said. "But I'm not using it."

"Great, tremendous!" Charlotte hopped with glee. "Stick it in your pocket and forget about it. But later on when you see some injustice, or if you're remembering some child you couldn't personally help, fish it out. Log in and see what's possible."

She bore in her message with a look. Jamie felt a rush of affection—for her energy, her belief, for how perfectly her childhood thirst for fairness—applied to dolls or action figures or brownie splits with Jamie himself—had matured as an adult.

He took the card. They hugged again.

Maybe he would check it out. *NetHuman. A little oxymoronic, but I'm sure she polled it thoroughly.*

Now a pair of teens, a boy and a girl, hurried past with staplers and red flyers.

"Thank you, Yoders—nice work!" Charlotte called after, but they were already through the stone arch to the street.

Jamie squinted. "Yoders? That isn't...those can't be Aunt Cecily's kids, can they?"

"The very ones," Charlotte said. "They're helping with the redistricting fight. Connecticut has a reform bill on the ballot to get rid of gerrymandering."

"They can't be any older than, what, sixteen?"

"Fifteen."

"And they're gung-ho into redistricting?"

Charlotte shrugged.

The Yoders, twins Jamie and Charlotte used to roll Hot

Wheels for in the Nantucket greenhouse, popped back into the courtyard for more flyers.

The fact that they were twins made it somehow worse, Jamie thought. Like the clan was stamping out its army in pairs, swelling methodically to keep its various missions staffed.

Watching the Yoders' passion now as they darted back outside with fresh flyers, Jamie felt nauseous.

His phone buzzed. A text from Sam.

need to talk quick if u can. meet daily cafe?

He stared at the phone. A new queasiness took hold of his stomach.

What could she want? Why the urgency? Had he left something behind? He swiveled his head and confirmed he was wearing the rucksack.

Could she have thought of something important she'd meant to tell him?

Feelings she wanted to discuss?

"I need to go," he said.

Charlotte clearly took this as being about the Yoders. "Lighten up, big brother. It's just a phase. If it wasn't politics, if they were in another family, they'd be wild about Nascar or Pokemon Go—"

"I get that," Jamie said. "I do, Char. I just need to go."

She smiled and made a point to help him put the NetHuman card in an outer front pocket of his bag, closing and snapping the flap.

"Use it, okay? Log in and join a project. *Start* a project—it's easy. Promise?"

Jamie smiled, too, hitching the rucksack over his shoulder.

"Sorry," he said, and left.

Jamie saw Sam from the sidewalk, through the chic, spider-cracked window of the Daily Cafe. Even from a distance, she looked frazzled—hunched forward on a black bench, face taut, sitting across from her daughter with elbows jutting out like protective spikes.

He had never seen Sam Lessing like this. Not when they'd been busted painting horns on the stone Puritan pointing a musket at the Native American outside Sterling Library, nor at any point during Sam's mother's chemotherapy.

The daughter kept peeking at the bathroom.

Jamie pushed through the cafe's heavy door and weaved his way to their corner table. His strides felt too light, as though his feet might either keep flying up to the ceiling or drop through the floor. A psychedelic wall clock—numberless with concentric circles of primary colors spinning opposite each other—was scrambling his thoughts.

What am I about to hear?

After having confirmed he could meet at the Daily, Jamie had gotten back *"ok"* by text. Only those two letters to guess at. He couldn't imagine some large relationship news like divorce would arrive like this. If there had been an accident, surely she had closer friends she would've called first.

Also, that: she'd texted instead of called.

Before Jamie's neurotic speculation could go further, he arrived at the table.

"Jamie!" Sam pulled his sleeve, slamming him onto the bench beside her.

He started to ask what all the intrigue was about when his eyes found an object in a Ziploc bag on Sam's far side, against the wall.

"We found something."

With painstaking delicacy, Sam pulled the object onto her lap. She peeked past Jamie to make sure no other tables were spying —paranoia that was, again, totally out of character.

The Ziploc had frost print on its front, a labeling space that obscured its contents. It looked brown or maybe deep red, and was heavy judging by how it sat upon Sam's thighs.

Something about this moment—the energy, the secrecy—made Jamie wish he'd stayed at Charlotte's dry-run.

He asked, "What is it?"

In racing whispers, urged on by her daughter's bugged eyes, Sam explained they had found a brick in the God Quad—where Rock Pruitt and Derek Dickerson had lived freshman year. They'd pried a board loose in the fireplace. The space had appeared to be undisturbed from twenty years ago.

As Sam spoke, she kept her fingers off the bag as though scared to contaminate it.

"I—we put it in plastic. I stayed in the room and Joss ran to RiteAid...we'd moved it already, or touched it I guess, and I didn't know what the police or whoever would—er, how to preserve it...and Henrik Schumer saw us leave but I—but hopefully he didn't notice the bag..."

She seemed to want Jamie to take over the thread, trailing off, looking at him earnestly.

Jamie shifted to keep her lap obscured from other customers. "You're thinking it's relevant to..." How to call it? *Crime? Murder?* "...to Derek Dickerson?"

Sam nodded. Her daughter was biting her nails.

He asked why.

Sam bent to the tabletop and spoke into her sleeve.

"Blood."

Jamie shrank involuntarily.

She continued quietly, "*It's streaked with blood, and look at these ridges...maybe fingerprints.*"

Joss said, "I think they *are* prints, there's a pattern!"

All three looked into Sam's lap at the brick. Through the frost print, Jamie saw one end was caked black.

He felt like an anvil had landed on his head.

He was right back in the feud.

Maybe it had been too much—coming back to the States, showing up at this reunion. He'd thought it could only be positive, seeing Sam and reconnecting with his family beyond his mother and sister. He hadn't returned for vengeance or to seek a position of power.

But then there'd been the pomp and circumstance of Gallagher College. And now a bloody brick in a fireplace.

"The police searched that suite up and down," he said. "And—and the media, even that long ago, the scrutiny was intense. How would they miss a thing like that?"

Joss deflated at this. Immediately, he wished for the words back.

Sam said, "I know, it's weird. But remember when they boarded up those fireplaces. Freshman year? Maybe it got done right after the crime."

Jamie still hadn't regained his equilibrium. "Even so, the police—"

"The police were being controlled!" Joss said. When her mother made a dial-it-down gesture, she continued, lower, "The master said the Pruitts influenced the investigation—they probably bribed them *not* to look!"

As Sam and her daughter waited for his reaction, Jamie steepled his fingers. Right and wrong chased through his mind. He recalled the pressure and emotions of freshman year, when Dickerson's death had dominated the news.

Sam said, "Rock could've even done it himself. He knew the fireplaces were getting boarded up—maybe he did it that night. Maybe he saw an opportunity."

The cafe fell into a quiet moment, other tables apparently sipping or taking a collective breath. One barista polished his gleaming espresso machine while another read off her phone.

Jamie wished he was doing that—polishing, or reading, anything at all but this.

"Sam, I don't—er, I want to stay out of this."

"But we have him *nailed*! Did you hear he's running in Virginia? Who knows what awful things he'd do in the Senate? We could stop him. We could put him in jail!"

"I used to think about it like that," Jamie said. "It feels good—you feel like you're stopping the other side, thwarting them. But it's just not me right now."

He stood and inched away from the brick as though it were glowing hot—as though it were one of those ancient pinebox relics people believed in.

"God. I want every good thing for you, Sam."

Her face soured. Jamie realized at once he'd said another wrong thing. She was either taking it to be condescending and paternalistic, or as an insult—implying she was dumb for thinking the discovery would amount to anything.

Neither had been his intention.

The words had simply been in his heart, so he'd said them.

CHAPTER 11

ROCK WOKE UP SOLID. HAVING FAVORED COKE OVER BOOZE LAST night, he had only a minor hangover. He breakfasted on eggs and hash browns from his favorite campus grease pit. He stalked up and down Elm Street with chest out manfully, daring anyone to tell him he wasn't the baddest hombre in the land.

He'd owned the Choosing. Theresa Velasquez was toast. She had rushed from the Grand Hall after the mass text and peeled out in her driver's car. Someone said she'd punched her husband, too, but that was unconfirmed—and when Rock had crossed paths with him later in the inner courtyard, he'd seen no mark.

Bryce seemed to have guessed who'd done him in. "Auditioning for North Carolina, huh?"

Rock had tittered. "Aw, you got the lay of your life. Big wins all around."

Bryce had looked ready to fight, but when Rock flinched and chomped his teeth, the paunchy house-husband slinked off.

Later, Rock had found Jonathan Pruitt pacing in the library, talking heatedly with an adviser.

He'd whistled his entrance. "Then there was one."

The former president had smiled thinly.

Jonathan hadn't guaranteed Rock the clan's support in Virginia, but hell, the writing was on the wall like "redrum" in blood at the Overlook Hotel.

One more coup, like the very one he was planning for this evening, would seal the deal.

Rock knew whatever he pulled for the Gallagher College ceremony would be huge, but he didn't quite know the shape of the hugeness, the way you know a porn video is going to absolutely annihilate from the preview image, even if you aren't sure of the precise acts inside.

It would involve Owen Gallagher.

It would involve intense humiliation of the Gallaghers.

Political blows usually come from an angle, Rock knew. Campaign apparatuses are girded for those fraught news-anchor questions, but it's the veteran's elderly mother at the town hall who blindsides them. You need mud bubbling up all sides, a splash here for misdirection, a smudge there to make the coming slop-bucket-to-face credible.

You need a range of initiatives. You need agents acting with vigor and malice, programmed to go until the desired damage is inflicted.

You need tools.

Rock found tool *numero uno* eating a late lunch at Commons: Jamie Gallagher.

"Chicken Cordon Bleu—you're joking!" Rock said, tapping Jamie's plate on his way to the chow line. "Can you still squeeze the patty and make it squirt juice? Ah, they probably backed off the breading, the commies."

Before Jamie could make sense of this, Rock had nabbed a tray and moved into the cafeteria flow. He shot back a thumb-forefinger gun through the salad's transparent sneeze guard, assembled a plate, and returned to Jamie's table. To make space for himself, he bounced a few nobodies to the next bench.

"How're you finding civilization?" Rock asked, spearing his

chicken. The fork penetrated clear to the plate without making a drop of juice. "See? Told you, everything gets ruined."

Jamie was eating with the same two he'd been with earlier, the bohemian chick and the younger, inky-haired hottie. All three were about done with their lunch.

They were looking at him...funny. *Weren't they?* Rock was used to sidelong and even hostile looks, like the ones these very three had given him yesterday.

But something was new. In their careful eyes, there was restraint—almost like a buddy could be standing behind him with a whipped cream pie, finger raised to his lips, urging them not to spoil the prank.

Rock's instinct was so uncanny that he reconsidered last night.

Let's see, the Choosing...then home on Marshall's chopper...then straight back to the room, right?

He felt 93 percent sure he hadn't gone anyplace else.

Jamie Gallagher said, "What do you want? We're eating here."

"I see that, so am I." Rock waggled a forkful of broccoli. "We're two classmates having lunch, chewing the fat."

"You're after something." Jamie's scarred forearms leaned into the table, taking all his torso's weight. "What?"

Rock gagged on his broccoli, which tasted like drywall. "*Blecht*! I'm done eating on campus. I'm taking the rest of my meals at Mory's."

He spun his tray away, kept looking at Jamie.

"I've told you," his adversary said, "I'm out. I don't want to debate you, or box you. Or anything."

Rock guffawed. Boxing or debating Jamie Gallagher—which would be easier?

Tossup.

"I'm just here for camaraderie," he said. "As you know, it's not easy finding peers when you're a Pruitt or Gallagher—people who understand what you've been through, faced the pressures you've faced."

Jamie downed the dregs of his milk. Nearby tables were looking, ignoring their food to see what had brought the two pinebox principals together.

Rock stood and yelled, "Quit staring, people! Have you never seen your betters divvying up the spoils of the planet before?"

To a few titters, he sat back down.

"Listen," he said, back on Jamie. "You're sick of your clan, I'm sick of mine. We're both outcasts. Let's bury the hatchet. Let's just exist as a couple of dudes who're done sweating the past."

The phrase felt so self-helpy off his tongue. Rock grabbed himself hard under the table to keep a straight face.

Jamie Gallagher did seem to soften, sighing ponderously.

Before Rock could capitalize, the bohemian chick said, "Rumor is you got picked to run for the Senate in Virginia. Doesn't sound like you're exactly on the outs with the family."

Piss.

"Where'd you hear that?" he said. "Virginia blows. Did you know Virginia accounts for 10 percent of the country's vanity plates? I have zero desire to represent those doofs."

The three of them continued to look at Rock like he was slime on the bottom of a shoe.

Time to face facts. This wasn't going well. Maybe he should abandon the mission, save further embarrassment. Sometimes you swung and missed—that was the nature of these forays.

He could return to Gallagher College and scout around for weaknesses. He could ping Marshall's guys and see if any of them were up for a flash operation—

"You two should go," Jamie said to his companions. "Joss shouldn't be around for this. Go ahead to the art gallery, okay? I'll catch up."

The bohemian chick and her daughter—Rock finally noticed

the family resemblance, there in the mouth shape—left to bus their trays.

Rock watched them off. "Hot, right?"

Jamie started gathering napkins and silverware on his tray. "I won't talk about Sam like that."

"Good, me neither," Rock said. "I meant the daughter."

Jamie frowned. Rock slapped the table grandly.

"But the mom's not half bad herself," he said. "And you have an art gallery date with her? That's nice work, brother."

Jamie bristled. "Have you ever seen a female and just thought, 'Wow, a person. Another person just like me, with hopes and fears?' Instead of going immediately to the gutter."

"Nope," Rock said, "and neither has any other red-blooded male who's honest about it. But you keep on fooling yourself."

Jamie rubbed the corners of his eyes. "How did this happen to you? When did women stop being mothers and sisters to you? Is it just grade-school us versus them you never outgrew? Did you watch too many *Porky's* or *American Pie* movies?"

Rock started to answer, but the dweeb was rolling.

"I saw enough overseas to know the West doesn't have a monopoly on chauvinism," Jamie said, "and neither does the ideological right. And maybe all you are underneath the bluster is a small, scared, insecure boy? Who think it's funny? But that doesn't make the harm you inflict upon the world any less horrific."

Rock laced his fingers together primly. "Are you done yet?"

Jamie closed his eyes.

Rock said, "You realize she's in a crap marriage, don't you?"

Jamie stiffened like a kid whose parents had just found his sock-drawer candy stash.

"Ah, don't pretend," Rock said. "It's all right there on the front cover. The skirt, the attitude. Fact that hubby stayed home."

"Plenty of spouses skip the reunion," Jamie said. "They don't know anybody, it's all Yalies. Doesn't mean anything."

Rock liked this: a genuine verbal response with no discernible revulsion. By telling Jamie exactly what he was dying to hear, Rock had gotten his foot in the door.

"It means plenty," he said. "You've been living with Bushmen for a decade—you've lost your feel for First World social cues. She's on the market. I promise you that."

Jamie's expression turned inward, in what could only be a consideration of how to bag her.

Stray concepts floated through Rock's brain. Could the chick be leveraged? Made into bait of some sort? How quick could he get Marshall's guys here? Ah, but that'd be messy…

He tabled the ideas. "Have you had a chance to meet Owen Gallagher yet? I've heard he's impressive."

Rock watched closely for Jamie's reaction, and was pleased to detect ambivalence—a curdling of the face.

Still, Jamie said nothing.

Rock continued, "Great on the environment, isn't he? Wants solar buildings, solar transit! Why not? I'll bet he understands the developing world up and down, coming and going."

Jamie kept quiet, but Rock could tell he wanted to talk. He had something to unburden himself of.

Rock said, "I'm only farking you. He's a dolt, isn't he?"

Jamie's mouth kept a straight line. "Politics today doesn't reward thoughtfulness. It's not what elevates a candidate."

"Amen." Rock ate a fingerling potato whole and said with his mouth full, "They want the loudest and the worst. It's amazing I haven't been elected president yet."

They bemoaned the degradation of civility. Rock played it soft, reading Jamie's body language, agreeing often but mixing in enough profane dissent to be believable.

Rock returned again and again to Owen Gallagher. Wasn't it stunning he'd risen as high as he had on *zero substance*? Didn't Jamie think he oughta come down a peg or two?

Despite his best efforts, Rock began to sense he was playing a losing hand. He wasn't going to convince Jamie Gallagher to act against his own clan. To join some kind of sabotage. Rock had come in with half a hope Jamie's marbles were scrambled, that somehow Rock's superior intellect could bend Jamie to his will and make him do a rash thing.

Rock saw now that was a bridge too far. Jamie wasn't nuts. He wasn't going to be hypnotized by a swinging pocket-watch.

As the discussion petered out, both their plates clean and departure imminent, Rock cast about for a plan B.

Planting some secret microphone...goading him into saying more about Owen and recording it...hmm...would tailing him from here get you anywhere...?

"I need to get out to the gallery," Jamie said, standing, picking a plastic milk bottle off his tray. "Was there a cans-and-bottles bin inside, did you notice?"

Rock snapped out of his plotting.

"Uh, dunno," he said. "I save mine to toss directly into the ocean. My personal gift to all those stuck-up dolphins."

Jamie frowned again—the joyless crank—and left to deposit the various trash and non-trash byproducts of his meal in their proper receptacles.

As he passed out of sight, Rock's gaze dropped underneath the cafeteria table.

The rucksack.

CHAPTER 12

BEFORE THE DAILY CAFE, BEFORE THE BRICK, JAMIE HAD PROPOSED going to the Yale University Art Gallery. He suggested—and Sam agreed—it would be a nice break from the wall-to-wall reunion schedule, whose many events could leave your feet sore and head numb from so much nostalgia.

As Sam strolled from the European to the Asian collection, she supposed he'd been right. It was a nice break. The ten minutes she'd sat in front of Stella's *Brooklyn Bridge*—a brilliant deconstruction of the vista she saw every day—had done her mind and body good.

Joss loved it, too. She'd been fascinated by the shimmering van Gogh and earthy Gauguins. *When was the last time I took her to the Met?* Sam thought. The gallery wonders were of a piece with the other experiences she'd had this weekend—the lecture, the architectural tour de force. Joss was growing before her very eyes, and Sam was loving it.

But she also felt that brick should get to the police.

"Mom, it's *gold pigment* on silk," Joss said, marveling at a hanging scroll. "It's fourteenth century! Can you even believe they made this six hundred years ago?"

Sam stepped closer and examined the scroll beside her daughter. She'd taken several art history courses and now felt that expanding of the mind she'd almost forgotten—the peace and possibility of being in a quiet place, considering another human being's masterwork.

It was nearly one-thirty. She and Joss had left Jamie and Rock Pruitt alone in Commons an hour ago.

Where was Jamie? Were they still talking? If so, about what?

Sam felt sure that whatever Rock had wanted from Jamie, its underpinnings were sinister.

A dim corner of her brain worried Rock knew about the brick somehow. Had he been looking at her funny? Maybe the Pruitts had been following her—following her because they'd spotted her with Jamie earlier. How many operatives did they have available for that sort of thing?

What if their people were busting into her room this very moment, tossing her drawers until they found her smoking-gun evidence?

It was fantastical, but the pinebox vendetta had produced plenty of fantastical episodes over the years. Daring thefts. Forgeries in the halls of Congress. Murder. It was said Nathaniel Gallagher had secured a deal with Britain to circumvent the War of 1812—until Virgil Pruitt riled up cotton farmers for the sole purpose of denying the Gallaghers a political victory.

When Joss had seen enough of the scroll, they found a staircase and walked back to the ground floor, entering the Ancient Art collection.

"Holy cat," Joss murmured.

A seven-foot-wide lion of glazed brick stopped them in their tracks. The animal looked wicked—sharp teeth, oriental-style face.

Sam flinched. The thing looked ready to pounce from its backdrop and eat them.

Footsteps approached from behind.

"I always think he's looking sideways, at you," said a voice. Jamie's.

Sam staggered back a step, and Jamie caught her. Joss, examining the lion's crosshatched mane with her nose just inches from the piece, didn't see.

"Whoa," Sam said. "Thanks."

Jamie lingered letting go of her. "No problem. Art can be scary, huh?"

"Apparently."

She smiled and returned the favor with her own touch, clutching him for balance longer than was strictly necessary.

She felt relieved to see him here, with the familiar rucksack on his back. Relieved he was away from Rock Pruitt. She'd had time to think since the Daily Cafe, and decided she understood his reaction—his resistance—to the brick. Escaping his family's never-ending fight with the Pruitts was why he'd fled to the Peace Corps, why he'd made his life in Africa.

He'd seen the feud up close and didn't want Sam and Joss embroiled in it.

He'd been protecting them.

This simple fact renewed Sam. The fact of his existence, this man she'd thought dead for ten years, renewed her. Sam felt alive. Even the brick, as heavily as it weighed on her, fed this new sensation that life mattered again. That important events were happening and she was steering them—or at least driving in the same car.

"So," she said.

"So," Jamie answered.

"What happened at Commons? What was Rock trying to pull?"

"I don't even know." Jamie stepped closer to the lion, squinting as though it might contain some clue to their classmate's motives. "But I'm not going to worry about it."

He grinned back at her. Their fingers brushed. Sam couldn't have said who initiated the move.

When Joss shifted to consider a different perspective on the lion, she spotted Jamie. Her face brightened and she gave a half-wave. Jamie raised a palm.

The gesture was nothing really, but its modesty warmed Sam through. She felt grateful he'd suggested the art gallery. Grateful he'd shielded Joss from whatever crass things Rock had said at lunch. Grateful he'd ditched his family to spend his day with them—to make their humble pair into a trio.

She said, "I forgot how much I loved this place."

"It takes you out of your world," Jamie agreed. "I remember Norah used to come here, just about every weekend."

Sam gave him a teasing look. "That's the second time you've mentioned Norah Fowler. Were you hoping to bump into her here?"

He shrugged. "I hoped I'd bump into a bunch of people."

The look between them was a little too intense so Sam asked, "Did you visit galleries in Africa? Or museums?"

"Just the Johannesburg in South Africa. It's an impressive collection, but museums aren't big in Africa. Not in my group of friends, at least."

He said this without a hint of preaching or superiority.

"Did you like living there?" Sam asked. "When you think of settling, is that—er, do you..."

She didn't finish. Jamie looked at his shoes, twisting on the gallery floor.

Sam's face flushed as she realized the discussion had reached a precarious spot. *Why did I say that? "Settling?" God, I sound like I'm projecting some future, don't I?*

Maybe the whole weekend had been too quick. Whose idea had it been to hang out so much?

Had they been trading invitations or had she been driving this? Who'd invited whom to Commons for lunch?

Sam couldn't remember.

She hadn't started out intending to spend every free moment with Jamie Gallagher. Whenever there had been a choice or a fork in plans, the best option—for Joss, for them both—had always included Jamie.

Was she in the wrong?

Was she leading him on? Leading *herself* on?

Jamie plunked down on a gallery sofa. "I think I'll settle here."

Like that, the moment was defused.

Sam could've fallen into his lap. Rock Pruitt and the bloody brick seemed a million miles away. Ditto for Abe and her Five Year Wait, even though these bore directly on her feelings. Her husband's sharp spite, all the bitternesses between them—it all felt small and light now.

Sam took a fresh look around. She was surrounded by centuries of art—millennia of it. Lifetimes funneled into ideas and canvases, artists who gave everything for a thing they believed.

No more petty, she thought. *No more negative.*

Inwardly, she chuckled. *What are you, turning into a life coach?* What did any of this mean—in concrete terms—for her and Abe? For Joss? She didn't know.

Falling into a crush didn't make the stakes any lower.

Sam said, "I imagine the janitors do a nightly sweep." She leaned into the back of the sofa. "It's doubtful they'll let you camp among the art."

Jamie snapped his fingers in mock chagrin.

Sam realized her daughter, standing nearby, had caught the tail end of this flirt. By instinct she summoned a neutral expression—replacing whatever dreamy face she'd had before—but Joss never saw it. She was already off, prancing ahead to the Indo-Pacific wing.

❧

Sam noticed the man in the lobby. He wore a jacket despite the balmy June weather, clean-shaven, hair combed back from his temples in perfect horizontals. His strides were careful and measured. He wasn't looking at art.

She avoided eye contact with him as they exited the lobby. Neither Joss nor Jamie seemed to notice.

It's nothing. So what if he doesn't look like a student or a professor?

He could be an insurance salesman on lunch break. He could be gallery security.

Wouldn't gallery security be in uniform, though?

Her fear mounted on the walk back to Silliman. A second man, browsing a newsstand, struck her as too ordered and circumspect. And how long had that car been idling there, one stoplight back on Chapel Street? When it abruptly turned left—the direction of the dorm—Sam imagined a pair of eyes tracked her out the passenger-side window.

She walked faster. A gap of several sidewalk panels opened between her and the other two. Joss had started complaining her legs were tired from all that gallery browsing.

Sam kept silent about her racing concerns. She didn't want to spook Joss. Or Jamie, who surely had no appetite for cloak-and-dagger feud talk.

It's nothing, she told herself again.

When they reached the college gate, Sam couldn't help speeding through and ahead to the entryway. Jamie had a key, he could let them in.

She galloped upstairs two at a time. She dashed through the common room with a smiling "Hey!" to Laurel, burst into her and Joss's bedroom…and knelt at the bed.

The brick was there, underneath, in its Ziploc.

"Breathe." She gripped the university-issue dresser, its knotty wood comforting in her fingers.

The Pruitts can't know about the brick. You found it yesterday.

They would've had to have the God Quad bugged or some kind of surveillance on Henrik Schumer.

She reminded herself it had been twenty-three years since Derek Dickerson's death. Not even the power-hungry Pruitts could maintain surveillance for two decades.

Right?

Sam laid down on the bed, allowing herself a moment. Her ribs and lower back hurt. Her feet felt gross—she slipped off her shoes and socks and kneaded her soles.

What a day.

She tried relaxing as voices drifted through the wall. Joss was raving to Laurel about the gallery, asking Jamie whenever she couldn't think of an artist's or piece's name.

The brick was safe. She would have to take it back to New York, she realized. Rushing decades-old evidence to the New Haven police on a Sunday made no sense. She'd have to think more about which law enforcement channel to pursue.

For now, she would keep recording audio, keep amassing material for the documentary.

Would the brick's discovery go into the documentary? Sam wasn't sure. If the authorities didn't believe her, or the trace evidence was somehow beyond DNA analysis, she supposed it could. It might serve as that one bit of new information, that buzzworthy nugget that raised the project's profile.

"Mom! Where ARE you, Mom?"

Joss's voice from the common room.

Sam sat up and stretched, twisting in place.

"In here!" she called. "Coming…"

She slipped on sandals and joined the others.

Joss was hyper, pirouetting in the middle of the common room. "What're we doing tonight?"

She blinked several times, eager. Clearly she had a specific answer in mind.

"Our plans are in flux at the moment," Sam said. "Why?"

Joss peeked to Jamie, who glanced away retiringly. "Can we go to the naming ceremony? He said we could."

Jamie quickly added, "I'm obligated—I told my sister I would."

"Can we?" Joss had been on her tiptoes a full ten seconds. "They're having speakers—*Owen Gallagher* is speaking!"

She argued that reunion events were basically over, when would they have another opportunity like this?, c'mon Mom…

Sam looked between her daughter and Jamie Gallagher. She couldn't ask Jamie in what capacity he was inviting them—that would be too forward, like her utterance about "settling" at the gallery.

Still, she worried if they accepted, they would be attending the ceremony *with* Jamie. She didn't think she should give that impression to him or Joss.

Laurel was folding clothes she hadn't worn this weekend, packing for home.

Sam said, "Are you going to this ceremony, Laurel?"

She figured Jamie would've extended the invitation to her. If they all went as a group, there would be no pressure or assumptions.

Laurel looked to Jamie.

He said, "Like I said, you're more than welcome. The more the merrier."

Then Laurel looked to Sam and, angled such that only Sam could see, made her brow into question marks.

Sam gave a tight nod.

"Sure," Laurel said. "I have a late flight, might as well. What time does it start?"

Jamie said three o'clock.

Joss jumped in, "When does Owen Gallagher speak? He's the main speaker, right? He must go last."

As Sam mouthed *thank you* to her former roommate, Jamie fielded Owen questions from Joss. Did he really play the bass guitar? Wasn't his position on gun control so courageous?

"I...am sure it is." Jamie took a step back against her zeal. "I've only talked briefly with him."

Joss faced Sam again with her best pleading, the-world-is-sure-to-end-if-you-don't-say-yes-to-this face.

"Oh, give your calves a break," Sam said. "We'll go."

"Yay!" Joss twirled once more and hugged her ferociously.

The warmth of her daughter's body washed away Sam's last concerns about propriety and not wanting to crowd Jamie.

It *was* an exciting opportunity for Joss—a memorable capper to a weekend that'd lived up to both of their lofty hopes. It wouldn't be fair to put the kibosh on this just because Sam felt squishy about the Jamie situation.

Jamie suggested they meet at the new college, say 2:45?

All parties agreed. He grinned, told Joss he'd reserve them front-row seats, and took off.

Sam yawned wide. She looked at the clock and was just considering snack strategies when loud voices began in the courtyard.

An argument.

"—excuse me, what's that?" one said.

"I said, *what were you doing up there?*"

The first speaker hesitated. "I, we were only making arrangements about—"

"I'll bet. I'll bet those arrangements were marvelous."

Sam's heart plunged. She took a step for the window, then decided not to look.

Her ears were on fire. Laurel watched her with a pinched, pitying expression. By a stroke of luck, Joss had gone to the bedroom to fetch headphones.

In another minute, Abe burst in.

He looked like death warmed over. That flannel with rips in both elbows. His ear and nostril hairs flared in every direction, like he'd purposely teased them out. He stormed to the center of the room.

"I thought he was dead!" roared her husband. "Huh? He's supposed to be dead."

Sam felt wobbly. So much was wrong. That Abe was here at all. That he seemed to prefer Jamie's being dead. That she—Sam —seemed to be getting blamed.

"But you—I didn't think you were coming. It's already Sunday, the reunion is over—"

"Sorry to screw with your plan." He made an obnoxious face. "How long have you known Jamie Gallagher was alive? How many years?"

"Seriously? I can't even—"

"Were you planning to leave straight from here? Hop the family jet to Nantucket? Well, you're not taking Joss. You want to abandon us, you're sick of us? No prob. But Joss comes home."

Sam felt stung and punched and sapped of will, but once he uttered their daughter's name, all these emotions gelled to anger.

Joss had come in. She'd heard—of course she had. Now she hid in Laurel's arms, sobbing.

The last time Sam had heard such plaintive sounds from her, they'd been in line for the roller coaster at Deno's. Joss had been ten. The switchbacking queue had become suddenly cramped— maybe some kid had pulled out the separating rope. Bodies pressed. Yelps turned aggressive. Joss began to hyperventilate, wheezing and gripping her sleeves.

Sam squared to her husband.

"You. Don't. Know. *Anything.*" She brought her face very near his. "Let's go talk. Let's go talk in the bedroom so she doesn't—"

"The bedroom!" he cut in wildly. "There's a novelty. Nothing's happened in *the bedroom* for years."

"You…idiot," she managed, disliking the word but finding no other.

She grabbed him, yanking at his flannel like toilet paper off a roll, pushing him ahead, away. In a wall mirror, she saw Laurel stroking Joss's back.

Out of the room, door closed, Sam hissed, "What are you doing? That is our daughter out there!"

"You think I don't know?" Abe's voice cracked. "I'm the one who packs her snack for dance class every day. I'm the one who taught her F chord! I think I know our daughter."

"Okay, and why would a person who's invested so much of himself into her—why would her *father*—say those things? In front of her?"

Abe smirked. "She knows. You don't think she sees the situation between us?"

Sam couldn't answer. Her throat felt like a gaping maw, air crashing in so fast that no words could escape the other way.

The horror of all this laid bare, after years of ignoring and festering, was like some grotesque wound breaking out of its cast. Raw and moist, tender—a thing too vile for the outside world.

He continued, "She's fourteen years old. Not eight."

"Stop."

"I know you don't spend much time with kids, kids were never your bag, but a fourteen-year-old and an eight-year-old have different conceptions of—"

"Please stop," Sam said.

Something in this quiet request did stop him.

They faced each other in the small dorm bedroom, their feet on hardwood, the window open and a balmy summer breeze wasted.

"For you to walk in here," she began, "and make an assumption like that—"

"Assumption! Yep, that's what it was, an assumpt—"

"—assumption like that," Sam persisted, "is so reckless, so cynical. And it does impact Joss. No matter what she…knows, or doesn't know. It does impact her."

Abe seemed to consider a few responses, now raising a finger, now animating different parts of his face hotly.

He took a retiring step back. "You win, I'm terrible."

"Abe."

"No, let's tell the truth. You're smarter than me. After all, you went *here*." He crooked his finger overhead. "Why argue? You're better. You're always going to win."

Sam's despair deepened. She'd almost forgotten this tactic of Abe's in the years they'd been skating around each other. It had been common in earlier days. Sam wasn't right—she just argued better. She was a better fighter. Conflict didn't come naturally to Abe. He preferred the high road.

"Look, I just..." She held her forehead. "There's an explanation here, about Jamie. But I almost don't want to give it. I don't think you deserve it."

"You're right, hundred percent. I absolutely don't." Abe spread his arms wide. "I have no idea what compels you to keep hanging around a piece of human trash like me."

He dropped his arms and pouted. Sam had a dozen bad urges —to yell at him, to tear those elbow rips to the cuffs, to walk right past him out the door.

But she contained them.

The situation looked fishy to him. Maybe it *was* fishy—after all, what had those touches with Jamie at the gallery been?

Oh, who cared? Whether Abe's case here was weak or staggeringly weak? That he was being small-minded and graceless? The man had flashed these traits for so long, with such consistency, that they'd lost their capacity to shock.

Against all this, Sam steeled herself the same way she always had: by remembering herself at seventeen, the day she'd learned her parents were divorcing.

Her mother told her in the car. Sam had just finished an *Arsenic and Old Lace* rehearsal, plunked down in the passenger seat with a granola bar, and Mom looked across the center console and said, "Your father and I broke up."

She then explained Sam could choose who she'd like to live

with, and they would work the housing/moving-out situation to fit her desires.

Patting Sam's hand like, *Look how considerate we're being.*

Sam had reared up in shock. She couldn't get her seatbelt off —it felt like a flat snake squeezing her torso. The car was running. They were in a high school parking lot.

Sam's entire world had bottomed out that day. For months she couldn't lay her cheek against a pillow without thinking of it. She dropped out of *Arsenic.* She stopped doing the reading in English—how could you care about made-up people from two hundred years ago *after this?*

She wouldn't do it to her own daughter—not at fourteen. At nineteen, maybe. Not at fourteen.

"Let's start over," Sam said, stooping at the bed. "Joss and I found a brick…"

CHAPTER 13

THEY ALL WENT TO THE RENAMING—SAM, JOSS, LAUREL, ABE. SAM didn't see an alternative. She had told Jamie—and more importantly Joss—they would go, and to back out because Abe had shown up would've been to acknowledge some transgression on her part.

Since the blowout, Abe had adopted a kind of pushy fatalism. "You want to take *me* to the Gallagher gala?" Raising one holey sleeve again like a shield. "Really?"

Sam shrugged. "We can buy you a shirt. If you want."

She'd chosen the floral yellow dress herself, simple stud earrings, and half-inch heels.

The whole situation was bizarre and hard to process mentally, but stable. Joss had hugged them both as they'd emerged from the bedroom, her body so light, feeling like reeds in Sam's arms.

"Yeesh—college, right?" Sam had said. "Too crazy."

From there forward, everyone had just feigned amnesia. Tomorrow, next week—there would have to be a reckoning, but not here.

Now the group walked to Gallagher College. Campus had surrendered its shine in the reunion's waning hours. Trash bins overflowed. Two maintenance workers walked Orange Street with the tails of their shirts out. The stone facades looked a shade grayer to Sam.

Laurel made small talk with Abe about NYC music acts. He, to his credit, engaged Joss about her trip, asking what-all she'd seen and whether she wanted to follow in Mom's footsteps now.

Near the college, they saw network news trucks jammed bumper to bumper. A camerawoman moved her silver-foil shade behind a broadcaster. A huddle of people was stapling poster board onto wood sticks. *Some kind of protest?*

It was strange, these streets Sam used to walk in sweatpants hosting a national event.

A national battle.

She texted ahead to Jamie, who met them at the gate.

"I got us seats," he said with a wink to Joss. "Right up by the stage."

He and Abe ignored each other as they all moved into the courtyard, which glittered with banners and balloons, passed hors d'oeuvres, hair. Here came Charlotte Gallagher breezing between groups, orchestrating with deft hand motions. There were Joan and Bernadette Gallagher, the bookend legislative bulwarks, anchoring boisterous discussions.

"Dad!" Joss said, pulling her father's hands into her own lap. *"It's Lem, Lem Gallagher!"*

Abe noted the presence of a singer-songwriter he used to call "formative for my own stuff" with a nonplussed nod.

He said, "We're among the Beautiful People."

Sam groaned and was thinking what she might say to counteract the effect of his snarkiness on Joss, but it wasn't necessary.

Because Joss had found Owen Gallagher.

"Other side of the stage, look!" She tugged Sam's dress, straining for a better view. "We're so close—I can't believe we're so close."

Owen was shaking hands with a woman in hijab and two men in suits. His off hand roamed familiarly along their shoulders and down to the elbow. A thousand-watt grin never dimmed on his lips.

The group mingled ahead of the speeches, following Jamie through the festivities. He introduced them as "my dear friends" and found ways to bring them into topics—"Maren, you're still managing the endowment for the Joffrey? Joss here is quite serious in ballet…"

Sam had the thought that Jamie was adjusting awfully well to the scene—then reminded herself Juba was no primitive village. Who knew what Jamie had been doing the last ten years? Maybe he'd been doing functionary work on the clan's behalf, writing grants, attending cocktail parties.

Sam didn't think so. But he could have been.

"Good good, you made it."

Claiming this voice with a hustling step into their circle was Jamie's sister, Charlotte.

She quirked her brow at Sam. "Davenport ninety-six, right? I was four years behind in Trumbull."

As they traded smiles, Sam couldn't decide whether it was modest or ridiculous of Charlotte to provide her year and college affiliation, as though a person of her global stature needed contextualizing.

Ah, cut her some slack, Sam decided. *It's modest.*

Sam said, "And these people with me are Joss…Laurel…and my husband, Abe."

"Pleasure to meet everybody," Charlotte said, giving only the merest doubletake at Abe's appearance. "Has Big Bro given you the tour?"

In school, Sam had known Charlotte only in passing. Now she liked the younger woman instantly, her energy, her appetite to lead—not an aide or minion in sight.

Charlotte Gallagher made things go. Herself.

"And you remember our mother, Joan?" she said, pulling over the Massachusetts senator. "You did a sail with us in Nantucket, didn't you? Would've been your senior year, April? Chilly."

Sam nodded, amazed by Charlotte's recall. It was said she could name any employee in SmartWidget's Silicon Valley office within a week of their starting—a claim Sam had found outrageous before but made sense now.

Joan Gallagher's shake was brittle. "Of course. The daffodils were radiant, as I recall."

Jamie, ever attuned to insincerity, said, "They never met. Mom was in Washington that entire semester, busy with immigration reform."

Charlotte puffed her cheeks at Sam conspiratorially. *What a stickler, huh?*

Sam said, "Thank you so much for having us to the ceremony. This is tremendous." Her eyes traveled the bunting, the balloon arches, the temporary steel stage. "Are you both speaking?"

"Just Mom," Charlotte said. "I'm better in the bowels, toiling away with the plumbing."

Jamie rolled his eyes. "You're laying it on a little thick, Char."

She punched his arm. The interaction cheered Sam, the powerful Gallaghers behaving like any pair of siblings.

She allowed a wispy daydream to sprout, visions of life in the clan. Seasonal New England meals, leek and potato soup on verandas. Talk of art and education reforms, boys in suspenders ducking under picnic tables, girls doing each other's French braids.

Sam wasn't in these scenes, exactly, more of a floating-eye observer, soaking in the mood, smelling centerpieces, the Atlantic crisp on her neck…

Abe's voice pierced it all:

"Do they know about the brick yet?"

Jamie's face lost two shades. Charlotte broke off gesturing to a stagehand.

Sam said, "It really isn't—I mean, we're still trying to figure out the best way to—"

"Brick?" Charlotte said. "What brick?"

Abe grew louder as the spotlight seemed to find him. "The brick Rock Gallagher used to kill that guy. That guy—his Yale roommate, wasn't it?"

Nobody spoke up to confirm or refute this. Fortunately the courtyard was buzzing, the speeches about to start, and other groups didn't seem to be listening in.

Abe continued, "Sam found it. It was boarded up in the fireplace—their dorm fireplace. She's got it in a bag in her room. He's a fascist. Pruitt. We can put him away."

Sam experienced these words as falling, slow-swerving knives. She reached vaguely for her husband, touching his shoulder, unsure if she wanted to stop him or steer him or what. The courtyard felt small.

Charlotte faced her brother, the lightheartedness of seconds ago gone. She seemed angry. *Is she upset Jamie didn't tell her earlier? Or something else? That he brought us here at all?*

She said, "This isn't an ideal place to talk."

Abe asked if she had ideas about what to do.

"Do about what?"

"About the brick," he said. "Who we take it to."

"Look, this—this is the first I'm hearing of it." Again Charlotte glared at her brother. "I take it you knew about this?"

Jamie looked queasy. "I told them I didn't want to pursue it. Nothing good would come."

"*Nothing good?*" Abe repeated. "What're you smoking? You can use this—you can nail Rock Pruitt. And Sam found it. You should be on your knees thanking her."

He sneered at the Gallaghers. It was an expression Sam had come to loathe, but now? She felt herself lining up behind Abe. She and Joss *had* found the brick—then delivered it right to them. Why *wouldn't* they be grateful?

"That was a long time ago," Charlotte said. "Physical evidence…I mean, you're talking twenty years…"

A chuckle escaped her lips, which irked Sam. She felt suddenly ashamed—for the pride she'd felt in her discovery, for the hope. For daydreaming about leek and potato soup.

She felt ashamed on her family's behalf.

"He's not wrong," she spoke up. "If this could stop Rock Pruitt, why *not* shout it from the rooftops?"

"I'm sorry—you're right," Charlotte said. "This is all new. It's a lot to assimilate." She kneaded her fingertips into one temple. "Clearly it's useful information, I—I shouldn't have been dismissive. I apologize."

Before Sam could accept or not accept, the first speaker mounted the stage: Kalifa Babajide, the former U.N. chief and longtime Gallagher ally.

Charlotte excused herself to hustle stragglers into chairs. When Jamie began ushering them to the front row, Sam balked—but Joss was already heading that way with a floaty smile.

As Babajide tapped the SmartPodium and began, tension rippled through their six padded folding chairs. Laurel, at one end, kept peeking down the row.

Jamie folded and refolded his arms, seeming uncomfortable at how the discussion had ended—or not ended.

Did he feel torn between acknowledging Sam's discovery and steering clear of the feud?

Was he irked they'd mentioned the brick in front of Charlotte, worried she was going to take it and run? She sure hadn't seemed eager to run.

Kalifa Babajide gave a dynamic vendroduction to the Gallagher legacy, regaling the audience with tales of ideas championed and rights bills passed. His formal accent and sober appearance—black dashiki with gold trim, shaved head—imbued his message with gravity.

"The world over, there exists one surname that all peoples

know stands with the seekers of progress," he said. "That name—the name this fine institute of learning honors today—is Gallagher."

Eyes forward, Sam checked Charlotte Gallagher in her periphery. Charlotte looked at ease, following Babajide's words with smiling nods.

Maybe there wasn't any tension here. Maybe Sam was only conflating her own emotions—about the brick, about Abe and Jamie—with the Gallaghers' confused reaction.

Charlotte Gallagher was dealing with presidential politics, a clan of incorrigible loose cannons, the reemergence of her only sibling after pretending he was dead for a decade—all on top of her day job, running the second-largest technology company on the planet.

Would she really sweat some brick in a bag?

Babajide spoke beyond his allotted ten minutes, and Lisa Vance after him went even longer—the warrior for child welfare, a rising star in the Democratic Party. This pushed Joan Gallagher's scheduled 3:20 speech back to almost four o'clock.

Charlotte caught her mother on her way to the stage.

"Might trim the middle section," Sam heard her say. "Make sure we get Owen on before the evening news cutoff."

The senator took this under advisement with thinned lips.

Charlotte sat down muttering, *"By all means, everybody do whatever the hell you like..."*

Sam glanced up the row to check on Joss. The speeches were solid but probably less than riveting to fourteen-year-old ears. Sam figured she might've slipped off a shoe for some idle piano-toes stretches.

She hadn't. Joss seemed to be drinking in every detail, the positioning of cameras, tonal cues from the SmartPodium. And, above all, any preparation surrounding Owen Gallagher—who was just visible through a pair of stone archways, getting makeup feathered onto his face.

During Joan's speech, Abe leaned over. "How much audio have you taken?"

Sam squinted. "Audio?"

"The documentary," he said. "You recorded some background clips, right?"

She nodded, wondering about his interest. *Is he excited for me? Or just seeing dollar signs?*

"Who cares about the Gallaghers?" Abe's hoarse voice didn't quite lower to a whisper. "Go straight to the cops, we're golden."

Beside her, Jamie leaned forward in his chair. Sam inhaled, moving her chest and shoulders between the two men.

Again, she wasn't sure quite what Abe was about—what was driving this sudden support of her.

Finally, it was Owen Gallagher's turn to speak. Crisp strides carried him onstage, whipping the fabric of navy suitpants. He dipped his brow and jutted his chin at media personalities in the crowd.

"Thanks, thank you," he began. "It's my great honor to be here at the christening of Gallagher College. And this weather, man! Almost feels like we could be at my alma mater."

Polite chuckles met the reference, which Sam believed was to Stanford.

Amid flash pops, shutter clicks, and the SmartPodium's dull *blups*, Owen launched into the meat of his talk. He emphasized the importance of scholarship, of supporting the Academy— whose primacy to the culture had never been challenged the way its foes were challenging it today. He used an earnest thumb-forefinger point for emphasis. He sustained eye contact. He sprinkled in stories of Iowans or New Hampshirites he'd met who worried about the affordability of higher education.

Joss listened without blinking.

Abe huffed every few minutes.

Sam felt tired, and great and awful at once. She could barely conceive of being back to work at WNYC tomorrow.

"...like to conclude by thanking my dear friend, Kalifa Babajide," Owen was saying—nearing thirty minutes in. "Or, as I like to call him, my little brown cheerleader."

Sam stiffened out of a light doze. For a moment, she thought she'd heard wrong—but one look around the courtyard told her she hadn't.

Camera operators rose up from their viewfinders. Charlotte Gallagher's teeth were a foot tall.

Onstage, Owen looked like he'd just swallowed a goldfish. His eyes zipped from side to side, scanning, searching. The general panic caught to him. A knot of confusion—or heat, or calculation—came into his forehead.

After several moments, seeming to fear any more silence, he looked back to the SmartPodium.

"Er—we Gallaghers rely on black votes," he resumed hurriedly, as though hoping to talk over the bizarre mistake, "and we are 100 percent committed to perpetuating class division through affirmative action, welfare, portraying inner-city police as racist pi..."

He trailed off mid-word.

Owen's face was a mishmash of pains. His eyes bulged at the podium screen. The corners of his mouth sagged like dripping mops.

The audience was fevered. Gasps, groans, sharp intakes of breath—Sam felt the courtyard teetering, lifting off its cobblestones. She was in the middle of a funnel cloud.

Cameras popped rapid-fire.

The buzz settled to a thick, hard, sad silence.

PART III

CHAPTER 14

THE GAFFE NEEDED NO ACCELERANT. ROCK CONFIRMED WITH Yanni the footage had been captured ("Yes, exquisitely") and was circulating online ("like wildfire through California forest"). They agreed to sprinkle a few social media flakes, making sure Owen's governing of whiter-than-white New Hampshire made its way into the discourse, but by and large, this one drove itself.

Rock celebrated at Mory's, drinking cup upon cup upon cup with whoever showed up—Nicky Kirkpatrick, Eric and Yoran from Rugby, Bethany who'd never let him in her pants and didn't now, but brought a friend who did.

Rock gave it to the friend—Cora? Terri?—in the same staff bathroom he'd had the undergrad the first night of the reunion. He put every ounce of joy from his triumph into the effort, kissing the woman full on the lips—which he rarely did—and taking the whole affair slow, sweet, all ten fingers splayed.

He was in orbit. Success coursed through his veins, sharpened his senses, burst from his orifices.

He'd beheaded the reader. He'd vanquished Theresa Velasquez. He'd fitted the Gallagher's preferred presidential nominee for a dunce cap.

Is anything beyond me?

Could I reverse time if I tried?

Leaving, he tossed the staff bathroom key to Johnston.

"Everything in order?" the ancient barkeep asked.

Rock said, "If there were complaints, I didn't hear."

He and his partner headed back up to the Captains' Room. The windows here afforded a view of Sterling Library and the lush lawns of Cross Campus. He looked out over the pewter, rum-stinking lip of another cup, exultant.

Suddenly he needed to be outside, to stretch his legs over these freshly conquered territories. He finished the cup and told Terri she belonged among the gods and ran by Johnston, out the door.

He pranced through campus, free, jolly as a schoolgirl. He didn't even suffer that lurking fear of apprehension—like he would sometimes after a mission for Marshall, looking over his shoulder for the FBI or Interpol.

Because this hadn't required fists or a picklock. He'd used nothing more than a computer. A puny black laptop, since incinerated.

Not a shred of evidence remained.

He looped between Morse and Stiles colleges. He lifted weights at Payne Whitney Gymnasium, adding fifteen pounds to his personal-best bench press.

His wife called while he was eating a chicken.

"What's up?" he answered.

"Rock Junior has an ear infection," she said. "He has a 103.5 fever."

"Put him -n," he said through a bite of drumstick. "L-t me talk to him."

Rock Junior came on. He said in a small vibrato, "Hi, Daddy."

"Hey, Bud! How you feeling?"

"Not very good."

"*Not very good?*" Rock made a buzzer noise. "Wrong answer. Try again—how are you feeling?"

"G—good," Rock Jr. said.

"There she is! You're not gonna let *an ear* get you down. Right?"

The line was silent.

Rock said, "Right?"

"Right, Daddy," Rock Junior said.

"Ears are made of cartilage, Bud. You could chew cartilage—you could cut it with a knife and fork and put ketchup on it."

Rock Junior didn't respond.

"I love you, Bud," Rock said.

"Love you, too, Daddy."

After dinner, he found Marshall at Skull and Bones. The tomb felt wetter than the other night, like a dank basement—the Bonesmen in their frames either sweating or pissing into the room.

"Impressive," Marshall said, wheeling forward to clutch Rock's wrist. "Perfectly tailored to the man. Hard to say whether it's a fatal blow, but this will stay with him for the duration of his career."

Rock sat open-thighed, basking in the praise. "Can you believe he made it all the way to 'racist pigs?'"

Marshall chuckled mutely. "Remarkable."

"All I wanted was the brown cheerleader bit—that's why I stuck it in first."

"Shrewd."

"How close do you figure he came to saying that line about eugenics, calling for more funding?"

Marshall did not engage the question. "We have an active file on SmartPodium." He regarded Rock through slit eyes. "The boys bought one. Expensive. We kicked the tires on hacking in but never could."

Rock rubbed his knuckles boastfully on his chest. The old

man was asking him to show his magician's trick. Rock might've played coy in other circumstances, but he was riding too high now for modesty.

"Jamie Gallagher," he said. "That NetHuman thing—Foxy Charlotte must've granted him full access to all their campaign documents."

"You stole his credentials?"

Rock nodded. "Recovered them from that filthy rucksack of his."

"When."

"Today. I waited for the last second to change the text of the speech. Figured Owen's babysitters would be rehearsing with him right up until he went live."

Marshall folded his hands, the fingers joining in a shriveled nest.

"This is how we beat the Gallaghers. With creativity. With details. The finances favor them now. But the *details*"—his cheeks hollowed with vigor—"favor us."

Rock said, "Cheers to that."

"There is opportunity here. For years, I've pushed for heavier investment in spycraft—the dirty, exotic sort." His eyes gleamed in their sockets. "I believe the efforts deserve formal designation, to be an entity under the Pruitt umbrella."

"Don't you already have a budget?"

Marshall scoffed. "Dimes that fall through the cracks. I want resources commensurate with the grandest goals, with changing the course of human history."

Rock felt some giddy-up in his gut at the language, but no burning interest in the topic.

He hadn't come to gripe about clan priorities.

"Makes damn good sense. Anybody asks my opinion, you got my vote."

A complicated look passed Marshall's face. "I thought I might have a bit more than your vote."

This put Rock on guard. The cadaver in front of him had gotten what he'd wanted from the worst strongmen in South America and the best diplomats of Europe.

What does he want from me?

Was he calling in his pound of flesh for bailing Rock out of the Sterling Library mess? Already? Did he want Rock to press Jonathan Pruitt on this matter of black-ops funding? *Why?* Jonathan cared nothing about Rock's opinion—a fact Marshall knew full well.

Rock didn't want head games. You played head games with Marshall Pruitt, you ended up in a rubber room.

"I'll do what I can," he said. "Tell me what you have in mind."

Marshall said, "I need a leader."

Rock didn't understand. "Leader of what?"

"Of this new entity. I need a man to launch it, to define its mission and culture. Somebody with the requisite force of will."

"That's…flattering. But I don't see it fitting into my career right now."

"We can adjust the title," Marshall said. "CEO. President of the Board—we can incorporate, structure the thing to your liking."

Rock felt a thrum beginning in his brain stem, some disorienting mistake at the core of this discussion.

"Again, I'm much obliged, Marshall," he said, "but I'm gonna be busy as a cross-eyed boy at a circus. I'll be out campaigning soon."

As he looked into the older man's face, Rock's thrum became a violent shaking. Marshall's expression—soft, the corners of his mouth drawn back—contained a sentiment that always made Rock's blood boil.

Pity.

Rock asked, "What did Jonathan say? You talked to him, right?"

Marshall nodded.

"Before or after Owen Gallagher?" Rock was talking very fast.

"Did he *see* what I did to Owen Gallagher? I did that. Nobody else —*me*. I did that."

"Yes. He knows."

"He doesn't care? And he doesn't care Theresa Velasquez has a husband running around on her with strange chicks on beaches? None of that matters?"

Marshall gripped the handles of his wheelchair as though preparing to push out of it and console Rock, then remembering his legs.

"Jonathan was never going to put you on the ballot." His tone was somber. "Not in Virginia. Not anywhere."

Rock swore profusely. He stalked to a wall and put his fist through the Bonesmen of 1926.

"I have pictures!" Rock said. "We have pictures! Bryce on his back, Bryce on his knees, Bryce brushing sand off his—"

"This is a blessing in disguise," Marshall put in. "Senators don't matter. Governors don't matter, even presidents. Politics is in a new phase, Rock. Today, you can *make* the facts. That's where the power is."

"Yeah? Does Yanni Jovanovic get a lot of ass, you think?"

Marshall pushed forward to Rock's hip, wheels crunching over the broken 1926 glass. "This is the superior play."

"It's a slap in the face," Rock said. "You're positive his mind is made up? There's nothing to be done to budge him off Velasquez?"

Marshal confirmed there was not. Jonathan Pruitt had been troubled by Bryce's actions. He appreciated Rock's energy—at the Choosing, and in exposing Owen Gallagher for the pretender he was—but there was simply no chance.

Not while Derek Dickerson still hung from his neck.

Rock left the tomb with acid in his heart. He'd done superhuman things this weekend, and the clan was essentially yawning.

It had been like this Rock's entire life. As a child, excellence was expected. His father's pet saying had been, "Is that all you got?" His mother's had been, "We're different, honey. You might as well prepare." Rock had devoured awards, owned every honor worth owning. The rare times he'd failed—or succeeded less than completely—he had been mocked.

Rock's father, holding a state runner-up trigonometry trophy with two fingers like trash: "Couldn't beat the Indian boy, aye? He's never had steak in his life, you know. Cows are sacred there. We fed you ribeye last night."

Campus taunted Rock now. The spires of Branford and Old Campus laughed, their skinny stone shoulders twitching in the night. Stained-glass windows made cruel mirrors, showing Rock just what he was: a mid-forties nothing with receding hair. An indifferent father and husband who possessed no great or marvelous position that justified indifference.

The acid worked down Rock's chest, eating channels between ribs and forging chutes into his lungs. When he moved, it moved, sloshing, fouling fresh tissue.

The only thing for it was alcohol and narcotics.

CHAPTER 15

IN THE COURTYARD OF GALLAGHER COLLEGE, A KIND OF surreality took hold after Owen's speech. He had finished out reading a paper copy—rushed to him by a heady staffer—amid graveyard silence. He delivered his parting promise to "keep fighting for progress, for people, and for you," and then brushed sandy hair off his temple.

It bounced back in his eyes.

Joan Gallagher rushed on stage to examine the SmartPodium, squinting, drilling her fingernail into the screen.

Charlotte stayed sitting beside Jamie. She'd already run through the gamut of reactions: shock, denial, rage, and now resignation.

"That'll be all she wrote for SmartPodium," she said. "Mother will be glad."

Jamie barely registered the gallows humor. His gears didn't turn as quickly as his sister's. Perhaps he just wasn't as accustomed to the speed and scope of their fight.

He'd been confused at first, angry at the grotesque sentiments, wondering how or why somebody allowed Owen to write his own speech…but once he realized the words hadn't been Owen's,

Jamie had needed only a few moments to figure out who'd engineered the sabotage.

The Pruitts.

It could only be the Pruitts.

And he, Jamie Gallagher, had been sitting across a table from one of them not five hours earlier.

Now, weakness exploding down his arm, he reached under his chair to the rucksack and checked the front pockets.

Empty, every last one.

The NetHuman credentials Charlotte had given him—given him with the expectation he would use them to do *good*—were gone.

Blood rushed to Jamie's face. He thought for several minutes how to undo the damage. Jump in front of the cameras outside— the cable news outlets were breathlessly reporting Owen's nightmare—and tell the truth? Claim full responsibility? Explain how he'd been duped?

Hunt down Rock Pruitt? Confront him, accuse him? Jamie had a strong instinct to do just that, to pin him against some wall by the lapels and wring a confession out of him.

All around, Gallaghers were in damage-control mode. *They'd been hacked—no question the podium had been hacked. Could they float the likelihood of Russian involvement? Chinese? Frame it as a malicious attack on democracy, foreign governments emboldened by lax Republican oversight?*

But how to handle the main problem? The podium had been hacked—fine, that could be sold to the public—but how did you explain why Owen had *said* those things? Why there hadn't been some filter between the teleprompter and his mouth?

Hands groped in pockets.

A Portland cousin had commandeered a Beefeater bottle from the caterers and was passing it.

Owen waved him off. The presumptive nominee stood apart from the frantic deliberations looking dazed, his rugged face a sheet of clean typing paper as friends and family strategized how to deal with his complete and unquestioned stupidity.

Jamie was angry, and a piece of him—a growing piece—yearned to jump into the fray. To avenge Rock's stunt and his own negligence, to go find that wall and those lapels…but he resisted.

He thought of ten years in Juba. He thought of Sam, of his reasons for coming back.

And he decided not to jump in front of cameras, nor to hunt down Rock and fight.

Laboriously, he pushed up off his knees and stood. He dreaded calling attention to himself, stepping into the spotlight, but he knew what had to be done.

"Owen," he said, stepping around Charlotte and others formulating counter-moves. "This is my fault. They used my credentials to change the speech."

He explained lunch at Commons, how he'd been joined by Rock Pruitt. How he'd left his rucksack unattended—probably the NetHuman card had been visible without undoing a single snap.

How Rock had looked into Jamie's eyes in parting and thanked him.

"I respect your moral compass," Rock had said. "You're living life on your terms, brother. That's priceless."

Rock had beaten him. Outsmarted him, exploited him—pick your pejorative.

Owen heard Jamie out, then draped an arm over his wiry shoulders. "This isn't on you. At all."

"The credentials were mine. I should've never—"

"Nah, I appreciate you telling us," Owen said, "I own this. The buck stops here, with me."

Chest full, he clapped Jamie on the back and told the courtyard at large they'd be fine.

"We will get past this," he insisted. "Don't lose heart."

Listening, Jamie felt he'd misjudged Owen—or at least judged him unkindly. Owen wasn't some privileged brute who felt entitled to lead the free world because of this last name. He was a decent, mostly competent man thrust into circumstances beyond him.

He was the boy who faints at the sight of blood but can't escape joining his parents' veterinary practice.

Owen finished by telling the crowd today was not about him, but about Gallagher College: their family's legacy of progressive achievement. This speech hiccup? It was a blip.

Charlotte didn't look like she thought it was a blip.

"Rock Pruitt is an absolute—" She strung together four or five curses, a sequence that suggested extreme bodily contortion. "The first thing we do, the first damn thing, is cram his—"

She painted another profane image. The Portland cousin's face curdled.

Jamie's mother said, "Where are they running this cycle? Besides Pennsylvania-sixteen, I know Penn-sixteen. *Where else?*"

"Florida-twelve and California-seven," Charlotte answered from memory, whipping out her phone. "Virginia Senate of course. And I hear that twerp T. Jonas wants to be attorney general of New York."

"Okay. Okay." Joan Gallagher paced between the stage and first row of seats. "Double the oppo research on all Pruitt candidates. Triple it—if there's even a whiff of dirt."

Charlotte was already swiping out texts. "Absolutely. What else? Let's make some trouble in Georgia, shall we?" Warren Pruitt was governor there. "I feel a labor issue coming on. What's their minimum wage? Pretty sure it's five-fifteen. *Five*"—she swore—"*dollars*, can you imagine? How're there not protesters on the governor's lawn every single day?"

Next there was a call for scandals-in-waiting. Someone thought Pruitt Capital had a diversity problem in the executive ranks. Someone else said there was gold in Jonathan Pruitt's presidential library donor list, if anybody would just take a few weeks to mine it.

Jamie shook Owen's hand and said, "You're being very gracious. I hope it is a blip."

Next, he approached Charlotte, who was scowling and stabbing out hate-texts on her phone.

"Stop, Char," he said. "We can't keep doing this. We can't keep plowing resources into fighting the Pruitts."

This sounded naive, Jamie knew, but he didn't care. The two families kept running each other through with spears, knocking off whoever dared raise their head, the count of ruined lives growing every year.

It needed to stop. Somebody needed to end the cycle.

Charlotte raised her brow toward him and, after a final peck of her screen, gave her eyes, too.

"Couple things," she said. "One? This isn't your fault. I designed SmartPodium. I gave you superuser access, which was the height of recklessness—there should've never *been* superuser access, where you could change other people's documents. Brutal design decision…"

She momentarily veered into arcane technical details, then broke off with a *fzzzt*.

"And two," she said, raising fingers, "we can keep plowing resources into this fight—because we have more resources to plow. In a war of attrition, *they lose*. They should know that. I think in fact they do know—I think Rock Pruitt went rogue. But I really don't care."

She finished with a tight, terrible grin. Jamie knew this expression from childhood. It meant she was feeling wronged—in Connect Four, in field hockey, in missing some academic prize or honor. It meant she was going to use this wrong. She was going to motivate off it, drive herself with the memory.

It meant she was going to win.

No matter that for a decade, Jamie had observed American politics from afar—he still saw the coming election cycle with perfect clarity. One retaliation after another, hitting and being hit, scandal and counter-scandal. Everyone sucked into the vortex, lower, filthier.

He had no standing to stop it from the Gallagher side. He hadn't been around. Whatever buzz his reemergence had created in the clan was forgotten after Owen's gaffe.

He could whisper in Charlotte's ear, but she wouldn't listen. She'd entered a zone impervious to suggestion.

Maybe Lem Gallagher would object, write some stark ballad about the pointlessness of ideological conflict.

Maybe the California wing would nudge the clan off the national tug-of-war, focusing on progressive solutions for the fifth-largest economy in the world rather than keep prosecuting culture wars against the flyover states.

None of this would matter. These were power centers, but lesser ones. Minor suns to Charlotte's supernova.

Should he head back to Juba? There Jamie had been doing unassailable good, improving the lives of disadvantaged children and the infirm. He could keep those missions alive. Physically removing himself from other Gallaghers and Pruitts would guarantee he didn't cause any further unintended harm—like he'd caused today.

Wouldn't it?

Watching the machinations play out now in the courtyard, Jamie couldn't be sure. He felt utterly incapable of living—of walking around, inhaling oxygen and exhaling carbon dioxide— without wreaking damage someplace.

Look what he'd done with Sam Lessing. Sam, the one pure thing in his life. He had started out cautiously this weekend, exercising discretion, but gotten too close. He'd put her in a compromising position with her family.

Look at me, Jamie Gallagher! All shiny and new! Money, power, romance without the bother or tarnish of real responsibility! Wouldn't you rather be here?

There was no mistaking that Sam and her husband had fought. They'd walked feet apart with their shoulders turned out. In Jamie's presence, they hadn't touched once. They talked to Joss in shifts, almost like a tryout for joint custody.

Jamie needed to do right.

Full of dread, he walked to Silliman College. Fading sunlight gave campus a mournful tint. Families stood next to bags on curbs, waiting for cars to take them to the airport or train station. The reunion was over. Silliman was in the throes of tearful sendoffs, strong hugs and swapped numbers, promises to keep in touch.

Jamie found the husband first.

"What do you want?" the man asked.

Abe, right?

"To talk to Sam," Jamie said, then realized how threatening that sounded. "And you, too. Things ended badly at the ceremony. I want to make it right."

"She went for a walk." Abe pointed north.

"Maybe up to East Rock?"

Abe flared a nostril, indifferent, ugly.

Jamie winced. *Of course—he doesn't know East Rock.*

"Did she go with anyone?"

"Our daughter."

Abe was standing outside the entryway of Sam and Laurel's room, leaning into a split-rail fence, not doing much. His shirt was a rag. He smelled.

Jamie tried for polite conversation. "How is Sam these days? Does she seem happy at WNYC?"

Abe narrowed his eyes. "It's not her life's ambition. But she has peers, friends there."

Jamie nodded, his chin's path to his chest feeling about a mile long. "And how are…you?"

Should he ask what Abe did for work? About Brooklyn? About what stuff Joss was into these days?

No. *She isn't some toddler discovering books or gravity.*

He decided to add nothing.

Abe's head ticked back and forth.

Jamie said, "It's just a friendly question."

"Right, real friendly," Abe said. "You're a Gallagher so you have to be friendly, right? Some kind of a plank in the platform?"

Jamie didn't respond.

Abe shook out his ratty sleeves. "I'm common as they come, aren't I? The perfect object of your charity."

Jamie took a half-step away. "Fine. We don't have to talk."

"We can just stand here? Stand here together waiting for *my wife*, you mean?"

The sallow skin under the man's eyes trembled. Jamie felt an extreme physical aversion, an urgent need to bolt.

He made himself stay. "I don't pretend to know anything about you. Or Sam. I just came to my twenty-year reunion. That's all I did."

"Is it? How innocent of you. How'd you end up chaperoning my wife and daughter all around New Haven?"

"That…I—I was keeping my distance from my own family."

"And Sam was just around?" Abe asked, incredulous. "You just happened to join up and become bosom buddies. Could've happened with anybody."

Jamie wondered what exactly Sam had told him about the weekend. "I didn't say that."

Abe hurled more accusations and veiled digs at the Gallagher name. He lolled his tongue mockingly and made vaguely effeminate gestures of the wrists. Several classmates were listening.

Jamie didn't care about the classmates, but Abe distressed him. Just being near him was oppressive—the constant aggrievement, the mantle of threadbare nobility he kept shoving under your nose.

What was it like to live with this man 365 days a year? He felt awful on Sam's behalf.

Still, Jamie had come here with a mission.

"I'm not going to argue," he said. "Things look one way from your perspective—I understand that. I'm sorry. I apologize for whatever I've done, or whatever you perceive that I've done."

The words, which Jamie had meant as an olive branch, seemed to flummox Abe. His sneakers shuffled sideways.

Jamie realized his extra words—all that "perspective" and "perceive"—had sapped the apology of its force. To compensate, he stepped closer and patted Abe behind the upper arm.

"What's going on here?"

Jamie turned.

It was Sam.

"What're you guys, pals or something?" she said, face tipped severely. "Man. I leave for ten minutes."

Jamie looked between husband and wife, feeling something like whiplash. Could he say or do *anything* without causing offense?

"We—I was just apologizing," he said. "This weekend, you know, I didn't come here with any big plan, it—things just happened and…"

He trailed off, realizing he had no idea what he meant to say—and finding his brain useless in the face of Sam's anger.

He managed, "You went for a walk?"

Sam seemed just as mad at her husband, looking between them like co-conspirators.

"Yeah," she said. "Yeah, just for air. To think."

Again, Jamie groped for a safe word or combination of words. Sam was a Sphinx now—quiet, her eyes fused to a laser beam.

He tried, "Rock Pruitt sabotaged the speech." *Surely we can all unite around this.* "It was my fault—he stole my login info and used it to stick that racist stuff in Owen's speech."

Neither Sam nor her husband said anything, nor Joss—who'd stalled out a few paces back.

Now Jamie felt *that* had been dumb to say, as though he believed this pinebox blow of the Pruitt's somehow trumped their insignificant family foibles.

"I'm sorry," he said again. "I really am. I'm sorry you got in the middle of the feud, I'm sorry this weekend got complicated. I'm sorry we—"

"Stop saying you're sorry!" Sam said. "I don't care about the feud. I really don't. I just feel like running that brick to the cops and…I don't care. Whatever happens happens."

Jamie folded his hands behind his back. Sam was peeved, no doubt, but he couldn't tell precisely what about. Did she think Charlotte had been dismissive earlier at the ceremony? Was this still about his seeming chummy with Abe?

For a while, everybody stood staring past one another in a circle of rancor.

The sounds of the courtyard were becoming diffuse, a caterer's hand truck scraping stone, a child whining for one last turn on the rope swing. Up Orange Street, a car horn faded.

It put Jamie in mind of another ending—twenty years earlier, their last night as undergraduates. That one, too, had turned at the very end.

Jamie had entered college with no plan, yet those four years still managed to feel like a series of ramblings away from some preset path. He paid lip service to his parents' advice to study history or political science for a semester, and then changed majors to philosophy. Outside class, he blundered from one mistake to the next, finding false purpose, correcting it, refocusing every few months on a new aspect of himself or the community.

Senior spring, it was people: these lovely people he was preparing to leave behind—and none lovelier than Sam Lessing. Jamie felt the subconscious restraint he'd always exercised around Laurel Trowbridge sloughing off, and Sam's too. As second semester wound down, he visualized a dozen ways it might happen.

On a bike trail, stopped for squirts of water.

Their knees touching at the dining hall—accidentally, then not.

Sitting in a rowboat at New Haven Harbor under a stone moon.

With each day none of these came to pass, his panic grew. *Would it happen at all?* Should he force the issue with some contrived meeting or declaration of feelings?

Instinct told him no, such clumsiness didn't fit Sam's style. It would end in a big botch-up, spoiling everything that'd grown up between them.

Could he really *not* try, though? Just let things whimper out? How cowardly was that?

Then, that final night in the courtyard, it put itself together. Their legs and hands intertwining, their Davenport classmates around like a chorus—some engaged in their own private heart-wrench, others acting young and dumb—as they followed the inexorable moment.

Jamie thought the entryway kiss might go further. His imaginings sure had. When it didn't, though, when Sam squeezed his hand and said, "You're perfect" before backing into her room, he felt no disappointment. He felt graced—by Sam, by this university he loved, by having graduated, which his classmates all took for granted.

Not Jamie. The kiss drove home this truth: everything in his life was a gift, one more golden bar on a pile that'd already risen to greater heights than he—than anyone—deserved.

College had worked out after all. If he got to kiss Sam Lessing tonight and fly to Macedonia to work on intransigent poverty in the morning? "Perfect" was exactly right.

He reached out to touch Sam's closed door. He laid two fingers against it, then rested his face against those knuckles and cried—with joy and relief and release and knowing life was pivoting on, moving ahead, and bringing Jamie Gallagher along.

Now, a minor lifetime later, he faced another sort of closed door. Sam's anger.

Reunion weekend was nearly over. This thing he'd forged with Sam must end, or shift, or snowball—but something. And right now, looking at this crease splitting Sam's forehead like black lightning, he didn't like his odds.

Sam was the reason he'd come to New Haven. The reason he'd resurfaced at all. Leaning against the grass-thatched mud, imagining the pain of returning to the States and giving up the life he'd enjoyed in Juba, Jamie had pushed through with visions of Sam.

Sam had gotten him on that flight to Khartoum.

He broke the group silence. "I refuse to be a negative. I refuse to hurt you, or be the reason—"

"Again, *damn it!*" Sam interrupted. "Again? Really?"

"All I'm trying to explain—"

"Hurt me! Hurt him!" Sam jabbed a finger toward her husband. "Or get mad at Rock Pruitt and help me nail him. Aren't you *enraged* at him?"

Jamie felt her breath's force across the circle.

Sam continued, "Life sucks. It sucks a lot—it's messy and soul crushing, but you still have to live it. You can't float through like mist and think you're never gonna upset people, or…you know, brush against anything."

Jamie didn't shrink from this, though his heart was twisting and numbness had overtaken his fingertips.

He met her eyes. He swallowed.

He needed to answer, but what could he say? Was there a word or even a single syllable that wouldn't provoke another torrent?

"You can't even speak," Sam said, and stormed off, gone again from his life.

CHAPTER 16

She was getting the brick from underneath her bed and taking it to a police station. Any police station. She wasn't going to think about which precinct or what timing would produce maximum impact. She wasn't going to wait. Jamie's hesitancy—and Charlotte Gallagher's skepticism—had confused the issue in her mind, fuzzed up her thoughts. But no more.

The brick wasn't theirs to hem and haw over. It belonged to her. Her and Joss. Maybe it would make Sam famous. She had plenty of footage and skill to produce a devastating expose on Rock Pruitt. The brick—and whatever legal action it spawned—would propel her work onto the national stage. Sam might end up on *Fresh Air* or *The Today Show*.

She didn't care if her thoughts were crass. She felt like being crass and selfish and letting everybody react to her for a change.

In the room, she found Laurel zipping her last suitcase.

"Aww," Sam said, her mood blunted. "When do you fly?"

"Nine thirty." Laurel stood and situated luggage over her shoulders, adjusting straps, balancing weight front to back. "Red-eye was the cheapest way to get home."

They embraced. Both sniffled at first, then chuckled when Sam couldn't find a way to wrap her arms around Laurel without upsetting a bag.

Sam asked if she was good getting to the airport.

"Uber's on the way," Laurel said. "Are you catching a train tonight? You and…Joss, I guess?"

"Yeah," Sam said. "I guess."

She didn't know what Laurel had heard of the courtyard blowup. Even if she had been packing and missed it all, she'd witnessed enough dysfunction from the Lessing-Isaacson family unit to know their situation had gotten royally scrambled.

"We should talk more," Laurel said. "I could really use it. Plus I need to hear all about your documentary and what Joss's dance teacher thinks about quarks."

Sam smiled and agreed.

Holding the door for her friend, Sam felt encouraged at the reset between them. When she'd imagined good outcomes from this weekend, Laurel had never figured into the picture. Their relationship had seemed beyond change, like some high-mileage car whose faults and maintenance costs you just learned to accept.

Laurel asked, "Did you hear if Jamie's sticking around? Or for how long?"

Sam shook her head. "I'm not sure he knows that himself."

Both their mouths turned down. Sam still felt anger toward Jamie, but saying goodbye to Laurel was filing off its sharpest barbs.

Sam shouldn't judge him. Jamie Gallagher was damaged. The pinebox vendetta had chewed him up, gripped him by its furious, hurricane arms and whipped him around and around until something broke inside. He wasn't the person she'd known at Yale.

Did that person still exist? Buried somehow, repairable? Sam didn't know.

Laurel stopped in the entryway. "Oh, did you need me to leave my key?"

Sam patted her front pocket. "No, I'm good—got mine right here. Why, did you find an extra somewhere?"

Laurel's expression turned quizzical. "I found the door unlocked earlier, when I came back. I thought maybe you'd lost your key and left it open?"

Sam narrowed her eyes.

Laurel went on, "I'll go find Joss and say goodbye. I have a few minutes before the car gets here."

As she disappeared to the courtyard, Sam felt her stomach bottoming out.

She started on shaky legs for the bedroom she and Joss had shared the past two nights. She'd been preparing to look up the address for the New Haven Police on her phone when she'd run into Laurel. Now she wasn't thinking about addresses or transportation or what hours the precinct was open.

She dropped to her knees on the hardwood floor. The bed skirt hung straight down—stiff, bulldog blue. She raised it.

Below the box spring was nothing but empty space.

❧

Sam couldn't stop the breaths from coming. One after another barged up her throat. She felt pressure in her ears, a high whinny destroying all sense of balance.

She staggered onto her side. Then—feeling watched, violated, marked—crawled across the room.

Maybe I put it back under the other bed, or Joss moved it there.

But the space under the other bed's box spring was bare, too. The brick had vanished.

Sam stayed prone on the hardwood, propped by her elbows, stomach flat to the floor. Her head dropped like the power had been cut. Waves of emotion crashed through her body.

Shock. Heartache. Rage.

Her worst suspicions about the Pruitts had borne out. Somehow they'd learned about her discovery. Whether they had the God Quad bugged, or had caught wind of Sam's project and tailed her, or by some other means—Sam didn't know. They had waited for her to leave the brick unattended, and then they'd taken it.

The naming ceremony had lasted two hours, plenty of time to pick a college dorm lock and find the evidence. Underneath the bed was probably the first place they'd looked.

Sam stalked to every corner of the room, checking for fingerprints or smudges or a left-behind crowbar, anything. Anything she could show the police.

She searched ten minutes. She ripped both bedspreads to the ground. She rattled drawers. She kicked walls. There was no logic to it, and she expected no results.

Finally, she laid on her back in the center of the floor.

Sam felt hatred unlike any she had known. All the stress, the ordeal she'd been through, the work she'd put into the project— which had become a shared experience with her daughter. Which had produced such cataclysmic downstream effects on her personal life.

Everything had been for naught.

This loss—this heist—would define reunion weekend. For Sam. For Joss.

It wouldn't be the weekend of quarks or New Haven boys or breaking through with Laurel. When they thought of this weekend, they would think of Rock Pruitt first.

Always.

Sam thought of his smug face. The uncouth jokes and language Rock believed elevated him over the caring, empathetic herd. He thought he was better than everyone he laid eyes on. He thought he could get away with anything. Maybe he could.

She wished for every bad thing to happen to him.

A rustle sounded in the common room. Sam instinctively cast about for something to defend herself with—cover, a weapon. The best she could find was a sharp pencil.

"Sam? Sam, you in here?"

It was Abe.

She unclenched her fist around the pencil. "Yep. You found me."

Her husband looked beat, his eyes unfocused, taking short steps like a nursing-home ward missing his walker. His hair seemed sparser.

Sam remembered his band's last gig. Seven, eight years ago. They had been at Arlene's Grocery, a dive they'd played often over the course of their thirty-odd year run. Abe's voice held through the first set, but during "Your Shoes Are Stupid!" in the second, it thinned out and became like (as Abe later put it) dogs whimpering for table scraps.

Afterward, he looked offstage to Sam. Things weren't super between them at that point, but they were still offering support and discussing plans with each other.

His face then—weary, hangdog—reminded Sam of his face now.

He saw her tears, then saw that both beds were upset. "What —what happened? The brick?"

Sam nodded.

She felt suddenly—unexpectedly—glad it was Abe who'd come rather than Joss or, God forbid, Jamie Gallagher.

Abe knew disappointment. This shared life of theirs had been one—and for as crummy as it had turned out, they had lived it together. On the same tired carpets and mattresses. She had seen him through liver disease. He'd been there when her mother had died, in the maddeningly plain hospital room that'd been her world for the last months of life.

They'd even loved each other once. For eighteen months—in

that hovel she'd lived in on Broome Street, eating at restaurants with five tables.

Eighteen months was the shelf life of Abe's cool, detached cynicism. His looks lasted longer—those rough, young-Keith-Richards edges that felt good to rub against even if they gave you blisters—and Sam tried desperately to keep loving him for another four years. She fought and stayed.

Then, for another four, she convinced herself this was simply what marriage was. She learned to not fight, and stayed.

Which took Joss up to eight years old.

It had been this shared history, Sam realized now, that had compelled her to stick up for him in front of Charlotte Gallagher.

He asked, "You didn't give it to Jamie?"

Sam swallowed, gathering herself to speak.

But Abe continued first, "Because I think that was dumb, if I'm being honest. They have no obligation to take it to the police. They might just keep it, use it for blackmail."

She inhaled and, again, was about to correct him.

But he kept talking. "See, you're nothing to them. They don't care about you—whether some documentary gets made or not." Pacing now, like he was working out the chorus for some new song. "You should've gone straight to the cops. Now you'll never see that brick again. What did you think, the Gallaghers would lavish praise upon you?"

He finished with a nasal huff. Or seemed to finish—maybe he was only pausing to think up more invective.

Sam felt her blood rising, pushing at its veins. She'd shifted up onto her knees and now had visions of launching herself like a missile, of driving her head through his mouth—through that small, disingenuous mouth.

Instead she said, "Go."

"Be mad at me all you want, but don't say I didn't tell you exactly—"

"Go!" She got to her feet and pointed to the courtyard. "This is my school, my place. *Was* my place. And I want you out. I want you the hell out now."

"So you can be with Jamie, right?" Abe backpedaled into the common room as he spoke, parceling out more hurt. "Did the bloody brick seal the deal—you're back together, like it was supposed to be twenty years ago? Ready to take your rightful place with the Gallaghers?"

"Please go. Just go."

"Of course, yeah. I'll go. I'll get out of your—"

"*Now*! Get on a Goddamn train to Brooklyn and hole up with one of your Fiverr ladies, and suck the life out of her—or yourself. I want away from you. You're poison."

Classmates in the courtyard listened through open windows, craning their necks to see who was screaming—and what about.

Abe said, "You've been checked out of this marriage for years. You've faked it forever."

"How could I not? Tell me—*how could I not*? You cheat, you're indifferent."

"Let's talk about indifference. Let's talk about how you completely lost interest in me once the NYC music scene passed me by."

Passed him by? It was just too Abe—the self-importance, all of it.

"Believe it or not, I couldn't have cared less about this…music scene, whatever. I just wanted to sit across a table Saturday mornings eating eggs without hating each other."

But Sam didn't believe this. She was grasping for words, for any plank of wood to hold up against his arrows.

The summer evening was quiet as death. Any courtyard farewells had paused so people could rubberneck.

Of course, this was the least of Sam's worries. Her life had imploded. Her marriage, this fragile rigging off which hung schedules and insurance forms and last names, was done. She'd protected it so studiously over the years that its dissolution stunned her.

How did this happen?

What do we do now?

It'd been dust, sure, but they needed that dust. Losing it shook Sam as deeply as if her apartment or WNYC had burned to the ground.

Her family. Her whole identity.

Finally Abe stood in the door, holding his toiletry bag.

"Personally, I'm glad," he said. "I'm ready to get out and live my life. Meet people. I woulda never put this on Joss, but hey, it's all about you. Right? All about you."

And off he went, not quite managing to keep a stiff lip.

❦

Joss.

She'd been lurking in Sam's mind, right below the tumult and sting of the fight, but as soon as Abe said her name, Sam stopped hearing anything else.

She rushed to the windowsill—dimly aware of her husband leaving—and leaned out into the courtyard to find her daughter.

Here was Troy Fickert, watching unabashedly from the cobblestone path. A dozen others seemed to have just averted their eyes, ambling away, holding onto a suitcase or child's hand.

Where is she? Sam leaned through the open window.

"Joss!" she called.

More classmates looked over. Sam was about to shout again when she spotted a red hoodie by the gate.

"*Joss!*" she tried again.

The hoodie—and the slender, skulking form inside—kept moving for the street. Sam ran from the common room, pounding through the entryway, possibly brushing by Abe—if she did, she didn't know or care.

"Come back, Joss, *hey…*"

She caught up on Wall Street, Joss kicking a deli wrapper.

"Listen, I'm sorry." Sam circled ahead of her daughter. "You shouldn't have heard—er, had to hear a thing like that, your parents…"

She was at loss for how to describe it. *Severing ties? Shattering their own lives and yours in one last sad burst of acrimony?*

She flashed back to herself all those years ago, in her mother's car after *Arsenic and Old Lace* rehearsal.

Was this any better?

"I just…am so, so sorry we did that to you," Sam managed. "Me and Dad."

Joss clutched her elbows even though it was seventy degrees out. "You were really loud."

Something in her eyes—was it irony?—gave Sam hope.

"I know, we were so, *so* loud." Sam felt about three inches tall, but she knew she had to keep explaining, keep fighting. "There's some bad stuff between me and Dad, and you—and it has nothing to do with you, or how we feel about you—"

"I know, Mom."

Again, there was an encouraging note here—an airiness you wouldn't expect from a teenager experiencing the worst moment of her life, which Sam feared she'd just inflicted.

"You know…that we love you?" Sam said. "That even if things aren't great between us, between ourselves, that we'd both do absolutely anything for you?"

"Well, yeah." Joss twisted the ball of her foot into the sidewalk, the start of a nervous pirouette. "I know that."

"Because that's important."

Joss inhaled at length and looked up with a pinched expression, like her six-year-old-self saying she didn't want to play soccer anymore.

"He's horrible to you," she said. "I mean, seriously, you two are an awful match."

Sam had a panicky instinct, like she'd walked onto the balcony in underwear, but made herself pause before answering.

"Getting married was different than…I guess, living together," she said. "Being a married couple, it's not easy. At least not for us."

Joss started forward, and they hugged. Sam cried into her daughter's hoodie, crying for old mistakes and lousy life outcomes, but also with relief, because Joss was crying mostly for her—for Sam—and not herself.

Sam knew this from the strength of her daughter's clutch. It had happened in smaller moments before, the child comforting the parent. When Sam had lost a cousin to cancer. When her Nicaraguan bird trade film hadn't won the IDA award it'd been nominated for—so not a big deal, but Joss had picked up on Sam's disappointment and eaten every bite of asparagus that night.

It had always surprised Sam, the capacity of this girl whose diapers she'd changed to think beyond her own needs and wants. It surprised her now.

"Thank you," she croaked.

Joss stepped back. "You should be happy, Mom. Like this weekend? You've been so totally alive, it's been amazing watching you here."

Sam nodded. She felt spent, and like she could sleep forever—but also looser in the shoulders.

It wasn't the same, Joss now versus herself a quarter-century ago. Joss was stronger, or at least more ready to accept a world where her parents weren't together.

"I want you to be like this *all the time*," Joss said. "I wish…I mean, I just wish…"

Her face bent and scrunched and got red from straining.

Sam pulled her into another embrace. "We're going to figure it out. Families deal with lots worse. I love you. And he loves you."

After several rickety breaths, and complex looks, and hand squeezes that stood in for further words, they started back to the dorm room.

Sam told her about the brick.

If Joss took the other news easier than expected, this news proved there was no predicting teenagers: it walloped her.

"*Gone?*" she repeated. "It can't be! You hid it under the bed, we made sure—"

"They stole it from the room," Sam said. "The Pruitts. I think they were following us. At the gallery, there was this guy, and then a car...I don't know. I don't know how they did it. But it's gone."

Joss's face cycled from disorientation, to fear, to anger.

"The Pruitts took it?"

"It's my fault. I should've never left it alone."

By now, they were back in the dorm. Joss looked to the corners of the room, up to the ceiling, along the plaster moldings, arms stiff at her sides.

When the brick didn't materialize or otherwise present itself, she looked back to Sam. "We have to go to the police!"

"How? With what?"

Joss stomped about with none of her typical dancer's grace.

"We can...testify!" she said. "We saw the brick—we found it. This is insane! We can describe where it was and testify they took it."

"The police aren't going to—"

"Mom, we have to! We can't let them—we can't let *him*"—her face blanched at the reference to Rock Pruitt—"just erase our evidence. *We can't.* We have to fight this!"

"Fight it how?"

"I dunno, maybe we could figure out where they have it! You said the Pruitts were big into that one secret society, right? Skull and Bones?"

Sam, who'd traveled these same rhetorical paths herself after discovering the brick missing only to end in despair, sighed.

Joss went on, "Or get him to admit it on tape! He's such a bigmouth. He loves bragging—I'll bet if we told him what we found, he'd admit it! He'd brag. As long as we keep the recorder hidden…"

Sam laid a hand on her daughter's back, feeling quick breaths rise and fall.

"He's not going to admit anything, baby," she said. "I'm sorry. We aren't living in some movie."

As Joss railed they had to do something—*something!*—Sam walked them back to the common room and looked out upon the courtyard again. The lawn was deserted.

She'd come here hoping to reclaim her life—to find friends, to find some spark or new purpose.

Had she? It was hard to say in all the rubble. Her life had changed irrevocably. Abe was probably gone from the picture. They'd recovered from lots in the past—screaming fights, thrown mugs—but always Joss had brought them back together.

Without the brace of her welfare—the presumed apocalypse binding them—they were free.

So her life…was what? Reclaimed? More like blown up.

"There's nothing to be gained fighting people like the Pruitts," Sam said, and found she believed it. "They thrive off fighting. They're built for it. We're not. We're built to live. So let's just live, okay? We can watch them on TV."

The words had the intended effect on Joss, who leaned back into the window sill and closed her eyes, seeming to accept the brick's disappearance.

"After all that work, you're just scrapping the documentary?"

"Not necessarily," Sam said. "I still have plenty of audio. I could do something like I was thinking before—smaller, atmospheric."

Joss exhaled without opening her eyes.

"I know, I know," Sam said. "It stinks. Rock Pruitt gets off. Really, though—who cares? The guy he murdered was a jerk. Two jerks. Better we stay out of the whole jerky thing."

This, finally, made Joss smile. Mother and daughter both wiped their eyes. Joss dangled one foot above the hardwood floor and, after a long beat of apparent thought, smiled bigger.

It was release, Sam thought, finding humor in that too-human inability to change the world. Joss was growing up. She had accepted the situation—accepted all the situations, like Sam had, and finally understood they were going to muddle through. Maybe with less, maybe not taking the route they'd planned, but they would survive.

CHAPTER 17

Joss told her mother she needed to meet a boy to say goodbye and exchange numbers, then stood around the common room fussing with her skirt, pulling strands of hair behind her ear.

Come on, come on! she thought. *Go use the bathroom. Or duck away to text your friends. Anything.*

Mom noticed she was stalling and asked if she wanted her to walk her downstairs. "You're just meeting across the street, that coffee place?"

"Right," Joss said. "No, it's okay. I don't want to be, you know, too on the nose. Time-wise."

Her mother smiled like she understood how it was, and Joss—fresh off seeing her go through basically the end of her marriage—felt a little guilty.

So she wouldn't have to look her in the eye, Joss busied herself packing, cramming dirty clothes into the plastic reunion bag Mom had said was for laundry, finding her butterfly necklace and spending way longer than necessary doing the clasp.

Finally, her mother left to get their toothbrushes and stuff from the bathroom. The second she disappeared to the entryway, Joss got to it.

The Zoom recorder was in Mom's duffel bag. She snagged it from the main compartment, re-fluffed nearby items to cover the hole, and stashed it in her jangly purse—which she'd brought in case Saturday night was dressy.

Nice call on the over-packing.

She buttoned the purse's buckle and puckered her lips in the mirror.

This is so insane, she told her reflection. *Are you seriously doing this?*

Her mother came back with a baggie of toothbrushes and shampoo. "Heading out? Has the proper interval of time passed?"

"Think so," Joss said with a hollow chuckle.

"Do you need cash?" Mom pointed to the jangly purse. "I could give you some, you could pick up a snack for the train."

"Um, thanks. No, that's okay. The purse...I just, you know, was trying to look a little nicer."

Mom gave another *I gotcha, no need to explain* smile, and Joss felt another guilty pang.

It passed.

"And remember," Mom said, "the train leaves at 8:32 p.m. Zero wiggle room."

"Got it," Joss said.

"If you get held up or need something, does he have a cellphone you could borrow to reach me?"

"It's okay to use someone else's cell, just not my own?"

Mom gave a wry grin, and Joss knew she was good. With all Mom was going through—Dad, Jamie Gallagher, the brick—deceiving her was cake.

"Eight thirty-two," Mom said again. "Zero wiggle."

"Zero wiggle," Joss repeated.

Leaving, she held her purse tight to her left side so Mom

wouldn't notice the bulky Zoom. She didn't take a room key. She felt tingly from her belly to the base of her throat.

The courtyard had gotten dark in a hurry. The tire swing's rubber blended into night, and the square's size—which had seemed ginormous to Joss only two days ago—didn't faze her. The first time she'd stepped over these stones, she hadn't been sure of her place here. She hadn't been sure she belonged.

She was sure now.

Where can I find him? How long do I have before Mom comes searching? An hour? Half an hour?

The first place she wanted to try was that windowless building Mom had pointed out, the Skull and Bones tomb. The Pruitts had deep ties there, she'd said. They might even have the brick there—but the brick wasn't Joss's main goal.

Her main goal was Rock Pruitt.

The tomb was in the same block as the ballet-physics classroom. Joss hurried, breathing hard, skipping ahead of a car preparing to leave a stoplight.

The building was short and ugly, made of black, gray, and dark red bricks. Its two halves were separated by a small arch, the halves and arch all topped with smashed-triangle roofs. The structure took up its whole yard like some fat bully hogging the playground.

Joss stepped over a low chain and walked up both sides.

Yep, no windows, she confirmed.

She walked back to the front entrance. The black door had a keycard reader like other campus buildings.

Suddenly, Joss felt stupid. What had she thought, Rock Pruitt was going to be out for a stroll? That she would just slip in through some screen door somebody forgot to close?

She didn't have a watch or—clearly—a phone, but it felt like about twenty minutes she'd been gone. Mom would be getting antsy.

Her next idea, actually her last idea, was the restaurant-drinking club Mory's, which Rock had mentioned at lunch. Joss had no ID, but friends had told her she looked twenty-one. Maybe if they negged her, she could say she was just eating?

She hurried away from the tomb, up the side street, left onto Elm Street. The sky had gone full dark. The dirty-yellow streetlights watched her. These people hanging around at the corner didn't look like students. An older woman pulled her head back as though wondering why Joss would be out by herself.

Okay, maybe she wouldn't pass for twenty-one.

Mory's looked like some stately colonial home, white with forest green shutters. *Is it even open?* Half the windows were dark, but the entrance was lit so Joss hiked up the front path. The brass knob felt slippery in her palm.

She'd been to the Yale Club of New York once with Mom, on Vanderbilt Avenue in Manhattan, and this place felt the same. Chandeliers with ornate fixtures, lead-lined windows.

She stepped past a deserted hostess station and peeked into a side room that was lit.

Somebody was slumped in front of an enormous silver cup, supporting his own head with both hands. His hair was black as oil.

Rock Pruitt.

Joss felt like her chest would explode. Fright, shock, exhilaration—she'd actually found him.

Alone.

Drunk. Wallowing in something.

It couldn't be more perfect.

She looked in a mirrored wall and reflexively tugged her skirt down. She sawed her lips side to side, feeling the stick of lipstick.

Nobody was eating in this main room. The tables had cream cloths and exactingly-placed silverware.

A bartender who looked eighty—at least—stopped polishing a beer tap.

"Kitchen's closed," he said.

"O—okay actually I'm not eating," Joss said. "I'll just sit if that's okay?"

His wrinkled face got wrinklier. "We aren't a sitting club, Miss. We're a drinking club. And you're not of age."

Well, that settled that.

"I can't order, like, a Coke? Or a glass of water."

The bartender breathed, making himself taller. Joss snapped her heels together to seem, she guessed, more grown-up.

The bartender wasn't reaching for a glass.

"Hey, *hey*—it's Jamie Gallagher's friend!" called a warbling voice. "There y'are for a surprise. A damn fine delightful surprise."

Rock Pruitt staggered in from his side room. Grinning. Trying to leer downhill at Joss, but his eyes couldn't hold their focus. One tail of his pressed white shirt flapped loose. His fly was down.

The bartender looked from Rock to Joss, then back to Rock. "I was just showing this one the door. Kitchen's closed."

Rock farted with his lips. "She didn't come for food. Food sucks here anyway." The *f* words ran together with his slurring. "Did you?"

Joss felt the impact of his eyes and ragged voice together, like a dirty rake reaching across the room.

Still, she said, "I was actually looking for you."

He spread his arms wide. "Well come on, then. I have a whole"—he hiccuped—"big whole room to myself. Please join me."

It was unreal, Joss thought, how easily he'd accepted her presence here and the ridiculous idea that she—or anyone—would *want* to be with him in this state. It said so much about his ego.

It said so much about why he had to be stopped.

Joss looked to the bartender, who'd started polishing taps

again. His gray, lipless mouth moved without making words. A dishrag squeaked under his thumbs.

He seemed to want to stop Joss—to stop them both. But when she started for Rock's room, he stayed behind the bar.

She passed underneath a nameplate that said *Governors' Room* in gold letters. The room was wrecked. Chairs on their sides with legs tangled. Those big silver cups tipped over, red or orange or purple liquid dribbling out. The wooden table was covered in jagged carvings like the tables at that pizza place. One groove near where Rock plunked down was full of white dust.

Joss had only seen cocaine once, at an older kids' party in Queens. This looked the same.

"Pardon my mess," Rock said, picking a chair off the ground for her. "Been blowing off steam. Inherently, that's gonna be messy."

Joss's nostrils pinched reflexively. She examined the chair's upholstery and smoothed her skirt.

Rock said, "Scout's honor, I didn't puke on it." He scratched his neck. "To the best of my recollection."

She sat.

When he pulled over a cup and tipped it high for a drink, obscuring his face, she pulled the Zoom from her purse—the snap gave her trouble but only for a second—and set it on the next chair, which was pushed underneath the table such that Rock couldn't see.

Then she pressed *Record*.

"Why are you blowing off steam?" she asked, hoping it sounded casual.

Rock looked at her blurrily, red spittle on his chin.

She prompted, "You said you were blowing off steam?"

"Oh yeah, yeah yeah—I was. Am." He thunked the side of the silver cup, smiling. "Family crap. Word of advice, never count on family. Families will"—he swore—"you over every time."

Then he told this weird, rambling story about being denied

the chance to run for the Virginia Senate seat. Joss remembered Mom's friend saying Rock had won that "Choosing" contest, but apparently not.

It was hard to figure out exactly what had happened—Rock would repeat parts, then skip way forward in time—but the basic idea was that another Pruitt relative had beaten him.

As he scowled and groaned on, Joss thought about how to get him talking about Derek Dickerson. Rock was bitter about how his family had treated him, and the root cause of this unfairness (in his mind) was Dickerson.

If she could just nudge him there, nudge him into discussing that incident…

"But you know what I say, honestly?" he said. "No spin, no bull—but *honestly?*"

He swooped closer to her, then farther away. A dress shoe fell off. He left it off.

"I say piss on 'em. The whole bunch. Even Marshall. Wants me to run his spy scraps," Rock mumbled at his collar, then abruptly jerked back. His other shoe fell off. "Piss on 'em. Piss on every last one of them."

He shoved a silver cup over to Joss. "I've been hogging. Here, you go 'head. That's Velvet. Best one they do. I re-sampled them all to be sure."

She looked over the cup's brim. Inside, it was like a small swimming pool of peach-colored, sharp-smelling liquid. Some hair or fuzz floated on the surface.

If I don't drink, he'll know I didn't come for the company. He probably already knows on some level. Maybe he figures it doesn't matter—if he gets me to drink enough.

She lifted the cup using its wide-apart handles. The liquid inside sloshed toward her, then away as she tipped, then back toward her, Joss struggling to sip without spilling.

She managed a small drink. It tasted like the hard cider she'd had at her friend Ryder's over spring break, only stronger and sweeter. She kept the cup held at that angle—her arms shaking—and gulped twice to make it look like she was chugging.

"Dang!" Rock said as she pushed the cup back his way. "Who says the youth today're all soft?"

He leaned low over the crack in the table and snorted violently, sucking up white powder. His eyes fluttered and popped.

"That'll cure what ails you," he said. "Where are my manners? Here, here y'go. It's world-class blow."

Rock scooted over, inviting her to try. Joss shook her head. She didn't think refusing hard drugs blew her cover.

"Suit yourself," he said.

There was silence now. Joss laced her fingers together, pushing them out in front of her.

This is the time. Do it—now!

"So…there was this thing Jamie told us," she began, speaking from the sketchy rehearsals she'd done on the way to Skull and Bones. "It was about, um, something that happened a while ago."

She paused to let Rock catch up. He'd started to wobble in place, tipping between opposite legs of his chair.

"Don't believe a word out of Jamie Gallagher's mouth. You have Gallaghers, and you have reality." Rock made two circles with his fingers and held them apart. "Mutually exclusive, okay? Never met a lazy poor person, or a banker who wasn't a crook. If only we turned it over to the commies, you'd get peace and love and unicorns sledding down rainbows…"

He tipped back and gestured airily at the ceiling. Then seemed to lose track of what he was saying.

Joss coughed lightly and was about to try another question when Rock seized her arm.

"How d'you know Jamie Gallagher, what's your connection?" he demanded. "*Why are you here?*"

Joss tried to free herself, but his grip—even drunk like this

—was iron. Her knee knocked against the adjacent chair, and she worried the Zoom might fall. Luckily she didn't hear a clatter.

"Like I said, I came to see you, to talk!" she said. "That's all! I like to think for myself, and Mom—er, my mom and Jamie Gallagher—I'm not going to just believe everything they tell me. I wanna hear the other side, other perspectives."

This had been part of her script, too. She'd figured it would be smart to appeal to his vanity—to his belief that his ideas were superior to everybody else's.

And Rock's face did relax now. Lines in his neck softened, and he let go of her wrist—but not without dragging his finger suggestively through her palm.

Joss choked back disgust. "So Jamie—yeah, he and my mom were talking about freshman year. That, um…thing? That thing that I guess a lot of people talk about? With you?"

His face changed again, but she couldn't read the change. Miffed?

Had she pushed too far?

He pulled the cup over one-handed and found it empty. "Johnston, my good man! We need another of the Velvet!"

From the main room came the sound of the bartender's shuffling shoes.

Rock lowered his voice. "*Derek Dickerson?* You came to talk about Derek Goddamn Dickerson? Get out. Get the"—he swore —"out now, before I throw you out by those chintzy little bra straps."

Joss felt a flash of fear, but also desperation at being cast away. "No, not like that! I'm not saying—I mean, you paid the price already. Your family—like you said, you paid the price for everything that happened or—or didn't happen."

He looked at her. He wasn't having trouble focusing now.

She continued, "I understand what it's like. Something happened to me, too, last year. I—one of my friends died and I was involved. I didn't…I mean, it happened real fast and stuff just got out of control, and none of us intended for her to…"

Joss stared into the table, trying to look anguished.

Rock Pruitt said, "People die every day," and touched her bare knee.

Joss's stomach turned into a pit of sludge.

The bartender entered now. Carrying its handles with handkerchiefs, he delivered another full cup.

He kept his eyes pointed away from the powder. "How are we doing here, Mister Pruitt?"

Rock was watching Joss intensely. She felt a sob starting behind her nose—partly going along with her phony story, partly from real fear.

"We're good," Rock said.

"Will the young lady be requiring a taxi?"

Rock still wouldn't look away. He grabbed the new cup with one hand but didn't drink yet.

"No taxi," he said. "I'll see her home safe."

The bartender seemed to be fighting himself. His temple twitched. One elbow tugged back toward the main room while the other stayed at his side.

Rock said, "I *will* see her home."

The bartender left.

When Rock asked Joss to join him in "drinking away the wrongs done unto us," she felt again she had to agree. It was hard faking sips with a full cup, and she took in more than she'd wanted to—more than she'd ever had in one sitting.

"Tell me 'bout this friend of yours," Rock said. "Who died. Y'say you *understand.*" He swirled the word around with his tongue. "I wonder if you do. Truly."

So Joss told her made-up tale, and drank more.

She lost track of the Zoom, where it was, how long it could record. The link between her brain and her mouth sputtered, but luckily she knew the story's details cold—because it was true. It had just happened to someone else, another girl at her school who'd spent two years in a juvenile facility after pushing a friend off a cliff in Trenton Falls.

"…said it was safe—it *was* safe, I jumped off myself! But now this thing follows me my whole life." Her eyes watered. She heard her voice soaring and sinking. "I feel awful literally *every single day*. What c'n I do? Whadda they want me to do?"

She had fallen into Rock's fuzzy speech. He was hunched close, leaning into her space like some ogre stealing her breaths.

The bartender poked his head in again.

"Another group has arrived," he said. "The crew team from oh-six. I thought for them, perhaps, the Cup Room."

Rock sniffed, seeming annoyed to be interrupted. "Swell, carry on."

The bartender looked out the window, fingering his collar. "Were the club to lose its liquor license, it would be a blow. Mory's might cease to exist."

Rock gritted his teeth but did pull away from Joss's chair now.

"Hell, you old ninny. Close the door if you want."

Johnston backed off. As he began moving away, he swayed in Joss's field of vision. She'd been grateful for his brief appearances —which made her feel protected, like there was another set of eyes here—but she had the sinking sense now he wouldn't return.

She watched the bartender pull a door she hadn't known existed from a wall recess. It clinked closed.

"So. You shoved her off a cliff?" Rock said, sounding almost sober. "That's rotten luck. But very different from what I did."

Joss squirmed away from his hand, which had found her knee again. "H-how so?"

He leaned in close—so close and so low to the table that if she'd had all her sense, Joss might've worried he would see the Zoom two seats over.

He whispered, "I never laid a finger on mine."

CHAPTER 18

SAM BREEZED THROUGH THE DORM, CHECKING SILLS AND DRAWERS for forgotten items. The bags were heaped by the door and ready to roll. They wouldn't make Brooklyn until eleven or so, which had bugged her while planning the trip—arriving so late on a school night—but didn't bother her one bit now. It would give Abe a head-start back at the apartment, a chance to fall asleep first. Or move.

She found Joss's Chapstick and stashed it in the duffel's side pocket. Then she checked the time. Seven-thirty.

They should be heading to the train station by seven-forty-five. Joss should be here.

Sam walked down to the courtyard hoping she would bump into her daughter, possibly bleary-eyed from parting with the boy.

But the courtyard was quiet. A custodial worker moved his ladder from one arch to the next, removing *Welcome Back Class of '96!* banners.

"Joss?" she called into the night.

Nothing.

A little irked—but understanding how all-encompassing

teenage trysts could feel—Sam left the courtyard for the coffee shop. She hated crowding her daughter like this, but the only train after the 8:32 was the 11:32, which would make for a brutal Monday.

The counter stools in the coffee shop's front windows were empty. So were the first tables. The pastry case looked bare.

Sam squinted at the frost-printed store hours. *It says they're open...*

She pushed the door and it did open. A chime sounded. The barista, his back to the register, kept watching his phone.

Sam took several steps inside, each quicker than the one before. The tables were all empty.

There was nobody here.

"Excuse me," she said in a voice higher than her own. "I'm trying to find my daughter. Fourteen years old, tall? Dark hair?"

It took the barista a moment to realize he was being addressed.

"Huh?" he said. "Wha'zat?"

"My daughter." Sam had an unkind urge to shake him. "My daughter was here, she would've been with a boy? They're fourteen—er, I assume he's fourteen, or so."

The barista yawned and scratched underneath a skullcap.

"Nah. We've been totally dead since five."

Sam was gripping the counter. "Nobody? Are you sure?"

He nodded. "Not a soul."

"She would've been almost my height, hair down? Skirt? Carrying a purse?"

He wet a towel and used it to wipe down a valve of the espresso machine, as though beginning his closing-up tasks. "No persons of that description."

Sam felt heat taking over her lungs—that horror unique to parents, which she hadn't experienced in years.

Could Joss have meant a different coffee shop? Did she go to the boy's room instead?

Where was he staying?

Why isn't she calling?

And, thoughts darkening:

Could this involve the Pruitts somehow? The brick?

Sam left the coffee shop adrift, buzzing, her shoes on the sidewalk feeling miles away.

Where now? Where did she go?

Turning around several times, she decided to return to the dorm. There she ripped open Joss's backpack and rifled through for…what?

A note? A receipt? Some clue.

She was just considering 911 when she noticed the duffel bag was unzipped. She had packed the duffel herself—to the gills, not a square centimeter free—and closed it tight. Overflow items were going in the Yale ninety-six tote.

She squatted to look inside the main compartment. At once, she realized what was missing.

The Zoom.

Joss had taken the Zoom.

The rest assembled instantly in her mind. Joss's anger at Rock Pruitt. Her rash idea of getting him to admit on tape to Derek Dickerson's murder. With awful clarity, Sam knew just what her daughter was up to.

She'd sneaked off to find him, to entrap him somehow.

Sam squeezed her eyes at the recklessness of this—but there was no time for blame.

Where would Joss look? Where would she go?

Sam didn't know whether Rock had been staying on campus in the dorms, or had nicer hotel digs. And if she didn't know, Joss wouldn't know either. A fourteen-year-old girl could not track down Rock Pruitt. Not on her own, not in a city of one hundred thousand-odd people. There was simply no way.

But what if she did?

The idea plunged from Sam's head to her core, sickening,

pulling every organ with it. She was on fire. She was never letting Joss out of her sight again.

She called Jamie Gallagher.

"Sam, hey," he answered. "I'm glad you called because I need to—"

"Joss is gone, she went after Rock!" Sam was knee-walking over the windowsill for no reason. "Help me find her. I have to find her. Where would Rock be?"

Jamie uttered half-syllables over the line. "I, w—well, I don't know. You can't just call her cellphone?"

Sam frowned. Apparently, her cellphone ban was as strange by African norms as by American. "No cell."

They quickly established how long Joss had been unaccounted for, the farthest away she could be, the belief (Jamie's) that nothing too awful could be happening.

He said, "What're the chances she actually did it? Actually found him someplace?"

Sam considered. Imagining her only child out in the world—choosing and reacting, moving from one location to the next—was a near mystical thought exercise. Sam felt herself stepping off curbs, could smell odors rising from sewer vents.

"I just…think…she did," Sam said. "And I have to figure out where."

Over the line, Jamie allowed a pause. He didn't challenge her dubious conclusion. He didn't reassure her Joss was going to be fine, or tell her worrying wouldn't solve a thing.

Finally, he said, "I can think of one place."

CHAPTER 19

JOSS DIDN'T BELIEVE HIM. ALCOHOL ROMPED THROUGH HER HEAD and it'd gotten really hot, the ceiling seemed sorta sweaty, and his hand was a tarantula on her knee—but through all this, she didn't buy Rock's claim that he hadn't killed Derek Dickerson.

"I saw the brick—the brick you hit him with," Joss said. She shouldn't tell him this. Didn't he know already, though? "So what if you stole it, doesn't matter. We all know the truth!"

He looked at her funny. "Old Johnston must've slipped something into that cup."

"You're lyING," she hiccuped. "It's what you do, Pruitts, you make it up. Make up whatever facts you, urm…"

She lost what she wanted to say. She tried propping her chin in her hand and missed, hitting herself in the cheek.

"This is what you came for?" Rock said. "To accuse me of murder?"

"No," Joss said by reflex. "I just came to t—talk. I…I try to decide for my own, with politics—"

"And so you sought out the dastardly rival of your mother's friend?" Rock cut in. "To have a nice, reasoned chat. Yep. Makes perfect sense."

Joss gulped.

He said, "Why don't you gimme that bogus story of your friend taking a header off the cliff again, too?"

He shuffled into her space, smelling like grease and flame and ten kinds of evil.

She couldn't hold a thought.

"You killed him," she said.

Rock shook his head, slow, satisfied. "You're wrong. I'm 78 percent sure you're wrong."

"Wh—what? How could…what does 78 percent—"

"I drank enough whiskey to set the state of Kentucky back six months, but I'm awful damn sure. I never touched him."

"We heard—my mom heard the story of Dickerson pushing you into a fish tank. The witnesses, all the witnesses saw you fight, and that German poet—er, guy, told us how they tampered!"

"*Henrik Schumer,*" Rock sneered. "Always had it out for me. Now there's one I would kill, gladly."

Joss looked at the door. It was still closed. She could hear the group in the next room—a lacrosse team, or squash team?—but barely. And they were probably yelling and singing.

Should she yell? Who would hear?

What would she yell?

Rock continued, "He did push me into the fish tank—just like we planned. Poppy Johansen, what a pair of tits. I lured her over by the fish—wasn't so drunk yet. Then Dicks drenched us both. We made a show of it. Damn, was it ever brilliant. Those nips shining right through."

His face glowed at the memory. Joss's insides frosted over. From those pig eyes—boastful, superior—she knew the story was true.

There was no way, in his state, that he could've faked those eyes.

"The fight was, um, bogus?"

"Course. I said so after—nobody bought it. Not even my heartless parents. Dicks was the only one who coulda backed me up. We'd been wanting to see those boobies all semester."

He licked his lips. *So. Gross.* He seemed to get excited, crowding her, their thighs brushing, his eyes thirsty down her body.

Maybe worse than the physical threat was the mental shock. *He didn't kill his roommate?*

So…had Derek Dickerson really just fallen against their coffee table, like Rock claimed all those years ago?

"What's that?" Rock said, sitting up suddenly.

Joss thought he meant her butterfly necklace. She went to lift it off her chest, but his hand shot past to the next chair over.

"A recorder?" He grabbed the Zoom in one fist. "You're taping me? Taping *me*? Why, you dirty—"

As he unleashed a string of foul names, he slammed the audio recorder to the ground. The casing cracked and a bad-sounding beep fizzled.

"But—but I wasn't…" She struggled for some lie but came up blank. "Well, why does it matter?" she tried. "If you're innocent, what's the difference? Why would you care?"

"It matters," Rock said. "When you come after me. When *they* come after me?" He thrust a finger out the window, then up at the ceiling—jerky, like he was tracking invisible enemies. "That's an attack, and attacks must be answered."

Joss held her butterfly pendant tight, wishing now that she could fly.

CHAPTER 20

Mory's was halfway between Silliman College and the Latham Guest House. Jamie told Sam to meet him there, then grabbed his rucksack and dashed down two flights of stairs, through the inn's lobby and past its blackberry-infused water, and hit the street running.

What might Rock do? That the girl was fourteen wouldn't bother him at all. The rumors about his exploits in Southeast Asia—working for Pruitt Capitol in his early twenties—were abhorrent.

As Jamie sprinted up Dwight, he burned imagining that wisp of a kid, just becoming comfortable with herself and the world, at Rock's mercy. Because he had no mercy.

Jamie burned, too, at the thought of Sam finding her daughter —in whatever state—and blaming herself. Because he knew she would. From their rushed conversation just now, from the sacrifices she'd undertaken throughout her adult life. Sam would hump all the blame, every ounce of it. Even though, by rights, it belonged to Jamie.

He ran through stoplights and between dog walkers.

Rucksack slamming against his back, he knocked over a bike leaned against a tree and ripped his pants.

He skidded up to the Mory's entrance almost simultaneous with Sam.

"*Are they inside?*" she asked.

"I just got here!"

They pounded up a short flight of steps and through the front door.

Jamie felt cheered at first by laughter coming from a side room, sounding like a typical Mory's gathering.

Nothing much can be happening, right? With a big group nearby?

Then he saw the bartender, an elderly man with hair like fine silver thread, cut his eyes nervously toward the Governors' Room.

Jamie bolted without looking back to Sam, without considering the danger or forming one conscious thought. He didn't bother with the pocket door's handle, barreling through with his shoulder.

The door splintered and took one jamb down with it.

Rock Pruitt towered over Joss, froth in his face. Her chair, the old-style cane variety, looked ready to buckle under her shrinking form. Her eyes were glassy, which probably had to do with these empty silver cups, but she was clothed and seemed unhurt.

Thank God.

Pruitt and Gallagher eyes locked. Jamie barely registered Sam rushing past him and pulling Joss away.

"You sent a *kid*?" Rock gestured to an oblong device—smashed—on the ground. "To get me on tape? You're garbage. You know that? Pure garbage."

Jamie heard the words but wasn't processing meanings. He wasn't processing anything but hate for Rock Pruitt. His rucksack slipped to the floor.

He lunged for the bigger man.

"Oooof," Rock groaned as the crown of Jamie's head hit his midsection.

They crashed to the ground. Jamie smelled body and sour booze and felt fists slamming his shoulder blades.

"*Nobody sent her*!" Jamie said. "She wanted to stop you—people want to stop you."

He was talking into Rock's neck as they tumbled over and over, crashing against table legs, toppling chairs.

"People are idiots. You're an idiot."

Rock dug an elbow in Jamie's side—a sword piercing a pillow of nerves.

Jamie gasped and, shutting his eyes against the pain, punched Rock's mouth. Teeth gave with a satisfying crunch. Jamie's shirt was flecked with blood and spit. He didn't know whose.

"We'll bury your side," Rock said. "When we drop pinebox on you? *Finito*. There won't be another Gallagher in politics."

He'd worked himself on top of Jamie. His words came out with a whistle, owing to the fresh gap in his mouth.

Jamie bucked him off, knowing the fight was only competitive thanks to Rock's impairment.

"That's urban legend," he said. "There is no pinebox. No Revolutionary-era secret floating around out there."

They were on their feet again, crouched, circling one another.

Rock said, "Keep believing that."

Jamie stepped into a back kick that caught Rock square in the chest. The impact traveled up Jamie's leg, a pressure wave rippling from knee to hip.

Rock was flattened. He looked up with a smirk. "Learn that from the Africans? What else you pick up over there, AIDS?"

Jamie stood astride his rival. "More slime, more filth. That's how you play when you have no ideas."

Rock swung his knee through Jamie's ankles, sweeping him to the ground.

"*Ideas*." He gripped Jamie around the neck. "The idea is a given

—slime goes around the idea. You gotta fight for it. You Gallaghers think you draw it on a chalkboard and everybody should bow down. Bow down before the elites."

"Ah, shut up." Jamie squirmed free and punched Rock again.

In his peripheral vision, he saw faces crowding into the busted doorway. Not Sam's and Joss's—they must've gone—but men's faces. The group from next door.

Ruddy. Rapt. Intoxicated. Some had their cellphones out. None were stepping forward to stop the fight.

Rock hit Jamie back, a sloppy blow that Jamie turned around into a half nelson.

"*Pussies,*" Rock said, snapping his head against Jamie's forearm. "Can't take the ground fight. Without all little sister's tech money, those ad buys, big air war? You all'd be out of the game already…"

As Rock spewed nonsense, Jamie felt himself rising to the conflict. With his fists first, and then his mind. And now with his whole heart.

Guilt and rage had started him down the path, but he'd traveling the last leg on his own. He was ready to hate—Rock, all the Pruitts. He was ready to follow Charlotte into the pit.

"We'll win because *we're right.*" Jamie clenched his biceps, bending the beefy neck underneath. "We're on the right side of history: the side of progress."

When Rock again called them pussies, Jamie added his second arm to make a full nelson. He thrust his joined knuckles forward.

Rock's neck bowed dangerously. "*Man,* you wanna snap it? You wanna kill me, is that it?"

Jamie didn't answer, firming his grip. He did want to. He'd been born to want it. He'd been raised and educated to want it.

For two decades, he'd tried *not* to want it—but he had failed.

"*What would you have done if we hadn't gotten here?*" he hissed. "How many others? How many girls?"

Rock looked sideways out of the hold, a gleam in his eye.

The men glared at each other. Every muscle in their torsos and arms was flexed—half for escape, half to prevent escape.

"I should send you to hell," Jamie said. "For Owen and Joss. For all your victims."

"Do it, yeah." Rock smiled, his remaining teeth smeared with blood. "Snap it. Snap my"—he swore—"neck, you spineless wimp!"

Jamie muscled up and squeezed. Was he trying to end Rock's life? Maybe. Maybe he was only shutting him up.

Rock gasped and sputtered, but nothing dramatic happened to his neck.

"They're g—" Rock broke off, coughing. "Gone, you know. Your chicks. They left."

Jamie waited out his own breaths, which had become frantic as bellows. He looked around, keeping his grip, and saw Rock was right. Sam must've taken Joss someplace safe.

"What're we fighting for? Them?" Rock moved his head the tiny bit he could toward the gawkers. "Like gladiators? This is dumb."

Again, Rock was right. There was no point to this fight. Should Jamie detain Rock and call the police? What could they charge him with? Jamie didn't know exactly what had transpired with Joss before they'd showed up.

Even if he had bought her alcohol or worse, what prosecutor was going to bring penny-ante charges like that against a Pruitt?

Jamie released Rock and exhaled at length.

Rock slugged him.

"Damn, are you thick." Rock advanced on Jamie, who wobbled but kept his feet. "We're always going to fight. Every time. Every time I see you."

He slugged Jamie again.

Jamie slugged him back.

The fight spilled into the main dining room, the gawkers

spinning out of their way. Chairs crashed. Tablecloths flew, sending place settings clattering across the floor.

The elderly bartender cleared his throat.

"That'll do, gents." As he approached, he took a towel off his shoulder. "Nobody wants to involve the authorities."

Jamie had Rock pinned under his knees. "No, it *won't* do! He's got this coming. Everything I'm giving him now? He's earned."

"Mory's has a reputation to uphold, and I—"

"Mory's closes with one phone call from me." Jamie paused, his palm twisting Rock's chin into the floor, to meet the bartender's eye. "My family has a college named for it. You want to try, our legacy versus yours? Go ahead."

The bartender took a step back, crossing his arms behind his cummerbund.

Now Rock shoved Jamie off. He scrambled up and grabbed a water carafe by the neck, breaking it against a table. The body burst in a spray of water and glass.

"That's a senior citizen you're talking to," he said, wielding a ring of shards. "What happened to that famous Gallagher compassion?"

Jamie circled, feeling no fear, waiting for an opening. He was going to tackle this monster. He didn't care if he came away with a few nicks. He'd trade nicks for the chance to drive Rock into the hardwood.

And when he finished here—when the man in front of him surrendered or fled or closed his eyes for good—Jamie was going to find Sam Lessing and tell her he was moving to New York City, that he wanted her, that her crumb-bum husband didn't mean a thing.

He charged forward.

CHAPTER 21

Next door to Mory's, Yorkside Pizza still stayed open until one a.m., same as in Sam's undergraduate days. She helped Joss along the sidewalk, catching her when she faltered.

Oy, she's grown this year.

Sam headed them toward the buzzing neon beer signs of Yorkside, and managed to get Joss into a booth without toppling either one of them.

She grabbed an empty pitcher off a nearby table and set it before Joss. Just in case.

A waitress swung by.

"Water, please," Sam said. "Lots of water and an order of breadsticks."

Mother and daughter sat across from each other. Joss held the table with two hands, steadying, swallowing, burping, her eyes focusing alternately near and far.

Sam asked, "Are you hurt anywhere?"

Joss shook her head.

"Did he do anything to you?"

"Hmm-nn."

"Touch you?"

Joss shrugged. "My knee. It—erm, it was icky but I don't care."

Sam felt a flash of anger, but as it passed, she decided the news was good on the whole. Non-terrible.

"Okay. You're safe now, that's the main thing."

She took her daughter's hands in both of hers. They felt brittle. Sweaty. Slow spasms passed through Joss's body like escaping poison.

Sam didn't know if she would ever let go.

"I'm s—sorry I lost..." Joss tried.

"Lost what?"

Joss struggled to remember what she'd been saying, or maybe to find a word—Sam couldn't tell.

Now the breadsticks came. Joss waved them off with a pained expression but did take a drink of water.

"The Zoom!" she remembered. "I took it, it's gone. He smashed it."

Sam dipped a breadstick in marinara sauce and took a bite. She shook her head as she chewed.

"So doesn't matter," she said. "It's a bunch of plastic and wires."

"But the footage, the audio you took—"

"I can re-interview if I want, which I probably don't. What matters is you. That you're here, safe. That's it."

Joss twisted her mouth regretfully. Sam considered reading her the riot act about how risky it'd been tracking down Rock Pruitt, sneaking into a place that served alcohol, putting herself in such a dangerous spot.

Not tonight, she decided.

Joss, who would brighten every couple minutes at some new memory, said, "He pl-nned the fish tank."

"He what?"

"He pla-aaa-anned," she over-articulated, "the fish tank."

Her eyes were intense, trembling and serious. Combined with the phrase "fish tank," it almost made Sam laugh.

Sam said, "He who? You mean Rock?"

Joss nodded. The eyes became still more serious.

Fish tank, Sam thought. *Fish, fish, fish…*

Oh!

"The Derek Dickerson thing?" Sam said. "What Gabe Navarro said about them fighting the night he died?"

"Yes."

"They planned it? Rock getting pushed into the fish tank?"

Joss nodded again. "It wasn't a fight."

Sam could see her daughter felt the information was monumental, but she didn't want to discuss it. She didn't want Rock Pruitt and Derek Dickerson anywhere in her head. She didn't want to go backwards twenty years, to consider them at all.

"Ready for carbs yet?" She raised a breadstick.

Joss tentatively accepted.

Over the next fifteen minutes, Sam got all the calories and water she could into her daughter. She talked about whatever Joss cared to talk about. There was no rush. They'd missed the 8:32 train and had three hours to kill. If Joss missed school tomorrow, she missed school.

Unless and until Sam heard something more sinister when Joss sobered up, she wasn't involving the police. Could Joss face legal jeopardy for her Mory's jaunt? Sam didn't know, but it seemed at least equal to whatever they might manage to pin on Rock—and Sam had zero interest in taking on the Pruitts in legal realms.

They sat in their oregano-smelling booth and talked, and drank, and chewed, and let the night turn quiet and boring again.

Sam asked what her highlight had been for the entire trip. Joss, working on breadstick number three, said probably the dance-physics lecture. Or the art gallery. It was hard to pick. Both were cool in their own way.

At ten o'clock, a figure with a rucksack appeared in Yorkside's front window. His shirt was torn.

Sam tapped the glass.

Jamie Gallagher flinched to a ready crouch, then relaxed, seeing Sam. He closed his eyes and joined them inside.

He moved slowly, one elbow dragging behind, the opposite-side stride boosting up in a limp. Half his face was black-and-blue.

He was smiling.

"Yikes," Sam said. "What's the other guy look like?"

Jamie lowered his rucksack and himself onto Sam's side of the booth, wincing.

"About the same."

As he recounted what'd happened, Jamie kept wiping a cut on his neck, smearing blood onto his collar. The fight seemed still vivid in his mind. Even with blood vessels cracked through, the whites of his eyes glowed.

Sam asked what Rock had meant when he'd said the thing about burying Jamie's side. "He said they'd 'drop the pinebox' on you—it was the last thing I heard. What was that? Is there actually some ancient relic?"

"Nah," Jamie said. "It's a hoax. The dagger, the old coffin—it's never the same twice. Both sides have their kooks. Once this aunt told me and Charlotte there was some horse bone floating around that held the secret to the whole feud."

Sam kept pushing water on Joss. Once she'd gotten three full tumblers down, Sam said, "I should get her in bed."

Jamie offered to walk them back to Silliman.

Sam said, "Sure."

Campus felt majestic and brooding. Most of Sam's Yale memories were in cold or at least autumn-crisp weather, and experiencing it at the height of summer unsettled her. The thick air gave breath to the stone gargoyles of Sterling Library and menace to the quads' Gothic arches. She walked between Jamie and Joss, holding hands with one and smelling the other's wounds.

The journey was dim. Sam thought through the weekend's events, new information and old. Truths she'd learned about herself and the people closest to her. Some fit with what she'd already believed and filled her with pride, or sadness. Joss's determination. Abe's basic irredeemability.

Others didn't fit at all.

Sam used her key at the college gate. She asked a passing maintenance worker if the rooms had been re-keyed and he said no, the dorms were vacant for the next month—they could take however long they wanted.

Sam paused at the entryway bathroom, thinking Joss might need a trip, but she staggered directly inside for bed.

Sam pulled the covers up her cheek like Joss was a baby. She'd have to rouse her in a couple hours, but even a short rest would do her good.

Jamie waited back in the common room. When Sam rejoined him, he smiled easily—incongruous on that bruised, gashed face—and leaned against the windowsill.

He seemed different. The arm at the sill looked wiry, muscled—not skinny like she might've said yesterday. Since Mory's, he hadn't once said he was sorry.

"I was too hard on you before," Sam said.

"No." Even in this word, there was firmness. "I deserved it."

"It must be insane, all these emotions you've been through."

"Yeah." He hitched his bag up his shoulder. "But you've had stuff going on, too. Everyone does. I didn't handle it…" He shook his head thoughtfully. "I didn't handle it."

Sam looked into his eyes. She felt lucky. Every once in a while, filming in Nicaragua, riding the subway, she would feel it

—her advantage, the opportunities she'd been given. Everyday comforts. The lack of physical distress.

She had survived the bloody brick and Joss's flight. Her marriage had dissolved without a single broken dish.

Now she was talking emotions with Jamie Gallagher.

He said, "So your husband, Abe—he left?"

Sam glanced around, stretching her arms through the empty air.

"Then you guys're," Jamie began, "I mean, not to be presumptuous, but is it…"

"Over," she said. "Blessedly."

He bobbed his head, a sweetly goofy response to the news.

Sam decided it would be over-dramatic to leave off there, and explained briefly how she'd stayed in the marriage for Joss— toughing it out, switching off that part of herself—but it turned out Joss didn't need her to.

"Wow," he said. "That's a lot to figure out in a weekend."

She chuckled.

In a playful voice Jamie asked, "What now?"

"Hm, I don't know," Sam said with some pluck of her own. "How about you? Where do you go from here, back to Juba?"

"It can be hard to get a flight."

"Oh?"

"Very. Could be weeks, months."

Sam felt the ends of her mouth rising. Jamie smiled, too, and in that moment he was perfect: the grin animating his skinned-up face like somebody had taken the road rash he used to get biking —that he'd seemed to live for—and painted it across his best self.

He said, "What do you want, Sam?"

She teared up. "That's broad."

"I know."

"I—I think something. Pretty sure I'm going to want something."

He slipped off his rucksack and laid it beside his foot. "Seems fair. We all deserve something."

They stepped together and kissed. Her moist lips wet his cracked ones, a touch, another touch, then both their mouths opened. Sam's head fogged with heat and release from her first kiss—real kiss—in a decade. It unfolded like the opening images of your favorite film, slow-growing and wonderful. She gripped his back and felt him feeling her.

When their heads tipped opposite, the kiss broke for a beat and resumed urgently.

Sam lost her brain a little. When it came back and she found herself entwined with Jamie, not an inch of space between them, the world felt sharper. She saw more details. She saw connections she hadn't seen before.

She saw the fish tank.

She saw a fight that wasn't a fight.

The kiss finished. Sam opened her eyes. Her body felt brand new, awake, but the dorm was still eighty years old. The walls' plaster stayed in her nose. Dark-grained wood loomed from the mantle and recesses of the room.

She looked in Jamie's eyes. They were a mile deep.

She looked.

And now she felt, wrapping the softness inside her like razor-edged thread, fear.

She said, "The Pruitts didn't steal that brick."

The fingers of Jamie's left hand were still laced with the fingers of her right.

He paused. Calculating? Weighing options?

"No," he said. "Not the Pruitts."

Sam was glad he hadn't lied. Glad that their intimacy had been real.

"Charlotte?" she said.

He took a dispirited breath. "My mother, more likely. She has more of those people."

Their fingers stayed together.

Sam said, "Why did she leave the brick there all these years?"

"She never knew," Jamie said. "After I—er, it happened, I almost wanted to get caught. I thought the police would discover it."

"The Pruitts stonewalled."

Jamie nodded. "Then the university boarded up the flues."

Their hands had slipped to a fingertip grip—a sad, stubborn contact.

Sam wished she didn't know. She wished the feud was a relic instead of a pulsing, contemporary force, devouring its combatants like some smoke-belching factory eats gasoline.

She wished Jamie had grown beyond that seventeen-year-old boy, righteous, crazed by ideology.

But look at this face.

"Why?" she said. "To take down Rock?"

"No," Jamie shook his head insistently. "Dickerson—I knew one of his victims. She…was in my hall freshman year."

The name came to Sam at once. "Norah Fowler."

How many other classmates had Jamie asked for information about Norah this weekend?

He said, "I told someone in my family about the assault. About how dangerous Dickerson was."

"And I suppose," Sam began, "you would've mentioned he was Rock Pruitt's roommate…"

Jamie's mouth twisted. "Two birds. One stone."

The words chilled Sam—even though they echoed her own thoughts at the candle ceremony, of the paradoxical goodness of the crime.

"Who could even *suggest* such a thing to a seventeen-year—"

"Doesn't matter," Jamie said. "I did it. Me."

Sam stood rooted to the hardwood for a while, unable to respond. Puzzle pieces zoomed through her brain. That Jamie was taking responsibility, that he'd been motivated by Norah—both these counted in his favor.

Still, he'd killed a college freshman in cold blood.

Then he'd killed a second man with cobra venom.

It was insane. Maybe it wasn't insane in a world where podiums got hijacked and threats were made with ancient relics, but in Sam's world? The world she and Joss lived in?

It was. Insane.

"Goodbye," she said.

Their fingers separated. Jamie rubbed his eyes clear.

"But what if I…" He trailed off, then started over, "It happened so long ago, it's history. Couldn't we—"

"No," Sam said. "It isn't history. It's here."

Jamie lowered his head. Dishwater-blond hair fell across itself in tangles.

His disclosures hadn't stopped the questions in Sam's mind. They'd only started more. *Did an elder Gallagher feed him the idea to kill Dickerson? Did Charlotte? But Charlotte would've been thirteen.*

How did Jamie keep his secret those last three years at Yale without losing his mind?

Did *he lose his mind?*

As Jamie turned and slinked away—maybe forever, this time—Sam wanted all these answers. But she also didn't want them. Because these answers, she knew, came packed in two hundred fifty years of blood.

Sam locked the door behind Jamie and walked to the dorm bedroom where Joss slept. Her daughter looked tiny. Curled into a comma, a sheet twisted through the crook of her elbow. Taking breath after peaceful breath.

Sam felt tired herself, but also lighter.

Abe would fight for custody. She would have to fight back, or find a way not to. They'd both have to move—their two salaries barely covered one Brooklyn rent, let alone two.

She would have to remake her life, break through the

callouses that had grown up around so many of her parts. It would take courage, and time, and will, and friends holding her hand through the worst of it. It would be the great challenge of her life, and she didn't know if she would succeed.

She refused to be distracted.

Keep reading for a sneak peek
at book two in the Pinebox saga:

POWER RIP

POWER RIP

SNEAK PEEK

ON THE DAY KARL PEOPLES TOOK THE BIGGEST LEAP OF HIS LIFE, he woke at five sharp. The former governor of Michigan tiptoed out of the hotel room so he wouldn't disturb his wife, got black coffee from the lobby, and drove out to the Kirksville County fairgrounds. He parked in dirt, among the eighteen-wheelers that moved Peoples Carnival from one city to the next.

Here goes, he thought, stepping from his pickup. *All the plans, all the work. Time to show 'em.*

Karl stretched his six-foot-six-inch frame. He breathed the quickly warming air. In the distance, cows lowed and horses snorted. Karl smiled thinking of the 4-H kids freshening their stalls. He would've loved to sneak over to the barns and watch, but just now, he had his own chores.

The carnival covered twenty acres, and Karl walked every bit of it. He flicked out his tape measure checking clearances between rides. He made sure you could see Dizzy's Endless Flavors Ice Cream when you stepped off the carousel, and the craft beer tent from the Zipper.

When he came to the lone void, a huge stretch of bare ground in the dead-center of the layout, Karl stopped. He looked up and took a moment imagining.

There was just one ride still left on its trailers—on its *five* trailers. And it went here.

Power Rip.

"I thought I was early," came a voice from behind.

Karl turned to find a squat, thick-browed man wearing a Peoples Carnival jacket.

"Claire keeps saying I need to sleep more," Karl said slyly.

Bruce Frazier ambled up alongside, and the two men finished in unison—extending a joke they'd carried through hundreds of fairs and Karl's six years in the governor's mansion: *"Tomorrow."*

Their eyes roamed to the Power Rip trailers, which drove end to end on the interstates so the cabs spelled out *PowerrrRIP!* in giant letters.

Bruce gestured to a string of flags rippling by the Tilt-A-Whirl. "Don't love that wind."

Karl waved him off. "It's a breeze. We'll be spinnin' and grinnin' by ten."

The carnival opened at ten o'clock.

Bruce looked at his phone. "Forecast says thirty-mile-an-hour winds, gusts to forty."

Karl hooked his thumbs through the belt loops of his jeans. Power Rip was a beast, built far beyond code with American steel, but the fact remained it was the tallest ride Peoples or any other traveling carnival had ever attempted.

The taller the structure, the worse for wind.

"We'll get people from Osawatomie today, from Gratiot. Heck, Indiana." Karl clucked his tongue. "They're not making the drive for deep-fried Oreos. They're coming for the Rip."

The crew was gathering now, staggering bleary-eyed from RVs or pickup trucks of their own. Karl and Bruce slapped hands and got the big plastic coffee urns filled for them.

Section by section, Power Rip grew toward the heavens. The

ride's scale was staggering. Giant pistons and crossbeams and axles, all painted Peoples purple with screaming white text. The workers had assembled it on plenty of test sites, but even so, their eyes occasionally glazed over at the rising behemoth.

For the rest of the summer, Power Rip would go up like other rides, as soon as the carnival got into town. For Kirksville, its debut, Karl had wanted to keep the press from poking around and spoiling the moment. Already they'd skewed their coverage, taking a thing that should've been pure joy and making it political.

Member of Conservative Pruitt Clan Aims for Massive Thrills, But Is Safety Lacking?

Questions Persist Over Regulatory Bodies' Scrutiny of Power Rip...

Karl—a Pruitt despite the different last name—had no doubt who was behind these headlines.

The carnival hummed alive over the next three hours. Peanut roasters cracked their knuckles and prepared their ovens. Ticket vendors donned their caps and vests. Jorge, who ran the dunk tank, leaned down precariously from his platform to test the water temperature.

Karl said, "Good day for a swim, Mr. Sanchez?"

Jorge flashed that smirk that had goaded so many customers into forking over five dollars for a chance to drop him.

"Never better, boss!" he said. "While the rest of you are baking, I'll be a cool cucumber."

He pulled a serene face that drew giggles from Jill and Pammie at the water gun race.

Karl savored the team's spirit and industry. He regularly pitched in himself to stake a sunshade or hang stuffed-animal prizes from hooks. The attractions were all staffed correctly and the workers didn't need help, but Karl's presence made a difference. It set a tone. It felt good in his arms and back too.

He knew every face and most names. The exception today was at *Maison Magicale*, where an unfamiliar man nearly Karl's height but stockier was putting the fun house through its checks.

"Good morning there!" Karl called to him. "Looking sharp."

The man, disinfecting the hall of mirrors, said nothing but raised his spray bottle in greeting.

Karl was just making a mental note to ask Bruce later where they'd picked him up when a young African-American woman emerged from the parking lot. She held a clipboard over her chest like a shield.

Reaching Karl, she asked, "How many apple cider donuts?"

Karl raised his hands defensively. "Zero."

Maya Simmons narrowed her eyes. The hand without the clipboard held a ceramic tumbler labeled Motor City Brew.

"Unvarnished truth," she said. "Remember? That's the terms of my employment."

With his metabolism, Karl could've eaten for days and not gained a pound—Maya's concern was cholesterol. She'd been a fixture at his side during his time as governor, establishing herself as one of the top consultants in the region.

"I ate no donuts. I stand by that." Karl stayed deadpan a moment, then admitted, "But there's a local gal selling rhubarb fritters over by the antique cars."

Maya frowned. "Fritters. Deep-fried dough?"

He patted his stomach. "With rhubarb."

Her lips thinned in disapproval, then she raised her clipboard. "Fresh poll numbers, hot out of the laptop."

"Are we still happy?" Karl asked.

"We're happy, but seeing some slippage with independents." She moved a neat fingernail down the page. "This will-he-or-won't-he dance only plays so long."

Karl palmed the elbow of his button-down shirt. "Nobody likes a waffler."

She nodded. "Good thing you aren't one."

The decision about whether to reenter politics weighed on

Karl. The current governor was floundering, scrapping through the final year of her term. The Republicans were putting up a hardliner with strong ties to President Barksdale, the divisive man Karl's fellow Pruitts referred to as "the dick."

The race was shaping up nasty, and Karl felt division growing in the state—festering. Liberals told their supporters they were smarter than the dummies on the other side. Conservatives hinted that their godless opponents had a secret agenda of tax hikes and drive-through abortion.

Karl's own clan, the Pruitts, were as guilty as anyone. They fought the rival Gallaghers with the same bile and cynicism, as though the centuries-old feud between the two families was inevitable, a churning wheel beyond any control.

Karl knew it didn't have to be so. He'd governed Michigan with honor. He'd fought hard, but the times he'd lost, he hadn't impugned the process or his opponents. And they'd done likewise, establishing a tone of civility.

Could it be that way again?

Maya interrupted his musing, joining him at the Power Rip guardrail.

"Look, I'll do anything for you," she said. "You gave me my start, Mr. Peoples. I'm here. I'm here for whatever you need."

Karl turned from the ride to face her. They'd called each other Karl and Maya since her third week on the job; clearly there was a large "but" coming.

She said, "We're coming up on a presidential cycle. For a consultant, career-wise, it's where you make your bacon." Maya looked down. "You want to stay in a holding pattern, that's cool. But if you aren't going to run, you know, I just...I think another consultant could hold down the fort."

Karl crossed his wrists over the guardrail. "You need to be in the mix."

"Ideally," she said.

Karl bobbed his head sympathetically. "I'm sorry, I've been

distracted with Power Rip going live. Three years it's been my focus. But I'm close now. I do believe once I see her fly, I'll be there. I'll be ready to decide."

Maya's face stayed straight, but just below the surface, Karl read skepticism at this wifty pronouncement of his.

He said, "You think I'm a nutball."

"No."

"You do. Go ahead, say it—you think I'm a nutball. I oughta have my head examined."

Maya shook her head, chuckling. "We all should, for going into politics. But your head's better than most."

⁂

Peoples Carnival had few lines. Last year, Karl had switched them to a system of virtual queuing using cell phones, which required riders to sign up in four-minute windows for all the biggest rides. He'd been reluctant at first. Karl found much technology to be more fuss than benefit, and the Grand Rapids firm pushing the software had wanted an arm and a leg.

But the results had been clear as sunrise over Lake Superior. As the hour approached ten o'clock now, people roamed freely instead of jamming knees and elbows. They played ring toss or stopped to try their hand at dunking Jorge. They browsed jewelry kiosks. They ate their donuts—or fritters—without hurry.

The virtual queues meant more non-ride revenue streams, less sun beating down on the shoulders of people stuck in line, fewer whiny kids. It was that rare policy decision that just worked.

Usually.

"We want Power Rip," an elderly woman with ball-chain glasses said loudly to nobody in particular. "How do I sign my grandkids up for Power Rip?"

She squinted and tapped her phone as six children of various ages crowded her, boosting up on tiptoes to give their opinion.

She cried, "I tried that, I already tried! *Why does it keep saying to pick my first ride?*"

Karl excused himself from Maya to look over the woman's shoulder.

"Lemme take a crack," he said. "These things never work when you need 'em, do they?"

The woman handed over her phone. Karl navigated through the Peoples Carnival app, reserving six spots on the 10:12 a.m. Power Rip.

He pointed to the youngest kid, who wore a Detroit Lions T-shirt. "You in, bud? Not too scared?"

The boy spread his shoulders and said, "Yes, sir, I am!"

Karl, handing back the grandmother's phone, told her, "Manners. Tells me something about how he's been raised."

The kids whooped and twirled around in the grass. Having raised a large family himself, Karl understood the importance of all willing children being allowed to ride. During the design phase for Power Rip, he'd insisted on a forty-two-inch minimum height rather than forty-eight or fifty-two, either of which would've meant a simpler constraint system and less expense.

Maya stepped forward to continue their conversation, but a gust upset the papers in her clipboard. The sky howled. A nearby willow tree creaked.

Across the midway, Bruce Frazier caught Karl's gaze. Their eyes had a brief conversation, then Bruce strode up to the fairground stage where they would be announcing the kids' tractor pull later.

"Attention please, folks," he called through the public address. "The opening of Power Rip and the other big'uns will be delayed thirty minutes. I do apologize—we're gonna let these winds pass. Please start your day on the smaller rides and continue to enjoy our concessions, voted best in the Midwest seven years running."

Disappointment spread through the crowd. The kid in the Tigers shirt kicked the ground. Somebody said, *"Kiddin' me, first day and it broke?"*

Karl felt all this in his bones, like bad news from the doctor. He had an instinct to rush up onstage and take the microphone, tell everybody on second thought they were going to give it five—five minutes ought to do it, then they'd get rolling. The thirty-minute rule came from the Great Lakes Carnival Association, a bunch of nervous Nellies in suits. Karl built his rides to operate all the way up to level eight on the Beaufort wind scale.

Then he looked over at Bruce. Bruce was conferring with Kirksville officials, pointing at clouds to the west.

Deciding not to undercut his right-hand man, Karl turned to Maya instead. "Let's drill down on these polls. How do I look against Conley?"

"Plus twelve," Maya said of the matchup against the current governor. "Slightly better with moderates, slightly worse with women."

That squared, Conley being female herself and a Democrat. "What's the story when you put my name opposite Barksdale?"

"Ahead there too." Maya paged back in her notes—he'd asked her to take the temp versus the president so they understood where his support was coming from. "You're sitting at twenty-seven percent unfavorable to his sixty-nine. That's a winner every time."

Karl smiled, wondering if she'd intended the reference to the game runners here.

Step right up! Winner every time...

Michigan had been revving hard when Karl had left office. Unemployment low, charter schools closing the achievement gap in urban areas, rural communities spurred to innovate by his *AnywhereEconomy* tax breaks. He'd had a vision for turning the state into a full-on powerhouse in his next term. Then Lindsay had the accident.

Karl's oldest had been a freshman at University of Michigan. She'd been jogging with those earbuds they'd warned her about and crossed against a light. The SUV knocked her twelve feet, slamming Lindsay's head against the curb. She lay unconscious in the ICU for the longest six hours of Karl's life.

As he and his wife held their daughter's limp hand, Karl reevaluated everything. Since entering politics, he'd been a fleeting presence in the kids' lives. He'd missed Lindsay's graduation ceremony. He'd been duking it out with lawmakers over Asian carp regulations when Rory threw his no-hitter against Saint Francis Academy.

By the time Linsday woke up—broken wrist and collarbone but no brain damage, mercifully—Karl knew what he had to do. He would step aside after his term, letting the lieutenant governor be the next Republican nominee. He would return to his executive role with Peoples Carnival, which left him free during school months.

This was one of the many graces of having five children: if you screwed up with the older ones, you had time to right the ship with the rest.

Karl became a fixture at Traverse City gyms and concert halls. (They had two violinists.) The renewed focus on his own family fed back into work. More hip to trends, he diversified beyond carnie staples into bubble tea, laser tag, silent dance parties. Most importantly, he rebuilt his relationships with his children, the youngest of which had just flown the coop to college.

Maya said, "I got some takes on the constitutional issue, whether you can serve a third term."

Karl patted his breast pocket. "And?"

"Because you were appointed first and only *elected* once," she said, "most scholars believe you're in the clear."

"But it's ambiguous enough that somebody could make trouble?"

"Oh, somebody will make trouble."

Maya didn't need to say who. They both understood: the Gallaghers.

The Pruitt-Gallagher feud, widely known as the pinebox vendetta, had gotten hotter in the last months after an embarrassing gaffe by Owen Gallagher, the liberal clan's entry into the upcoming presidential race. The Gallaghers blamed his mistake on Pruitt subterfuge, which the Pruitts naturally denied.

Karl had no inside dope on the incident. He wasn't friendly with Jonathan Pruitt, the ex-president who still dictated the clan's strategy. But Karl knew that Marshall Pruitt, the old spymaster, had been in New Haven—the site of the gaffe—when it had happened. So had Rock Pruitt. Rock was daring, reckless, ruthless: just the type to hatch such a scheme.

The Gallaghers had money to burn thanks to Charlotte Gallagher, founder of internet-of-things giant SmartWidget. They'd been using it to attack Pruitts everywhere—congressional races, state attorneys general races, even benign diplomatic appointments.

Karl figured the negative press coverage of Power Rip was a shot across the bow, warning him they would be involved if he ran for governor.

"If we do this," he told Maya now, "it's going to be a fight."

"Always," she agreed.

Looking out upon the fairgrounds, Karl considered the risks of putting himself back in the public crosshairs and wading back into the muck. What he'd built here was good. He loved this carnival, dirt and gears and gobs of people. He loved watching the tattooed punks strutting around, trying to impress girls. He loved these mothers pushing one in a stroller and yanking another by the wrist and screaming at a third, "No, you can't have a candy apple—we spent enough already!"

These people lived tough all week. Here, they got to cut loose.

But good wasn't all Karl saw. He also saw a fat guy with a T-shirt that read, "Democrat (n.): An open-minded individual whose brain has fallen out." He saw trucks flying Confederate flags. He saw disrespectful slogans about Christians or President Barksdale.

A man in a trucker hat was telling a friend, "If they pick that moron Owen Gallagher over Barksdale next year—California, them liberal states?"

The friend pinched his mouth. "They will. And we'll get four years of dumbass socialism in the White House."

Karl approached the men.

"Fellas, let's find another topic of discussion," he said. "That's not the talk I like to hear at my carnival."

The men were flustered by the sight of their former governor. One fumbled his sourdough pretzel. Karl caught it before it hit the ground and handed it back.

The other recovered to argue, "All we're saying is the truth. Owen Gallagher's all foam, no beer."

Karl couldn't stop a smile. "You guys watch Zoe Pruitt?"

The men nodded. A small peanut gallery had formed—Karl's loud voice tended to attract an audience. The Zoe Pruitt guess had been a safe one. Her cable news show, *The America I Know with Zoe Pruitt*, averaged four millions viewers per night.

"Zoe's sharp as a tack," Karl said of his second cousin. "But understand, she's got bills to pay. Same as us."

A voice from the side asked, "You telling us she lies?"

Karl raised his hands forthrightly. "I'm saying she's in the entertainment business. She entertains. It's what keeps her ratings high."

The crowd went quiet. Maybe they were surprised to hear Karl criticize—even mildly—a member of his own clan.

He continued, "Owen Gallagher sacrifices his privacy, nights out with his wife. For a chance at public service. He deserves our respect."

A certain amount of grumping was unavoidable, but this constant knee-jerk stuff irked Karl. Regular people wasting time and breath running down the other side instead of what they should be doing, arguing Michigan-Michigan State, or Coke versus Pepsi. Or actually talking to one another with purpose.

Karl thanked the man in the trucker hat for his patronage, wished the onlookers a happy day at the fair, and took a fresh lap around.

He thought more about the choice before him. He imagined the next year and a half if he did run. The highs and lows. The vicious things his family would read in the press.

Finally, Karl came back around to Power Rip. The mighty ride sat idle, a soaring spiral of purple steel. Restless kids stepped in place along the guardrail. The grandmother he'd helped earlier was handing out baggies of raisins from her purse.

Her youngest, the Tigers fan, spotted Karl.

"Hey, mister!" he said. "We wanna ride, can you start it?"

His siblings chimed in. *Yeah, yeah, couldn't he?* An older brother wearing a hoodie pointed to the sky and observed the wind was hardly blowing.

As Karl looked down on their beaming, hopeful faces, he wavered. They sensed it and cheered harder. "Come on, *let's go!*"

Claire often told their friends that Karl couldn't say no when the kids ganged up on him. But that wasn't true. Karl took a firm line on questions of discipline or duty. There were times as a parent, though, when you ended up in a position that made no sense. You're road-tripping on a schedule, and a billboard for a hibachi joint pops up two hours before you planned to stop. The whole car's screaming about shrimp with yum-yum sauce, but you'd said dinner wasn't until seventy-thirty come hell or high water.

Many parents, especially fathers, will stick to their guns in these spots so as not to look weak. Karl didn't. When circumstances changed, Karl changed. Others could think what they wanted. His heart wouldn't allow him to elevate pride or vanity over logic.

Now Karl checked the tops of the trees. The older brother was right. They were still.

He cupped his hands to his mouth and called to the stage, "Bruce!"

Bruce Frazier found Karl through the crowd. Seeming to read his boss immediately, he glanced at his watch. It had been eleven minutes since his announcement of a thirty-minute delay.

Karl turned his palms up. Bruce's eyes crinkled at the corners.

The kids' cheered and cheered until Karl, feeling their gathering voices like exploding popcorn kernels in his chest, hiked his thumb high.

Bruce made the all-clear announcement. In another minute, the grandmother's phone dinged and her grandkids were hustling up the stainless-steel ramp to Power Rip, *thunk thunk thunk*. When the youngest reached the turnstile, the operator eyed him next to the minimum-height ruler. The kid visibly held his breath before being waved on.

The crew clambered around the side to get their own cage. The older brother boosted the youngest into a seat.

The rest of the cages filled quickly. Karl kept one eye on the operator locking harnesses and tugging lap belts, and one eye on the treetops.

They were rustling, just barely.

"Riders ready?" shouted the operator.

The riders shrieked, hooted, whistled. The operator grinned at parents and spouses watching from behind the guardrails, then pressed a large green button.

Power Rip's maiden ride began.

Karl's knees locked subconsciously as the primary arms jerked out to its sides, boosting the cages aloft in twin carousels. The family Karl had helped—the Fullers, he learned now from the grandmother—were in a bottom cage, which meant the stiffest, meanest G-forces at the jump.

Power Rip was briefly calm, a giant barbell of throats and

kicking feet. Then, with a silky mechanical whoosh, the two carousels began whipping around, faster and faster, hurtling their component cages through three planes at once.

When Karl had approached Wagstaff Coasters three years ago with his vision, he'd said, "I want to cross the Scrambler with the Ferris wheel, but tilting, way up in the air. At least two hundred feet."

The CEO had laughed and said, "Anything else?"

"Yeah," Karl had said. "Make it look cool."

Boy, did it ever. Power Rip blotted out half the morning sky, plunging, twisting, accelerating and decelerating riders. If a cage spun just right at the primary arms' horizontal, it got the perfect combination of forces to transport its riders nearly outside their bodies.

After seventy-four seconds, the Rip growled down. When the cages' feathery descent stopped, their occupants looked around —*did that just happen?*—and broke into spontaneous applause. The operator took a bow.

As the next group boarded, the Fullers sprinted around from the rear exit and mobbed their grandmother.

"Sign us up again, Granny!"

"Again, *we wanna go again!*"

The woman peered through ball-chain glasses at her phone. Karl hurried over to help, but she figured it out. In a few swipes, she'd successfully reserved six spots for the 10:52 Power Rip. The kids erupted with joy, and Karl knew—in that moment, in those perfect faces—he would run.

There was joy everywhere, Karl Peoples believed. Joy waited in a pair of sisters wanting to start a beauty salon but unable to bear the government's red tape. It waited in the unemployed twenty-two-year-olds whose dads had worked the lines at General Motors, who just wanted a paycheck and a beer softball league on Thursdays. It waited in the cities, all those youngsters craving opportunity instead of politicians' shell games—what they'd been fed for decades.

There was so much bottled-up joy that Karl turned around a full 360 degrees and grinned like a loon at every face he encountered—because he saw it now, that joy bubbling below the surface. Waiting to wash away the lies and bitterness, to restore trust and belief in common purpose.

Waiting for a leader.

Karl scanned the bustling walkways for Maya. He looked forward to telling her she could quit networking, quit printing up her resume. She was going to be busy for the next fifteen months—longer if he won.

He kept scanning, twisting around. Looking between hats and kids sitting up on their parents' shoulders.

Where was she? *Did she take off?* Maya only tolerated these carnivals, he knew. She would've rather been mountain biking or at some gallery.

Karl thought he'd last seen her around the bumper cars. He started that way, breezing past the vintage Old West photos and buttery elephant ears. He was vaguely registering the "This ride is temporarily closed for maintenance" sign on *Maison Magicale* when a big man seized his arm.

"Ow! Hey, what the—" Karl began as the man dragged him toward the fun house. "What is this? Who're you?"

The man moved quickly and said nothing. He wore the purple uniform, and now Karl realized it was that man from earlier—the face he hadn't known. Before Karl could wrestle free or shout for help, his feet were banging the counter-spinning metal panels of the entrance.

The action jiggled his knees apart. Karl fought to stay upright, staggering ahead into the hall of mirrors. His abductor's hand firm on his back, he slipped around two panes of glass before slamming into the third.

"Keep moving," the man ordered.

Karl chop-stepped through the rest of the maze, wobbling onto the buzzer panels and toward the smell room. He obeyed for now, unsure who he was dealing with. Kidnappers? Had they taken Maya too? Terrorists? The man didn't look foreign—in fact, something at the bottom of his voice sounded familiar.

The smell room doors separated like an elevator car's. Lilacs rushed to Karl's brain. He experienced a split-second of euphoria before rotten eggs came blasting from the next archway of air jets, shriveling his nose.

His abductor coughed, "Ack, *friggin' rank,*" and kept pushing.

Could he be a Gallagher? Or hired by the Gallaghers?

They squinted their way through the fog corner and onto the spiral escalator. Karl thought about going for his phone to dial 911. He thought about slugging the man, but the idea of violence here—on carnival grounds—killed him.

The escalator's railings curved opposite each other, turning Karl's long body into a swooping, tilting airplane as the escalator whisked him up to the second story. He and his abductor spilled out into the bright room: blinding white light, high-frequency buzz. Tom and Jerry cartoons raced around the ceiling and walls. The temperature was twelve degrees hotter here. Karl's forehead tingled and seemed to be pulling away from his scalp.

The man tugged Karl along, shoving him through a plastic flap leading to the spinning exit tube. The tube raised and dropped and raised and dropped Karl like a clothes dryer, finally ejecting him to the ride's last stop.

The wizard chamber.

At this point, an animatronic figure with a pointy hat and wizened eyebrows usually roared, "To the end you have come, my small adventurer!"

The figure was nowhere to be seen. In its place was a live man in a wheelchair.

Not a Gallagher.

"You should have a body man," said Marshall Pruitt.

As his abductor receded to the shadows, Karl took stock. Marshall Pruitt was here. The man who'd overseen the clan's black-ops wing for decades. Who'd infiltrated Mossad and the Black Panthers. Who'd seduced one of Fidel Castro's mistresses and was said to be dabbling now in uranium enrichment.

Why is Marshall Pruitt in Kirksville, Michigan?

"I walk the crowds," Karl said. "You can't tell anything about your customers hiding behind a bodyguard."

Marshall laced his skeletal fingers before his chin. "A reckless attitude."

"I don't fear," Karl said. "We don't get that sort at the fair."

The wizard chamber was dim, lit only by a blacklight that gave Marshall's neat white hair—together with the mechanized chair—an electrocuted look. His teeth were small and feral. Carnival sounds came through the fun-house walls, faint, disembodied.

"Running for the highest office in the land changes a man," Marshall said. "Not often for the better."

The comment chilled Karl. He felt a paranoid rush that the spymaster knew he intended to run for president—when Karl hadn't known himself until seconds ago. He had been playing possum with Maya and even Claire, feigning interest in the governor's job. He liked to shock people with goals greater than they were expecting, with moonshots.

He tried, "What makes you think I'm going after Barksdale?"

Marshall frowned like the question was beneath them both. "You aren't going after Barksdale. That is the purpose of my visit, to inform you."

Karl's emotions whipped from cold to hot. "*Inform me?*"

"Franklin Pierce in 1850 is the only sitting president to lose a primary challenge." Marshall's tone was professorial, grim. "Barksdale is weak but not weak enough to lose. We're sparing you the embarrassment."

Karl strode forward, towering over the octogenarian. "You don't give a damn about my embarrassment. What's in it for you? And why'd you bum-rush me with some thug? Got something to say, just pick up the lousy phone."

Without meaning to, he'd encroached into the space over the wheelchair.

"Back off, hombre. You're looking for a fight, I'll give it."

This came from the man who'd seized Karl outside. That familiar quality to his voice was stronger, and as he stepped out of the shadows holding a latex mask, the air became grimy.

"Rock Pruitt." Karl shook his head, stunned. "How long have you been here? On site?" He felt panicked, thinking of his female employees and patrons around this corrupt man. To Marshall: "I don't want this here—him, you. You got ten seconds, and then I'm calling the calvary to boot your a—"

"The matter couldn't be discussed by phone," Marshall said. "Discretion is of the utmost importance."

His sunken eyes traveled the chamber, seeming to delight in its oddness.

Karl said, "Tell Jonathan I don't care if he approves or not. I don't need the clan. I'll find my own money, I got a website."

Rock came swaggering between them.

"*You've got a website*," he mocked. "Well, la-de-da. Maybe you can raise some cash for Michiganders' dental work. I swear, there's a few out there I'd poke, but those mouths? Disgusting. You'd have to start around back and—"

"We are not here," Marshall interrupted wearily, "on Jonathan Pruitt's authority. And the reason you cannot run for president has nothing to do with money."

Karl kept his body squared to Rock but turned his eyes to the older man. "Okay. What's it have to do with?"

Marshall steepled his fingers gravely. He said, "Pinebox."

For a moment, Karl matched his solemn air. Then he sneered, "Aw, don't give me that bull. I'm from Michigan. In Michigan, we don't believe in ghost stories."

Rock rolled his eyes obnoxiously. Marshall gave a dry chuckle.

"The pinebox is no ghost," he said. "It's made of wood and brass. You can touch it." He lifted a finger as though caressing the conjured artifact.

Karl looked between the two men, a phantom and a devil—both blood relatives. Icy fear grew inside him. He ignored it.

"You came a long way, gentlemen," he said. "A long way for nothing."

www.ingramcontent.com/pod-product-compliance
Lightning Source LLC
Chambersburg PA
CBHW021111110726
47900CB00007B/2138